A BAD BREED

KAT ROSS

A Bad Breed

First Edition

Copyright © 2019 by Kat Ross

ISBN: 978-0-9997621-2-7

PROLOGUE

TUESDAY, JANUARY 15, 1889

The last rays of the sun were setting fire to the high peaks when he caught her.

She'd run for miles through the forest, fighting the black tide of the drug he'd slipped into her wine. Whatever it was made her feel as if she floated above her own body, weightless and without a care in the world.

If not for the bitter cold, she might have sat down in the snow for a spell.

The hard-eyed, sober part of her, which was not yet gone entirely, knew that would be a very bad idea.

So she ran, focusing on the tidal rasp of her breath, the metronomic ticking of her heart. After a while, the sounds of pursuit grew fainter. She dared to hope she'd lost him.

Then she'd twisted her ankle in an animal hole concealed beneath the snow.

It wasn't broken, though it hurt like the dickens even through the narcotic fog. At least the pain sharpened her wits.

I am so bloody stupid, she thought for the hundredth time, leaning against a tree. *I never should have....*

Should have what?

Her eyes lost focus.

What an intricate, miraculous thing snow was! She'd never noticed it before, each crystal outlined with perfect clarity. Deep cold was like swimming underwater....

Her fingers tightened to a fist, the nails drawing blood.

Drunk the wine, that's what. Bloody stupid of me. Now get a grip.

She studied the woods. Blue shadows gathered beneath the tall pines where the twilight deepened. All was quiet. But she sensed a presence, watching.

There were wolves in these mountains. She'd seen one that morning at dawn, standing on a rocky tor. It stared at her with yellow eyes, then turned and loped away. She'd felt a sublime grace in its presence.

She had no fear of wolves.

Yet her heart hammered in her breast as she limped down the path. She wore stout boots and a high-necked wool dress over layers of petticoats and a cloak lined with dark blue silk. The path followed a frozen creek, its edges brittle with ice. Frost lay thick on the ground and the boughs of the trees.

The light bled away as she reached the edge of the forest. A full moon rose, huge and bright. The nape of her neck prickled a warning.

She looked back. A silent shape glided through the trees. Not a wolf. Not a man either, though it moved on two legs.

In the distance, she heard the whistle of a train.

She scrambled down a steep incline. Her ankle throbbed, but she thought it would hold for a few more minutes.

A quarter mile off, the mouth of a tunnel led into the mountain. The tracks sat atop an embankment and she could see the glossy black engine chugging toward the tunnel. Light spilled from the windows of the passenger cars. The hood of her cloak fell back as she struggled through knee-high drifts. She tore a glove off with her teeth and freed the long iron blade sheathed at her waist.

The clatter of the train grew louder as it approached a curve and slowed down. She veered left toward the white expanse of an open field. If she cut across, she might still catch the train before it accelerated into the tunnel. Silhouettes filled the windows and she imagined the people on the train, reading books or sipping coffee, in the warmth and light.

She risked another glance over her shoulder. Whatever came was cloaked in shadow, but she sensed it speeding down the slope.

She was halfway across when ice cracked beneath her boots. Not a field but a lake — and not solidly frozen. She flung out a hand, scrabbling madly as she slid into the frigid water.

She tried to summon her elemental power but it drifted away on a black tide of tranquilizer. The train whistle sounded again and then it was swallowed by the tunnel.

And the last thing she saw was two golden eyes, bright as the moon, rushing toward her.

PART I

"If the loup-garou were only a natural wolf, why then, you see" —
the mayor cleared his throat — "you see we should think nothing
of it; but, M. le Curé, it is a fiend, a worse than fiend, a man-fiend
— a worse than man-fiend, a man-wolf-fiend!"

—*The Book of Were-Wolves: Being an Account of a Terrible Superstition*

CHAPTER 1

SUNDAY, FEBRUARY 10

Vivienne Cumberland lit an Oxford Oval and exhaled a stream of smoke at the ceiling. She'd been about to leave for an early supper followed by a play at the Adelphi Theatre when the summons came from 19 Buckingham Street. There was no time to change so she was dressed for an evening on the town, in a red silk dress with matching hat and gloves.

The hat had been tossed onto a side table. Fog pressed against the windows of the library, blurring the glass with chill droplets. A fire roared in the grate, but her hands still felt cold. She drew deeply on the cigarette, savoring the rush of nicotine.

"Anne's been missing for over three weeks and we've just been informed?" Vivienne asked with a frown.

Henry Sidgwick, president of the London division of the Society for Psychical Research, gave a small cough, eyeing her cigarette with disapproval. He wore a dark frock coat nearly the same color as his thick black beard. He had stern features, but his voice was gentle.

"The village was snowed in, Vivienne. It's a tiny place. They don't even have their own constable. Ten days passed before they could get word to the nearest real town. The authorities there contacted the British consulate in Bucharest, but they had no record of her. Anne neglected to bring her official identification. It took another two weeks to connect her with the Society."

Vivienne pondered this for a moment. "Where was she last seen?"

"At her rooms in Mara Vardac. The mayor ordered a search party when the innkeeper realized she'd gone, but they found nothing. The snow had erased any footprints." He clasped his hands together. "Her things were still at the inn." A pause. "At least no body has been found. The others were all left in plain sight."

Vivienne's black eyes flashed. "You should never have let her go alone."

He gave her a level look. "As if I could stop her. Anne is a bright, capable agent. For God's sake, Vivienne, you know how she is. She *prefers* to work alone. And you and Mr. Lawrence were preoccupied with the Clarence case."

This provoked a stab of guilt. "I know. But she's also my ward. I feel responsible for her."

Anne wasn't a child and hadn't been for a very long time, but part of Vivienne would always see her that way.

"What did her last letter say?" Sidgwick asked.

"Only that she'd stopped at Saint Sava College to pick up the books Cyrus wanted, and had arrived safely in Mara Vardac. That was January 12th or 13th. She seemed to think there was something odd about the place, but she didn't say what." Vivienne frowned. "How did we first learn of this case anyway?"

He pushed a slim dossier across the desk. "Anne came across a news article from one of the Bucharest weeklies about a series of strange deaths in the mountains. Three so far."

Vivienne opened the file and scanned the top sheet of cheap paper within. The article was barely two paragraphs, though a few phrases leapt out from the jumble of Romanian. *Savagely assaulted ... strange bite marks ... presumed madman.*

"The first victims were two children from the village, a brother and sister aged nine and twelve. Their throats were torn out." Sidgwick sighed. "Then a woodcutter was found outside his hut, badly mauled."

"Drained of blood?"

"No. Just mutilated. I don't have any additional details. Anne planned to look more closely."

Vivienne frowned. "That doesn't sound like a ghoul. They only want the blood. And why would the newspaper call it a madman? It sounds more like animal attacks."

He shrugged. "Most likely it's wolves."

"Do you believe that?"

His face was solemn. "I honestly don't know, Vivienne. But three violent, mysterious deaths in a tiny village? I agreed with her. We'd be remiss not to investigate it." He paused. "Is there any chance the Duzakh could be involved? Anne thought there might be."

"The Duzakh no longer exists," Vivienne replied tightly. "Not for a hundred years."

"A rogue necromancer, then."

Vivienne exhaled, considering it. "They're more than capable of such savagery, but they don't like drawing attention to themselves. Leaving the bodies to be found.... That's careless. Necromancers tidy up after themselves." Her face darkened. "It's why we've had such a bloody hard time finding any of them." She stood and paced to the window. "It's not the sort of assignment Anne usually chooses."

"No, but Central European folklore is one of her specialties and she speaks fluent Hungarian. She was the obvious choice."

"I suppose."

Henry Sidgwick cleared his throat. "My impression is that she was quite disturbed by the choice of victim."

"The children, you mean."

"Yes." He frowned. "What do you propose, Vivienne? I told the consulate to wait before taking any action."

She sighed. Henry was brilliant in his own way, but he could be quite thick sometimes.

"I'd better go to Mara Vardac myself. She may have followed another lead without telling us. She's done it before." In fact, Anne had done it many times, to Vivienne's exasperation.

Sidgwick nodded. "Take the dossier. It has the letter from the constable in Satinari. And be sure to bring your full credentials. I wouldn't rely on a warm reception from the locals." He paused. "What about Mr. Lawrence?"

"He's gone away for a holiday. After our last case, I can't blame him. But I've no idea where he is. Somewhere near Morocco, I think." She stood and pulled on her gloves. "I can handle this myself. "Cable Cyrus Ashdown if anything comes up in London."

Sidgwick nodded. "Field agents are supposed to report back regularly," he said with a feeble smile. "When you find her, tell her I said that."

"I will." Vivienne snatched her hat off the table.

He sighed at her grim expression. "She insisted on going, Vivienne. If you hadn't been preoccupied with Dr. Clarence—"

"I know. I don't blame you. Anne does what she pleases with little thought for those who might worry about her." Vivienne took a last drag and tossed her cigarette into the fireplace. "Tell Cyrus everything. And check in with your liaisons in Central Europe, all of them. Find out if any have heard from Anne."

"I've already done so. Nothing yet, but it will take a while for the inquiries to trickle through." Sidgwick gave her a serious look. "Be careful, Vivienne."

She nodded and left the S.P.R. offices off the Strand. It was just after five o'clock and already growing dark outside. Tendrils of mist rose curled around the streetlamps, softening them to dim smudges. Vivienne lit another cigarette. Her hand was unsteady and it took three tries to flick the wheel. If Anne had stumbled over something more dangerous than a ghoul or two, she could be in trouble.

But it was far more likely she'd gone her own way. Anne always had an impetuous, headstrong streak and it had grown worse over the years.

It was a short carriage ride to her townhouse on Park Place where the butler, Quimby, greeted her at the door. Tall and formidable, with a beaky nose and white side whiskers, he took her damp cloak and hung it up to dry.

"His lordship is in the conservatory, milady," he said.

"Thank you, Quimby."

Nathaniel. She'd forgotten about him. Well, he deserved to know.

Vivienne made her way to the glass-walled conservatory, an oasis of green facing the garden at the rear of the large house. The smell of living things filled the air, perfume from a dozen hothouse flowers and rich, moist earth. It was the one room where she never smoked.

"Darling!" The Marquess of Abervagenny stretched like a cat, his blond hair adorably untidy. Nathaniel spent most of his time at his family seat of Eridge Castle in Sussex. He'd come up to London that morning to see his solicitors and wore an elegant blue morning jacket, open save for the top button, over a single-breasted waistcoat. A newspaper lay open on his knee. He gave it a tap.

"I'm reading all about the Exposition Universalle. It opens in Paris in May. You must let me take you. Alec, too, if he ever decides to come back to us." His grin died as he studied her face. "What's happened?"

Vivienne sank into a wicker chair. "It's Anne. She's vanished again."

Nathaniel's vivid blue eyes narrowed. He was very fond of

Anne, and one of the few people she seemed to like in return. He folded the newspaper and jumped up to pour them each a finger of brandy from the sideboard.

"Tell me all of it," he said, handing her a glass.

Vivienne knocked the brandy back in one go and let out a sigh. "I don't know much. She went to investigate some killings in a remote Romanian village."

Nathaniel nodded, cradling the snifter in his hands. He already knew that part.

"Sidgwick thought it could be a ghoul. Anne wouldn't have had any trouble with one of those. She must have made some inquiries in the village since she was there long enough to post a letter. But then she went out and didn't come back. This place is miles from anywhere and it's the dead of winter…." Vivienne trailed off, unable to meet Nathaniel's gaze. "I must go after her. Immediately."

"Of course you must," he said soothingly. "And I'll come with you."

Vivienne gave him a tired smile. "It's kind of you to offer, but—"

"Nonsense." He leapt to his feet in a burst of boyish energy. "I *am* your husband. Isn't that what we're good for? Sickness and health, good times and bad. Ghouls and goblins."

She gave him a level look. Their marriage was one of convenience, though they enjoyed each other's company. Nathaniel had his dalliances — not of the female persuasion — and Vivienne had her work with the S.P.R. He knew some of what she did, but not the full truth of it.

"It's too dangerous," Vivienne objected, realizing too late that this was precisely the wrong approach to take.

Nathaniel got a glint in his eye. "Don't be beastly, darling. It's about time you let me help with one of your cases. And Anne is my ward, too. I promise I'll be well-behaved and do as you say."

To her surprise, Vivienne found herself actually considering it. If she traveled alone, she'd spend the whole trip fretting. And Alec couldn't be reached, damn him.

"I don't know how long it will take."

"It doesn't matter. The only thing that matters is Anne. I'll make all the arrangements."

Vivienne felt a rush of gratitude for their friendship. Beneath the façade of an idle lord, Nathaniel was as dependable as English rain. She rose and kissed him lightly on the mouth. He smiled.

"You're a gem," she said softly.

"Take care," he murmured. "I might have to make a proper wife of you."

She gazed into his eyes. They both burst out laughing and he strode off, bellowing for Quimby.

What have I done? Vivienne wondered. Now she'd have to protect him if they did encounter monsters, though he was big and strapping and could certainly prove useful in a pinch. The master of Eridge Castle was not one of those soft-bellied aristocrats who spent their time playing cards and drinking. He preferred the company of dogs and horses to his fellow peers — the ones he wasn't currently seducing, at any rate — and had the build of a middleweight boxer. At thirty-nine, he looked a decade younger. He was also charming and discreet. Lord Cumberland guarded her secrets and she guarded his.

Yes, Vivienne reflected as she set her glass on the sideboard, Nathaniel was a gem. The year-old marriage suited them both. Vivienne was rich as sin and she'd saved him from having to sell some of his lands to pay off debts. In turn, she'd gained a title and some measure of respectability.

Trusting her husband to arrange the details of the journey, she went upstairs to her bedroom where Claudine was airing out the bedding.

"Filthy weather out there, milady, you must be half-frozen. Shall I draw a hot bath?"

"Yes, please. It might be the last I get for days. And pack a trunk, if you would. My warmest things."

"Where are you going, milady?"

"The Kingdom of Romania. Three days' worth of clothes should be adequate. Nothing fancy. I intend to travel light."

Claudine didn't bat an eyelash. She was used to her mistress leaving at the drop of a hat.

"Will you take me along, milady?" she asked hopefully.

Vivienne smiled. "Not this time, Claudine. But I promise to send you a postcard."

"Very good, milady," she said with a sigh.

While the tub was filling, Vivienne climbed up to the top floor and opened the door to Anne's room, where she paused for a long moment. It was large and gave a fine view of Green Park but held few hints about the woman who lived there. The vanity was bare of powder or cosmetics. There were no photographs or keepsakes on the bedside table. In fact, it looked almost exactly as it had when she'd first moved her things to Park Place a year before. The only personal item was Anne's violin, which lay in a case on the window seat. She was passionate about her music, but she wouldn't have taken it along.

One of the wooden panels protruded slightly from the wall. Vivienne pressed it and it sprang open, revealing a secret book-shelf. She suspected this was why Anne chose the room. It held a small library of volumes on folklore and witchcraft. They were scholarly works one might find in any decent library and Vivienne never understood why Anne kept them hidden away, as though she were ashamed of them.

Vivienne traced her fingertips across one of the shelves. There were gaps where Anne had taken books with her — the most pertinent ones, she assumed. But she found one called *Transylvanian Superstitions* written by Emily Gerard and published only four years before. Vivienne flipped through the pages. They were well-worn, with creases on some of the pages, as though Anne had read it many times. Perhaps that was why she'd left it behind.

Vivienne tucked the book under her arm and closed the panel.

If anyone had harmed Anne…. Well, she would hunt them to the ends of the earth.

And so would Alec Lawrence.

For the first time in days, Vivienne opened herself to her daēva. She could sense him through the gold cuff around her wrist. He wore its match and little short of death could break the bond between them. Alec was well, though she felt the old ache in his leg. She wished she could send him a message, but the bond didn't work that way. And the farther he was, the fainter the sensations were.

Vivienne missed him more than she'd expected. Rather desperately, in fact. As much as she was loath to admit it, Alec was a part of her. But she wouldn't drive herself mad with worry over him, too. Alec Lawrence knew how to take care of himself.

He should be here, she thought angrily, though there was little real heat in it. He never went off on his own. But he had, and now she couldn't find him when she needed him. First Alec, then Anne. The sudden conviction that everything was falling apart sent a chill down her spine.

"There's a ferry service leaving for the Hook of Holland from Harwich in six hours," Nathaniel said from the doorway. "We can just make it if we go straight away."

Vivienne turned. "Thank you," she murmured. "For everything."

He came forward and folded his arms around her. He smelled pleasantly of aftershave and a hint of brandy. "It *was* rather mad that she went off unaccompanied," Nathaniel said. "Not because she's a woman," he added hastily. "But I thought you agents worked in pairs. I'm surprised Mr. Sigdwick would approve it."

Vivienne almost told him the truth then, that Anne was much more than she seemed, and Alec too, but it wasn't her secret to reveal.

"She's handled cases alone before. He had no reason to think it wasn't routine."

Nathaniel gave a mirthless laugh. "Not everyone would consider three brutal murders routine, darling. Well, I suppose I'd better help Quimby pack my things. We should get to the terminal at Liverpool Street as soon as possible. The train leaves at 8:30."

Vivienne took a quick bath and chose a blue woolen dress suitable for hard travel. Then she opened a valise and packed an assortment of iron blades wrapped in cloth. Two were short swords for close-quarter combat, as well five others of varying lengths she could stow in specially tailored slits in her bodice.

As for the rest of it, Claudine managed to cram everything into a single trunk. Before it was latched, Vivienne took a small oval portrait in a silver frame from her vanity.

It showed a serious-looking young woman who appeared no older than her late twenties. Her auburn hair was loosely upswept, covering ears that stuck out a bit. She wore a high-necked grey dress. Anne rarely smiled and she wasn't doing so in the picture. She had a small, straight nose dusted with freckles and a pointy chin, but the most remarkable feature was her eyes, which were large and unsettling.

It was the only photograph of Anne that Vivienne had.

She slipped it into the trunk, along with two small carved wooden figurines. The first was a woman with the skin of a crocodile, her patron, Innunu. The second, Kavi, had nine arms, each wielding a flail.

Vivienne worshipped the old gods and she could use all the luck she could find.

And hour later, they were racing in a carriage through the dark streets of London.

"We'll find her, Viv," Nathaniel said cheerfully, though she heard an edge to his voice.

Vivienne gave him a wan smile. "Of course we will."

CHAPTER 2

The night crossing to Hoek Van Holland was not an experience Vivienne cared to repeat. Nathaniel seemed unaffected by the violent pitching of the ferry, but she clung to the rail, wishing for death. She'd never liked ships, but at least her last voyage with Alec had been on a Trans-Atlantic luxury liner. The *Richard Young* was a 240-foot paddle steamer that waddled through the troughs of the Channel like a fat dowager with a gouty leg.

Half the passengers in the lounge were in a similar state and she couldn't bear to listen to their retching, though it was freezing on deck. Nathaniel gamely kept her company, distracting her with amusing stories about country life, and Vivienne was very glad he'd come.

Once on the train to Munich, she collapsed into their first class compartment and slept until they changed for another line to Vienna, and thence to Buda-Pesth. The train arrived near to midnight and they spent the night in a hotel near the station, then caught a local to Brasov early the next morning.

Fields and forests raced by out the window, broken by the occasional medieval walled town. Vivienne had the sense of moving back in time to a land untouched by the modern world. She stretched, wishing for coffee, and dug out the book she'd taken from Anne's room. It was a slim volume, bound in cloth with gold lettering.

Nathaniel had propped his long legs on the seat next to her and sat drowsing beneath the brim of his hat. Despite four days of constant travel, he somehow managed to look fresh as an English rose. Vivienne started reading and barked a laugh.

His sapphire eyes flickered open.

"Listen to this. *'Transylvania might well be termed the land of superstition, for nowhere else does this curious crooked plant of delusion flourish as persistently and in such bewildering variety. It would almost seem as though the whole species of demons, pixies, witches, and hobgoblins, driven from the rest of Europe by the wand of science, had taken refuge within this mountain rampart, well aware that here they would find secure lurking-places, whence they might defy their persecutors yet awhile.'"*

He raised an eyebrow. "One can hardly blame them. These poor people have been invaded by one army or another for centuries. I suppose clinging to the old ways is a tactic of quiet resistance."

"They're a proud people," Vivienne agreed. "I'm glad they finally gained their independence. It can't have been fun to live between the jaws of the Ottomans and the Hapsburgs. Not to mention the Mongols, Goths, Huns and assorted other hordes."

Vivienne herself had met Genghis Khan briefly — and under inauspicious circumstances — when she and Alec were trying to close a Greater Gate to the underworld in Samarkand in 1220 and the Khan arrived to sack the place. It was another experience she'd not care to repeat.

"Do you think there's any truth in it?" Nathaniel wondered. "Witches and hobgoblins and the like?"

"Of course there is," she murmured. "They just have most of the details wrong."

"Such as?"

Vivienne laid the book on her lap. "Ghouls are the spirits of restless dead who linger in the Dominion, the veil between the living world and what lies beyond. They have different names in different cultures. In Spain, they're called *brujas*. Your medieval ancestors called them incubus or succubus. In the Philippines, *mandurugo*. In Germany, *nachzehrer*. There are literally hundreds of words for the same thing. But ghouls don't appear randomly."

"Let me guess. Necromancers."

She laughed and dug out her Oxford Ovals. Nathaniel leaned over to light her cigarette with a match. "So you do know something."

"I overheard Alec and Cyrus talking in the drawing room," he admitted.

Vivienne blew a thin stream of smoke toward the window. "Yes, necromancers. Their power derives from human captives. When a captive dies, a ghoul comes through. Sometimes a wight. And when a *necromancer* dies, a revenant is born."

"Revenant?"

She made a face. "They're even nastier."

"So … a large number of ghouls in a given area is a sign there's a necro hanging about?"

"Often, yes, but not always. Once loosed, the creatures will travel until they're caught and beheaded. But here's the worst part. After they've consumed a few pints of blood, they gain the ability to mimic their victims. If you don't know the signs to watch for it can be hard to tell the difference until it's too late."

"That's what happened with the Queen?"

"Unfortunately, yes. Now there's a special division of Scotland Yard devoted to hunting them down. The S.P.R. works as a consulting agency in tandem with the Dominion Branch."

Nathaniel looked impressed. "Go on."

"I wondered if there might be a necromancer behind the killings in Mara Vardac, but it doesn't really fit their modus operandi. And ghouls drain their victims dry, but I've never seen one tear a throat out."

His smile died. "That's what happened in this village we're going to?"

Vivienne nodded.

"What do you think it is, then?"

"I don't know. But I'm sure the locals have their own explanation." She opened the book and flipped through the pages. "Here we are. The people of the Carpathians call ghouls *nosferatu*, blood-suckers. *'The living vampire is in general the illegitimate offspring of two illegitimate persons, but even a flawless pedigree will not ensure anyone against the intrusion of a vampire into his family vault, since every person killed by a nosferatu becomes likewise a vampire after death, and will continue to suck the blood of other innocent people till the spirit has been exorcised, either by opening the grave of the person suspected and driving a stake through the corpse, or firing a pistol shot into the coffin. In very obstinate cases it is further recommended to cut off the head and replace it in the coffin with the mouth filled with garlic, or to extract the heart and burn it, strewing the ashes over the grave.'"*

She closed the book. "That sounds like a standard ghoul. And I see they're familiar with the head-chopping part. The garlic is nonsense."

He patted the pocket of his greatcoat. "Well, I brought my Beaumont-Adams revolver in case we need to shoot up any coffins."

Vivienne laughed. "I feel ever so much better."

"Don't mock, darling," he said with a wounded expression. "I happen to be a crack shot."

A few minutes later, the train pulled into the town of Satinari. Nathaniel and Vivienne collected their luggage and paid a lanky teenaged boy to guide them to a tavern near the station. Like many of the larger houses, the walls and window frames had been painted with intricate, colorful designs, giving the inn a quaint gingerbread aspect. A few men in long wool coats drank beer at tables inside, casting surly glances as they approached the mistress of the place. Her eyes widened a little at the sight of Vivienne's brown skin, but she wiped her hands on her apron and bustled forward with a polite smile. Nathaniel greeted her in German, which she understood. But when he asked about hiring a carriage to go to Mara Vardac, she crossed herself and looked alarmed.

"Oh no, you mustn't go there, sir," she said in broken German. "It is a bad place. Very bad."

Nathaniel glanced at Vivienne. "We know about the attacks," he said gently. "We've come on official business. To help."

She didn't reply, only crossed herself again and turned away.

"Please, good mistress. A friend of ours disappeared. An English girl...." Nathaniel trailed off. The woman had retreated to the kitchen, slamming the door behind her.

He looked over at the men, who'd buried their noses in the mugs of beer.

"I have money," he announced, pulling out a thick wad of Romanian banknotes. "Fifty leu to the gentleman who takes us to Mara Vardac."

It was a princely sum. The men shifted, eyeing each other.

"A hundred."

"I'll take you." The oldest of the bunch rose on unsteady legs. He had a red, bulbous nose and his coat was worn and patched. He spoke in Magyar, which Vivienne had a smattering of. She knew dozens of languages, and hundreds of local dialects, though she tended to forget the ones she didn't use often.

His friends shook their heads. A low-pitched but heated argument broke out. The old man wouldn't be dissuaded, tugging his sleeve from their grasping fingers. One of them muttered something about drunk fools and made a sign to ward off evil.

"They say it is too late in the day," Vivienne murmured. "That

24

no amount of money is worth being caught out after dark near Mara Vardac."

Nathaniel frowned. "Well, it's hardly noon. How far is it anyway?"

"Only seven or eight miles, I think."

The man led them to a farm wagon behind the inn. He fetched a pair of roan horses from the stable and they all squeezed onto the bench. He cracked the whip and the cart lurched off at a brisk pace, passing through the town and up a narrow road that climbed into the foothills. The snows of late January had given way to a thaw and patches of green showed in the fallow fields and orchards. It was a spectacular countryside, riven by deep gorges and heavily wooded slopes of pine and spruce.

"Thank you for agreeing to take us," Nathaniel said companionably in German.

The man grunted, staring straight ahead, the brim of his black hat pulled low.

"We plan to stay the night. I suppose there's an inn?"

Vivienne translated the words to Magyar, though she knew he'd understood.

"Lock your door," the driver muttered. "And pray to Saint George to preserve you 'til dawn comes."

Vivienne relayed his reply to Nathaniel, who gave a respectful nod. "What do you think would disturb us?" he ventured.

The driver merely hunched his shoulders and gripped the reins with gnarled hands, driving the horses to greater speed.

The sun was bright, the sky blue, yet Vivienne felt a sense of foreboding as they left Satinari behind and ascended into the higher passes. The land grew more rugged and wild, the forests thick and dark. They passed above the thaw line. A blanket of snow covered the road with no sign that any other travelers had passed this way in weeks.

The driver kept glancing anxiously at the sun, cracking the whip above the poor horses' heads as it began descending to the west. The cart raced along, taking the curves at perilous speeds. Foam flecked the beasts' flanks, their breath plumed white in the air, and Vivienne was about to object that it would do them no good if the cart overturned when they rounded a bend in the road and Mara Vardac came into view. The driver let out a sigh of relief and slackened his grip on the reins.

At first glance, it looked no different from any of the other tiny villages Vivienne had seen from the train. Two dozen white-washed houses with tile roofs nestled in an open valley, a vista of snowy mountains rearing up to the north. There was a small church and a smithy with smoke coming from the forge. But as they approached, she saw the village was enclosed by a palisade of sharpened stakes, the wood still green. Stumps at the edge of the forest signaled where the trees had been felled.

The driver passed through an opening in the palisade and guided the cart down the main street, pulling up abruptly in front of an inn. It was an ancient-looking building made of mortared stones with a sagging roof. Nathaniel jumped down and offered Vivienne his hand. Faces watched from the windows of nearby houses, but no children played outside and the whole place had a desolate air.

The driver helped unload their trunks in an obvious bid to see them on their way as fast as possible. He quickly saw to the horses, filling a bucket of water from the well and rubbing them down with a musty blanket, every movement fraught with impatience. The instant Nathaniel handed him the banknotes, he climbed back onto the cart, not even bothering to count them. The journey had sobered him up, and she saw pity in his eyes as he gave them a final glance.

"*Isten vigyázzon rád*," he muttered.

God watch over you.

He shook the reins and the cart raced away toward the pass leading back down to Satinari.

"Charming fellow," Nathaniel grunted, hefting a trunk in each hand.

"He meant well. He's just frightened." Vivienne looked around. The faces had disappeared, but she saw curtains twitch and felt sure they were still being watched. "They all are."

The inn was dim inside and empty of custom, though a dozen tables and chairs were scattered through the common room. Heavy wooden beams, black with age, supported a low roof. The great hearth was cold and the place smelled of old wood smoke and beer.

"Hello?" Nathaniel called.

A door closed and footsteps approached. A middle-aged man emerged from a passage at the back, his dark hair shot through with streaks of grey. He stopped dead when he saw them, his face expressionless.

"Good afternoon," Nathaniel said in German. "I am Lord Cumberland and this is my wife, Lady Cumberland. We've traveled hard from London."

The innkeeper blinked. He glanced through the window as though hoping whatever conveyance had brought them here would still be waiting outside. When he saw the cart had left, his brows drew down in a frown.

"We'd like to take a room for the night," Nathaniel prompted.

"I'm sorry, we're full," he said in heavily accented but fluent German.

Nathaniel looked around. There was no one else in the common room and no indication anyone was staying there. The man was obviously lying. Vivienne found her patience wearing thin.

"My ward lodged here," she said curtly, taking the photograph of Anne from her pocket and holding it out. "Surely you remember her."

The innkeeper barely glanced at it. "You must leave," he said firmly. "Strangers are not welcome in Mara Vardac."

"Now see here—" Nathaniel began.

Vivienne touched his sleeve. He followed her gaze through the window to the street, where a crowd was gathering in front of the inn. They were all men and most carried shotguns. The innkeeper crossed his arms.

"You can walk back to Satinari," he said softly. "Or...." He shrugged, his face defiant.

The mob was swelling by the moment, its angry murmuring clearly audible. Vivienne reached into her cloak to produce her credentials just as the door banged open.

A roughly handsome man with thick, wavy black hair strode inside the common room. He was in his middle thirties, but grief lined his face, making him look a decade older. He hissed something in Magyar to the innkeeper, his eyes never leaving Vivienne.

She was used to hostile stares even in London, which at least had a small population of African descent. But here in the hinterlands of Romania, Vivienne guessed she was the first dark-skinned person this man had ever seen.

"We're not here to cause any trouble," she said calmly in Magyar. "If you'll just let me—"

The man scowled. He gripped his shotgun loosely, but Vivienne had no illusions that he would hesitate to use it.

Nathaniel moved to stand in front of her, his face pale.

"If any of you lay a finger on my wife, it will be the last thing you ever do," he snarled in German.

The newcomer gave no sign he understood — which was likely for the best. But then he forked his fingers at them in a sign to ward off the Devil, the watching crowd outside began to surge forward, and Vivienne felt the first stirring of true fear.

"What's going on?"

A small man with a prosperous belly and hard eyes pushed through the mob. Vivienne thrust the dossier at him, forcing her hand to steadiness. His words had been spoken in Magyar and she replied in the same language.

"We've been sent by the British Crown, with the full approval of the authorities in Satinari."

He eyed the papers with suspicion.

"Please, just take them."

The man snatched them from her hand and studied them for a long minute. One bore the seal of Queen Victoria, mounted on horseback and holding a scepter. It authorized the bearer to act in her name on behalf of the Dominion Branch of Scotland Yard. That letter was in English, which she doubted he could read, but the second was from the constable in Satinari.

The man read it through several times. His face softened a bit. "It is Dobrescu's mark. I recognize it."

Both the innkeeper and shotgun-toter looked startled, then abashed.

"I am the mayor of Mara Vardac." He handed the papers back. The tone was not precisely warm, but Vivienne sensed the tension ebbing. "I think we'd best speak privately. Excuse me for a moment."

While the mayor went outside to settle down the villagers, Vivienne showed the innkeeper the photograph of Anne again.

"Miss Lawrence is my ward. I understand she stayed here."

His shoulders slumped as he gazed at the cameo. "The English girl. Yes, she was here." He sighed. "We already told everything we know. I am very sorry."

Vivienne's gut tightened. "Has she been found?"

He saw immediately what she meant and shook his head. "No, no. But my wife and I…. We fear the worst. You know what has happened in our village? The curse?"

Vivienne nodded.

"Then you understand why we are not trusting." His eyes flicked to the picture again. "It was four weeks ago Miss

Lawrence came. Such a nice girl, very quiet and respectful. She must have gone out on her own. We warned her not to."

"No one saw her leave?" Vivienne asked.

Again, he shook his head. He beckoned them to a table by the window and sat down heavily. "She was interested in the old stories. She said she collected them."

So Anne had not identified herself as an investigator of supernatural phenomena. No doubt a wise decision.

"Tell me all you remember of the day she disappeared."

"Miss Lawrence took breakfast in the common room. Then she went up to her room. She liked to read her books there."

"What was the weather like?"

"Snowing a bit, not very heavily yet. I went out to help the blacksmith shoe two of my horses. Elena was in the kitchen baking for most of the morning. Miss Lawrence must have gone out then, though we didn't realize it until later. When she didn't come down for supper, I knocked on her door. There was no answer. The storm outside had grown worse by then."

He clasped his hands. "It made me worried when she wouldn't answer so I fetched Elena. She knocked again, then went inside. Miss Lawrence was gone, but all her things were there. We thought she must have gone for a walk in the village. Her Hungarian was very good and she had a friendly way about her."

Vivienne smiled. "Yes, Anne can be quite charming when she puts her mind to it."

"We expected her to return at any moment. It was snowing so hard. When it began to get dark…. That is when we grew truly afraid. We went around the village, knocking on doors, but no one had seen her. We saw no footprints, but if she'd left early enough, they would have been covered by the falling snow."

"But where could she have gone?"

"I do not know, Lady Cumberland. She said nothing to either me or my wife. By the next morning, the road was impassable. It was several days before we could summon help from outside."

"What about the other deaths here? Did she ask about those?"

For the first time, he looked away, not meeting her eyes. "Yes, she did. She said she'd read a newspaper report about them. I told her it was wolves. That they get hungry in the winter and she should be very careful not to stray far from the village."

"Have there been any more deaths since she disappeared?" Nathaniel asked.

The innkeeper crossed himself and shook his head. "Thank God, no. I still have her things, if you'd like them. The constable from Satinari looked them over but didn't take them." He looked up as two men entered with the mayor. "Ah, this is our priest, Father Cernat."

The priest wore a black cassock and large silver cross on a chain around his neck. He had a bushy red beard and long, sharp nose.

"My son, Andrei." The third was a young man in his mid-twenties with broad shoulders and his father's dark eyes. He crossed his arms, barely suppressing a scowl.

"And my name is Alexandru Korzha," the innkeeper said. He flushed. "I...I will help in any way I can."

The mayor gestured to a long table near the hearth.

"Please, sit down," he said.

Nathaniel held Vivienne's chair, then took one next to her.

"I apologize for the disturbance, but the timing of your arrival...." He shared a look with the priest.

"I don't understand," Vivienne said.

"It is the full moon tonight. Miss Lawrence also disappeared on the day of the full moon. And the children...." The mayor swallowed.

Vivienne drew a deep breath. "Miss Lawrence is not only my ward. She works for an organization in London called the Society for Psychical Research, as do I. We have experience in dealing with creatures of the Devil. I might be able to help you find whatever it is that preys on this village."

Father Cernat looked surprised. The son, Andrei, didn't appear to understand German, for he frowned impatiently, muttering something to his father in Magyar. The innkeeper made a quelling gesture.

"So you have such things in England?" the mayor asked. "In truth, I didn't expect you to believe." He seemed about to say something more, but fell silent.

"Oh, I believe," Vivienne replied dryly. "I've seen them myself. We call them ghouls. Spirits of the dead that return to plague the living."

The mayor nodded. "Yes, here we call them *strigoi*. But—"

He cut off as a plump woman emerged from the kitchens. She wore a loose white blouse tucked into a colorful embroidered skirt. A scarf covered her dark hair.

"My wife, Elena," Master Korzha said. "She has prepared an early supper for us."

Nathaniel gave her a charming smile. "Thank you, Mistress Korzha."

The innkeeper's wife brought out grilled sausage and cabbage soup, followed by a pork stew flavored with garlic and onions. A dusty bottle of red wine completed the meal. The food was plain but delicious. Nathaniel ate with gusto, praising Elena's cooking and declaring that he wished to bring the recipe back to his own cook. He did his best to make conversation, but there were few takers. Master Korzha wore a frozen, distracted smile. The mayor declined to eat anything, staring into his cup of wine.

Vivienne sensed mounting tension in the men, but it was no longer directed at her and Nathaniel. Andrei kept glancing out the window, his knee jittering beneath the table. The setting sun turned the sky a pale rose that tinted the snowy mountains and fields. Again, Vivienne was struck by the wild, desolate beauty of this country.

"Who found the children?" she asked gently, pushing her plate back half-eaten.

"Their father, the poor man," the mayor replied.

"Might it be possible to speak with him? I don't wish to intrude on his grief, but it's important that I know every detail."

The mayor seemed doubtful, but he nodded to Father Cernat.

"I will go ask them," the priest said softly. He rose and went out the door.

"Perhaps we can see Anne's room while we wait," Nathaniel suggested.

Master Korzha nodded wearily. "You may stay there tonight. I left it as it was. I kept hoping she might return."

He led them up a dark, narrow flight of stairs to the second floor and showed them into a surprisingly large room with a double bed and wardrobe. A wooden cross in the Byzantine style was fixed to the wall over the bed. A trunk sat against one wall. He pointed to it.

"That was hers. Please, rest and refresh yourselves." Master Korzha left, closing the door behind him. They heard his footsteps retreating back downstairs.

"He seems a decent enough fellow," Nathaniel said.

"He's hiding something," Vivienne replied, walking over to the trunk.

"Do you think he had something to do with it?"

"I don't know. At least he's human, though I wonder about the rest of them."

Nathaniel gave her a sharp look. "How can you be sure?"

"Ghouls are crude facsimiles. They can pass, but only in dim light and if you don't look too closely. They're the weakest spirits, preying mainly on animals, children and the elderly. Wights are more evolved. They're faster and stronger and a few can speak in their victim's voice. Both can be subdued with iron." She shrugged. "After you've encountered enough of them, you simply know."

Vivienne unlatched Anne's trunk and opened the lid. It held clothes and a toiletry case with a silver comb and brush, along with a stack of books. She piled everything on the bed and Nathaniel helped her sort through it. Knowing Anne's fondness for hidden compartments, Vivienne ran her hands along the sides and bottom, but it was only an ordinary steamer trunk. There was no diary or half-finished letter hidden away — no clue at all as to where she went.

"That was a beastly journey, and an even beastlier arrival," Nathaniel muttered, eying the bed with longing.

"I should have been better prepared for it," Vivienne said with a wan smile. "But don't get too comfortable, love. No rest for the wicked. Not just yet."

A soft knock came on the door, summoning them back down to the common room where Father Cernat waited.

"The family will see you," he said. "But we must go now, before full dark."

CHAPTER 3

Nathaniel fetched her cloak and his own greatcoat, and they followed the priest into the village. As before, the lanes were empty of people, but frightened, hostile faces watched from the windows, shutters banging closed as they passed. More than one made the sign of the evil eye.

"The father's name is Cristian," Father Cernat said. "But he doesn't speak German."

"I know some Hungarian," Vivienne said. "Will that work?"

The priest nodded. "Marius and Daniela were their only children." He crossed himself, touching the silver crucifix around his neck. "It is a terrible tragedy."

At last, they reached a small, poor house at the edge of the village. Smoke came from the chimney, which tilted at an off-kilter angle from the thatched roof. Two skinny pigs rooted in the muddy yard.

Father Cernat called out a greeting and the door was opened by the same man who had nearly shot them two hours before. He drew a sharp breath, studying Vivienne and Nathaniel with an intense stare, then took a step back and wordlessly gestured for them to enter.

The room was dark and cold despite the small fire burning in the hearth. A young woman sat staring into the flames. Her head turned as they entered, but her expression was one of utter weariness and disinterest. A very old woman sat next to her, holding her hand. A shawl covered her bony shoulders and her eyes were cloudy with cataracts.

"Thank you for allowing us into your home," Vivienne said in Magyar. "I'm very sorry for your loss."

There was no reaction from the younger woman, but Cristian nodded brusquely. "Father Cernat said you came to hunt this devil." His fists clenched. "If that is so, I am willing to answer your questions."

They took stools near the fire. Cristian stood next to his wife, one hand resting on her shoulder. She stared into the flames again, her eyes distant.

"How much do you know?" he asked.

"Almost nothing. Only that the children were killed by some kind of beast."

His jaw set. "Then I will tell you all of it. It was eight weeks ago, just a few days before Christmas. We had a dog, full-grown but still a pup. Around dusk, he went into a frenzy of barking. I went outside to see what had set him off, but he'd scrabbled at the gate and somehow managed to open it. The children were playing in the back while I chopped wood for the stove. Marius was twelve, old enough to be trusted. He wanted to go look for the dog, and I let him, God help me."

The young mother's eyes tightened for a moment. She seemed in another world, but she was listening.

"Daniela insisted on going, too. I told them to come back by dark no matter what. I figured the dog had caught the scent of a deer. When they didn't return an hour later, I went looking for them." He drew a deep breath. "It was a full moon and I could clearly see the tracks of the dog and the children in the snow. They had crossed yonder field" — he pointed out the window —

"and entered the forest. I'd only gone a short way into the trees when I found the dog."

Cristian drew a shuddering breath. "He'd been gutted. I found the children not much farther on. The blood ... it looked black in the moonlight. There was so much, I knew they were gone. But I touched them to be sure. The poor wee things were so cold."

He broke into a sob and Father Cernat rose. "If it is too hard, we can return tomorrow."

"No!" His voice was savage. "I'll not tell the tale again. Better to finish it and be done." Cristian wiped the sleeve of his threadbare coat across his eyes. "I ran back to the village and got help. A dozen men went to the forest with me and brought the poor things back. We put them in the church and set a vigil. The next morning, we oiled our shotguns and went out hunting the wolf that killed them. No fresh snow had fallen. In the light of day, the tracks were clear. Great paw prints leading deeper into the forest. We followed them, determined to bring the beast to bay."

He paused, an oddly defiant look on his face. "The tracks changed from paws to the bare feet of a man. Two dozen others saw them. They'll swear to it. The tracks led a mile or so into the woods and then vanished into thin air at the edge of a ravine."

"It is a *pricolici*," the blind grandmother said in a strong voice. "That much is clear."

Vivienne raised her eyebrows.

"A werewolf," Father Cernat said. He gave her a steady look, as if daring her to contradict it.

"An unclean thing," the grandmother muttered. "In the day, they walk as a man. But the beast lives inside. When the moon comes, it brings the change."

Nathaniel had gotten the gist of it. He shared a disturbed look with Vivienne.

"Do you believe the *pricolici* comes from this village?" Vivienne asked.

Father Cernat replied. "Naturally, the people were very afraid.

Suspicion fell on a woodcutter, a solitary fellow who lived alone in the forest not far from where the children were discovered. The men went to his house, intending to drag him back here for questioning. They found him dead, torn up in a similar fashion." He gave a sigh. "I examined the body myself. It was clear this was no ordinary wolf. The savagery...."

"And the children?"

"The same."

A terrible moan erupted from the young woman. She turned to Vivienne and Nathaniel with blazing eyes.

"Leave my house," she hissed, pressing her hands over her ears. "For the love of God and the Saints, I cannot bear to hear another word. Just get out!"

Vivienne stood smoothly, murmuring apologies. She thanked Cristian, who stared at his wife with pity and embarrassment. He did not reply.

"I'm sorry—" Father Cernat began as they stepped into the twilight.

"Please, don't be," Vivienne said firmly. "She had every right to throw us out. I wouldn't have troubled them at all if it wasn't necessary." She shook her head. "I can't imagine what they're going through."

"Do you have children, Lady Cumberland?" he asked as they walked back toward the inn.

All the shutters of the cottages were firmly latched now, glimmers of light coming through the crevices.

"No, though I think of Anne as a daughter."

He nodded solemnly. "And you believe us?"

"I do." She glanced at Nathaniel. "As does Lord Cumberland. Don't you, dear?"

He started. "What? Oh yes, of course."

She followed his gaze to the palisade of sharpened stakes. A group of men were driving a wagon into the gap where the road entered the village.

"They will keep a watch tonight," Father Cernat said. "With dogs. Cristian's must have scented the *pricolici*."

Vivienne nodded in approval. "Yes, dogs have a nose for the unnatural. They would give us a warning." She glanced at the priest. "Did they bark on the night Anne disappeared?"

"No."

She frowned in thought. "You said suspicion immediately fell on the woodcutter, but was anyone else unaccounted for at the time of the killings?"

He gave a tired shrug. "These families go back generations. Everyone knows everyone. Nobody was seen out that night, but it doesn't mean they weren't. By the time Cristian found the bodies, enough time had passed for the devil to creep back under cover of darkness." He stared out at the palisade, where men were lighting pitch torches and placing them around the perimeter. "There was no wall then."

"But surely the murderer would have been covered in blood," Nathaniel said.

"One would think so," Vivienne said thoughtfully. "It must have created much discord here."

"The fear is a poison that eats away at us," the priest agreed sadly. "Neighbors no longer trust each other. Old grudges are being aired. There have already been two drunken fights at the inn. Master Korzha stopped serving beer." His face darkened. "I pray this devil came from elsewhere, but if he walks among us, we will catch him tonight."

"What do *you* think?"

"I think the *pricolici* is an outsider," he said, although she detected a slight hesitation. "I cannot believe any of my parishioners could be such a monster." They reached the end of the lane and he pointed. "That is our church. We have a very beautiful organ." There was pride in his voice.

"Might we see it?" Vivienne asked.

Father Cernat hesitated.

"We won't stay long."

"For a few minutes," he agreed reluctantly. "Then you must go to your rooms and lock the door, as all godly folk will do this night."

The church was a humble whitewashed building, though it boasted a tall steeple. Vivienne's gaze lingered on the three fresh graves in the cemetery. Father Cernat saw her looking.

"The children were buried with silver crosses, to protect them. Their family is poor, but good Mistress Elena insisted they accept the gift."

"And the woodcutter?" Nathaniel asked.

"We drove a stake through his heart," Father Cernat replied grimly.

"*Does that work?*" Nathaniel mouthed at Vivienne as the priest strode ahead of them.

She shook her head.

They entered the church and he showed them the organ, which was indeed splendid. Bright, intricate paintings of various religious themes adorned the walls.

"What other villages are nearby, besides Satinari?" Vivienne asked.

"There is one about ten miles away, over the passes. And the Monastery of Saint George, of course."

"How many monks live there?"

"About thirty." He frowned. "What are you suggesting?"

"Nothing," Vivienne said quickly. "But I wonder if Anne showed any interest in it?"

He thought for a moment. "Not directly. She came to see the church and was admiring the paintings. I told her that Saint George's is famous for its frescoes." He smiled. "They're much grander than ours."

"Did she say anything about going there?"

He shook his head. "Not to me. It's a distance of about six

miles by the road. A hard walk in the snow." He looked at the door. "I think you'd best return to the inn now."

"Yes, thank you for everything, Father Cernat, you've been very kind."

"I wish I could have been of more help. I will pray for Miss Lawrence tonight." His chin lowered to his bushy red beard. "For all of us."

They stepped outside into the darkness. Six men were hunkered down around a fire near the wagon. One of them was the innkeeper's son Andrei, who looked at them without expression for a moment before turning away. Vivienne saw the gleam of shotguns. A pair of sheepdogs sat on their haunches nearby, tongues lolling.

Over the black wall of the Carpathians, a full moon was rising.

Master Korzha and his wife waited in the common room. The moment they stepped inside the door, he slid the bolt shut. "Did you speak to Cristian?" he asked anxiously.

Vivienne nodded. "He told us everything."

Master Korzha's shoulders sagged. "I'm sorry," he said. "I should have warned Miss Lawrence. Perhaps she would not have gone out if I had. But I feared she would never believe me."

Vivienne gave him a kind look. "It's not your fault. I'm sure Anne suspected the truth. It sounds as if she made her own quiet inquiry."

He nodded, relief on his face.

"I have to confess, I've never encountered this situation before, but I hope to get to the bottom of it."

"Do you think the beast will come back tonight?" Elena asked anxiously.

It might already be here, Vivienne thought, but she refrained from saying the words aloud. These people were frightened enough.

"If it does, I'm sure the dogs will catch the scent," she said reassuringly.

The innkeeper and his wife bade them goodnight and retreated to their quarters on the ground floor as Vivienne and Nathaniel climbed the stairs to their room. She lit the candles and dug out her pack of Oxford Ovals.

"Goddess, I've been dying for a smoke," Vivienne murmured, exhaling a long stream of smoke.

"Give me one of those," Nathaniel said. "I wish I had a tot of stiff brandy to go with it."

Vivienne smiled and took a silver flask from her valise.

"Darling," he sighed, lighting his own cigarette. "Now I remember why I married you."

They sat on the bed, smoking and sharing the flask.

"Shouldn't we be manning the barricades?" he asked.

"Those men don't want us there. If anything happens, we'll hear the barking."

"I might take the dogs from the kennel when I return to Eridge Castle. Let them sleep with me."

Vivienne laughed. "That old heap is already full of ghosts and they haven't troubled you yet."

"True. But this place is getting to me. When the old blind woman started talking about the *pricolici*, the hair on my neck stood up." He shook his head and took a long drag. "Why are wolf-men so bloody terrifying?"

Vivienne swallowed a swig of brandy, feeling the warmth spread through her chilled limbs. "They symbolize the beast that lurks in all of us. The one civilized society pretends doesn't exist."

He gave her a crooked smile. "The Earl of Pembroke is hairy enough to be half wolf. He left fur on my sheets."

She frowned. "You make a jest of everything."

Nathaniel sobered. "I know. Men like Dr. Clarence, you mean."

"He was something else entirely." She sighed, pushing the

bitter memories of her last case away. "I think we should go up to that monastery tomorrow. It's the only place of interest for miles and Anne clearly left of her own accord."

"I brought a guidebook, let's see what it says."

Nathaniel rummaged through his bag while Vivienne collected Anne's books together and reclined on the bed, scanning the titles.

"Korzha thought Anne was an innocent, but she suspected before she even arrived." She brandished *The Book of Werewolves: Being an Account of a Terrible Superstition* by Sabine Baring-Gould.

"Have you ever come across one? A real one?"

"No, but I've seen enough strange things in my life not to rule anything out."

It was quiet for several long minutes as they read in the flickering candlelight. Vivienne first scanned the book on Transylvanian superstitions she'd brought from London, searching for references to *pricolici*, then moved on to Sabine Baring-Gould.

"Find anything useful?" Nathaniel asked, tipping the empty flask to his lips with a disappointed sigh.

"Here's a relevant passage. *'First cousin to the vampire, the long exploded were-wolf of the Germans is here to be found, lingering yet under the name of the Prikolitsch. Sometimes it is a dog instead of a wolf, whose form a man has taken either voluntarily or as penance for his sins.'*"

"Who would voluntarily take the form of a wolf? And how would one even go about it?"

"Not a clue." She yawned. "Sell one's soul to the Devil, I suppose."

"I thought you didn't believe in the Devil."

"Not with a capital D." She thought of the Duzakh. "But I do believe in evil. Have you ever heard of Gilles de Rais?"

Nathaniel shook his head.

"The case is mentioned in here." She waggled the Baring-Gould book. "He was a French baron who lived in the early

43

1400s. Fought alongside Joan of Arc during the Hundred Years' War against your Lancaster ancestors. They eventually appointed him Marshall of France." Her gaze darkened. "He also had a taste for murdering children. His victims are thought to number in the hundreds. Everyone knew about it, but he was powerful enough to fend off justice for years. He was finally tried and hanged in 1440."

"Bastard. But why is he in the wolfie book?"

"I honestly don't know. He was never accused of lycanthropy. I'm merely making a point. There are plenty of human monsters in the world." Vivienne closed the book. "As for the others, it's mainly cases of lunatics who committed murder under the delusion they were wolves. The author isn't a believer, but he does pen a witty turn of phrase."

She lit another cigarette and read aloud in a plummy voice. *"The werewolf may have become extinct in our age, yet he has left his stamp on classic antiquity, he has trodden deep in Northern snows, has ridden rough-shod over the medievals, and has howled amongst Oriental sepulchres. He belonged to a bad breed, and we are quite content to be freed from him and his kindred, the vampire and the ghoul."*

"A bad breed," Nathaniel echoed softly.

"There's more…. *'Yet who knows! We may be a little too hasty in concluding that he is extinct. He may still prowl in Abyssinian forests, range still over Asiatic steppes, and be found howling dismally in some padded room of a Hanwell or a Bedlam.'"*

"You're giving me the shivers again, darling."

"So we could be dealing with a man who thinks he's a wolf." She closed the book with a sigh. "Or simply real wolves. Though I believe them about the tracks and those are rather hard to explain away." She frowned and looked over his shoulder. "What about you?"

Nathaniel cleared his throat theatrically and tilted the book so she couldn't see it. "The Monastery of Saint George dates back to the rule of Stephen the Great, mid-sixteenth century. Like Father Cernat said, it's quite famous for its murals. Scenes from the Old and New Testament ... blah, blah, blah. Here's something. It seems the Romanian princes were crafty buggers. When the Turks forbade them from building fortresses, they went ahead and did it anyway but claimed they were monasteries. Saint George's is one of those. It has enormous buttresses." He waggled his blond eyebrows.

"You're a silly man."

"I hope so, you'd be bored of me otherwise. Now listen. After Stephen died, all the provinces fell under Ottoman rule, but they permitted a large degree of autonomy. I bet lots of loot was stashed away in the monasteries to hide it from the conquerors."

"Are you game to ride up there and find out?"

"Of course." He paused and looked heavenward. "Though I'm such an awful sinner, God might strike me down if I try to enter."

"Just keep your hands to yourself," she laughed. "Half those monks are awful sinners, too."

Nathaniel grinned and crawled under the covers, setting his revolver next to the bed. Vivienne donned her nightgown, a white cotton shift with lace at the bosom. She unbraided her hair, which immediately sprang back into tight curls. Then she positioned an iron dagger so that she could roll over and grab it at a moment's notice. Vivienne blew out the candle and listened to Nathaniel's even breathing, but it was a long time before she fell asleep.

She thought about Alec and wondered what he was doing at that moment. She could sense him through the gold cuff around her wrist, but faintly. The permanent ache in his right leg was the strongest sensation. It was a product of the bonding process, which maimed Alec but not Vivienne. In theory, the cuff also gave her control over his elemental magic, though she never abused that.

Vivienne idly stroked the cuff, tracing the roaring griffin with one fingertip. It was the sigil of the Persian emperor Artaxerxes II, though few would recognize it now. She and Alec had been bonded for a very long time, yet there were parts of him she still didn't fully understand. His quiet demeanor masked deep currents. And their last case had taken a heavy toll on him.

Vivienne closed her eyes and tried not to think of Dr. Clarence.

In the small hours of the night she dreamt of a dog barking and lurched into wakefulness, one hand groping for the iron blade next to the bed, but all was quiet.

CHAPTER 4

A light snow was falling outside when Vivienne woke the next morning. She braided her hair and donned a high-necked wool gown and thick stockings. The water in the wash basin was freezing cold, but a quick splash to her face banished the last remnants of sleep. Nathaniel murmured groggily as she tweaked his ear, swatting her hand away.

"What time is it?" he groaned.

"Time for lazy lords to get up," she said, yanking the covers back.

He wore only a short linen nightshirt, open at the throat, and Vivienne had a fleeting but heartfelt pang of regret that their marriage was a sham. Nathaniel sat up, raking a hand through his blond hair.

"Nothing happened last night?"

"No, I'm sure we would have heard a commotion." She lifted an eyebrow. "Perhaps it's not what they think."

"Or the beast struck elsewhere," he said darkly, peering out the window at the drifting snow.

The wagon was still in place at the palisade, but there was no one about. The men must have headed back to their homes for a hot breakfast once daylight came. Vivienne could see the cold remains of the bonfire.

"I'll meet you downstairs," she said, lacing up her boots and sliding the daggers into hidden sheathes cunningly sewn into her skirts.

A fire roared in the common room and Vivienne held her palms to it, relishing the warmth. A minute later, Mistress Elena emerged from the kitchen and greeted her with a smile.

"Any news?" Vivienne asked.

"The men patrolled all night, but it was quiet."

"I'm relieved to hear it. Is Master Korzha about? I'd like to ask him something."

"He went out, but he should be back shortly. In the meantime, I give you breakfast."

Vivienne took a table by the window and Mistress Elena brought a bowl of porridge called *mamaliga*, along with fried eggs and thick slices of ham. Nathaniel wandered down and ate with her, his blue eyes bright with anticipation. He loved to ride and was no doubt eager to escape the stifling atmosphere of Mara Vardac.

"Master Korzha," Vivienne said as the innkeeper bustled in, stamping snow from his boots.

"Ah, good morning. It seems you bring us luck. The village was spared last night."

"It's a good omen. I was hoping to hire two horses. We plan to visit Saint George's Monastery today and view the murals. It's possible the brothers might have seen Miss Lawrence."

He frowned. "Are you sure it's safe to travel alone? The beast—"

"Strikes on the full moon, which is now past. It's not so far. We should be back well before dark. If not, we can stay the night there."

He innkeeper nodded reluctantly. "Come to the stable when you're ready, I have a pair of geldings you can take."

Nathaniel didn't bother haggling over the price, though it turned out to be exorbitant. They were Master Korzha's only horses and he seemed to think there was a fair chance he might never see them again. A short while later, they rode out through the gap in the palisade, turning north this time into the foothills of the mountains. A layer of fresh snow blanketed the road. Other than the tracks of birds and small animals, they saw no sign that anything had come near Mara Vardac in the night. The scene was tranquil, the sun occasionally breaking through the clouds.

"Maybe it was a wolf after all," Nathaniel said. "If the beast came upon the woodcutter and chased him, that might account for the tracks."

"They said the feet were bare."

"I'll admit that's peculiar. But we have only their word for it." He glanced at the village dwindling behind them. "I think those people were prepared to believe the worst. I'm not mocking them, but they are rather backwards."

Vivienne pulled her hood up. "Something terrorized Mara Vardac. And in my experience, it won't stop until it's put down."

She wondered if Anne had discovered the *pricolici*'s identity. If so, she could have gone out to hunt it in the forest and been hurt. It was a possibility Vivienne had to face. But the tracks indicated the work of a single individual and she couldn't believe Anne would fall victim to some jumped-up man-wolf. She was a daëva, faster and stronger than any human by many magnitudes. And she had her own powers, ones Nathaniel knew nothing about.

No, Vivienne decided, more likely she caught another scent and followed it without telling anyone. That would explain why there had been no more killings.

The road wound through a series of steep, wooded valleys and then rose toward the mountains again. Heavy clouds moved in and the snow grew thicker, settling in drifts that slowed the horses.

"I hope it isn't much farther," Nathaniel called over the wind. "The poor creatures are tiring."

Vivienne studied the crude map Master Korzha had sketched for them. "It should be just ahead."

They entered a sheltered pass where the snow was thinner. A few minutes later, the view widened again and she saw the abbey a quarter mile on, surrounded by hills of fir and oak. With its high stone walls, the Monastery of Saint George did indeed resemble a medieval fortress. Sturdy towers with thin slits for windows anchored the four corners. The road led straight to an imposing gatehouse with heavy wooden doors. They rode up, pausing to admire the archway and a painting above it, at least twenty feet high, of Saint George flanked by two angels. Nathaniel pounded a gloved fist on the doors until they heard a scraping sound on the other side. A moment later, a black-clad figure peered up at them through the falling snow.

"Good afternoon," Nathaniel said cheerfully in German. "I am Lord Cumberland and this is my wife, Lady Vivienne. We're staying down the road in Mara Vardac. We've come to speak with the abbot about a personal matter."

The monk cast them a quick, nervous glance. He was of middle years and wore a long beard like Father Cernat and a flat-topped black cap of the Romanian Orthodox style, which looked rather like a stovepipe hat without the brim. He opened the gates wide and they spurred the horses through the outer wall. Once they were inside the gatehouse, he dropped a heavy wooden bar into brackets to seal the gate again.

They trotted through a second archway and emerged into the monastery grounds. Vivienne looked around, her keen gaze taking in every detail. To the right lay a vaulted refectory built in the Gothic style. To the left was a low stone building that housed the stables, and beyond it, the church itself. It looked like a miniature fortress, very tall and narrow with ornate engravings and a soaring bell tower. Scattered other outbuildings stood in the church's shadow, the roofs capped with snow. The monk led them to the stables, where they dismounted and passed the reins to a teenaged boy who led the horses away.

Another wordless gesture signaled they should follow the monk to the refectory. Once inside, they passed into a deserted, bitterly cold dining hall. The monk signed at them to wait there and hurried down the corridor, turning the corner. They stood for a long minute, trying not to shiver.

"Chatty fellow," Nathaniel remarked. "Perhaps he doesn't speak German."

"Oh, I think he understood perfectly," Vivienne replied in a low voice. "When we see the abbot, you'd better do the talking. I doubt he'll be comfortable around a woman and I don't want to put him off."

"At your service." Nathaniel grinned. "You see, I told you I'd be useful—"

He broke off as the monk returned and led them from the dining hall and down a long passageway. The walls were bare stone but the floor was laid in a diamond pattern of intricately painted maroon and white tiles. The monk paused in front of a door and bade them to enter.

A small fire burned in a grate, though the room was still chilly. A stained glass window allowed daylight into the chamber, which was dominated by a large desk covered with neat stacks of paper. A man in his early thirties sat behind the desk, his black-sleeved arms resting on an open book. He had shoulder-length dark blond hair and a fine-boned, intelligent face, though his eyes were bloodshot as if he hadn't slept. A pale beard covered his cheeks.

"Brother Grigori says you came from Mara Vardac," he said in excellent German. "I am the abbot, Father Gavra."

"Thank you for seeing us. Lord Cumberland of Sussex, Father," Nathaniel said with a little bow. "And this is my wife, Lady Vivienne."

The abbot gave Vivienne a respectful nod. "It is a pleasure," he said, switching smoothly to English. "What brings you all the way to Saint George's? We have few sightseers in the dead of winter. This countryside is unforgiving if you stray from the road." He glanced out the window. "Snowing hard again. You were brave to risk it." When he looked back at them, his eyes held curiosity and a slight wariness.

"We traveled from London in search of our ward, Anne Lawrence," Nathaniel explained. "She disappeared from her room at Mara Vardac a month ago."

Vivienne produced the cameo and held it out so he could see.

Father Gavra's brows creased. "Of course, the English girl. You mean she didn't return?" He stared at them with a stricken expression.

Vivienne's heart beat faster. "Anne was here?"

"Oh, yes. She came on foot." He seemed a little bewildered by this. "Alone. She spent the afternoon here. I urged her to stay in the guest quarter and leave the next morning, but she insisted on going."

"What did she want?"

"She asked the see the frescoes, but she seemed more interested in our library. It is very fine and old." He hesitated. "All the brothers have taken vows of silence save for the two most senior who are responsible for the day-to-day affairs of the monastery. You are welcome to speak with them. Miss Lawrence spent most of her time here with our librarian, Brother Florin."

The abbot rose and led them out of the study into the passageway. "Forgive me if I seem distracted, but we suffered our own tragedy last night," he confided as they walked through the refectory. "Our infirmarian, Brother Adrian, was killed by a wolf. It is not unheard of, though never inside the monastery walls." He frowned. "No one saw or heard anything. We still haven't determined how the beast got in. One of the brothers must have forgotten to latch the postern gate."

Nathaniel shot a look at Vivienne, who nodded.

"Father Gavra," he said, touching the abbot's sleeve and drawing him to a stop. "Did Anne bring you any news from the outside?"

He shook his head, perplexed.

"There was an attack on Mara Vardac. Two children and a man are dead."

The abbot crossed himself. "When did this happen?"

"Late December, about a week before Christmas."

Father Gavra shook his head. "I'm surprised Miss Lawrence didn't mention it." He studied Nathaniel's face. "There's more. Was it a wolf?"

Nathaniel paused. "The villagers think there's a *pricolici* on the loose."

The abbot's brows lifted. Vivienne watched his reaction closely, but it was difficult to read.

"What is their reason for believing so?" Father Gavra asked evenly.

"They say the wolf tracks turned to those of a man."

"I see." The abbot fingered the silver cross around his neck. "Did you observe these tracks yourself?"

"No, but Lady Cumberland spoke with the children's father. He was adamant and said a dozen men saw the tracks and would swear to it. But that is not all. The attacks on the village occurred on the night of a full moon. Anne's disappearance came four weeks later — also on a full moon. And you say a monk was attacked last night."

The abbot shifted uneasily. His gaze grew distant. "Only Brother Adrian's footprints were visible leading out to the garden. I saw no other tracks, but assumed they were covered by the falling snow. He was not found for some hours."

Vivienne stepped forward. "Father Gavra, I must ask you to have faith. We came for Anne Lawrence, but also to find the truth of what happened in Mara Vardac. The village was spared last night, but it seems the hunting grounds have moved."

He gave a reluctant nod. "As I said, wolf attacks in these parts are not unheard of. The poor children.... Well, they would be easy prey. But it is rare for wolves to approach a full-grown man."

"Where are you keeping the body?" Vivienne asked.

"In the infirmary."

"With your permission, we need to see it." She fished a card from her pocket. It had *The Society for Psychical Research* in black cursive with the emblem of the Greek letter *psi*, which resembled a trident. "I represent an organization in London that investigates such things in collaboration with the Crown and the British government. Things beyond the scope of ordinary understanding. I don't know if it is indeed a *pricolici*, but I have dealt with similar creatures."

The abbot accepted the card, though he barely glanced at it. He looked shaken.

"My parents told stories — everyone has one, about the friend of a distant cousin who saw a *pricolici* or vampire — but I've always taken a more modern view." He gave a faint smile. "You are surprised? Well, we are not all still living in the Dark Ages, though it might appear so. I studied theology at Balliol College in Oxford." He sighed. "And yet now I find myself a child again, afraid of shadows in the night."

So that explained his fluency in English. Vivienne found herself liking Father Gavra. He had an earnest, open-minded quality that was far from what she'd expected in such a remote backwater.

"We won't disturb the body, only examine it," she promised. "Perhaps it will help rule out any supernatural explanation."

"I hope so," the abbot said wearily. "I cannot believe God would allow such a monster into his house."

They went to the infirmary, which occupied a separate building adjacent to the refectory. Like the rest of the monastery, it was frigid inside. Father Gavra gestured to the cold hearth.

"We only set a fire when there are patients to care for," he explained.

The rectangular room was divided into two sections. The closer part had shelving with jars and bundles of dried herbs hanging from the ceiling. The rear had six beds in two rows of three pushed against the wall. Five were empty. The last held a figure laid out under a sheet.

"It is a difficult sight," the abbot said quietly, making the sign of the cross. "Poor Brother Adrian."

"Perhaps you could tell us exactly what happened," Vivienne said.

"Of course." Father Gavra visibly gathered himself. "He was last seen at *Miezonoptică*, what you call the Midnight Office. The brothers assembled in the church for the service, then returned to their cells. When Brother Adrian did not appear at Matins, I grew concerned. He never missed any of the canonical hours. I stopped in his room after, but it was empty, his bed unslept in."

"What time was Matins?"

"About four-thirty. It was still dark out when it ended. I feared he might have fallen ill. A search was mounted, first of the church and refectory, then the outbuildings. Two of the brothers finally found his body in the infirmary herb garden, lying near to the stone wall. The body was blanketed in several inches of snow so he must have been dead for some hours."

"And no one else missed the Midnight Office or Matins?" Nathaniel asked.

Father Gavra shook his head. "But there was a period of roughly three hours when the brothers had returned to their cells to rest. He must have been attacked then."

"Didn't you wonder why he'd gone out to the garden in the middle of the night?"

"Of course. But it seemed obvious he'd been attacked by a

wild animal." Father Gavra's voice grew cool. "If I had known that three others were dead in the village, I would have ordered greater precautions. Your ward should have told us of the danger."

Why didn't she? Vivienne wondered. It was yet another piece of the puzzle that didn't fit.

"How long was Brother Adrian the infirmarian here?" she asked.

"About ten months now. He had his training from Brother Nicolae, who held the office for decades but is growing old and frail. When I saw Brother Nicolae's mind was becoming cloudy, I suggested he take on an assistant. He made no objection. That was several years ago. Over time, Brother Adrian took on most of the duties. I gave him the formal title…. Oh, I'd say it was last April or May. He was a bright young man. It's a terrible loss for all of us." Father Gavra gazed at the white-sheeted form and let out a sigh. "I suppose we'd better get on with it."

He gently folded the sheet back. Vivienne braced herself, but Adrian's face was untouched. He had thick black hair and sharp cheekbones. The skin was very white, as expected considering the degree of blood loss. Father Gavra drew the sheet down further and she saw his throat had been savagely torn, exposing the windpipe. It would have been an immediately fatal wound.

Father Gavra swallowed hard at the deep gouges across the monk's chest. The body had been washed and a set of four claw marks were clearly visible.

"It does appear to be consistent with an animal attack," Vivienne said.

"Bear or wolf," Nathaniel agreed. He drew a deep breath. "Though if it was driven by hunger…." He trailed off.

"Why didn't it eat him?" Father Gavra finished quietly. "I wondered about that myself."

He'd left the sheet covering the young monk's torso for the sake of decency. Vivienne studied the wounds. Ghouls drained their victims through puncture marks at the throat or wrist, but she'd never seen this kind of mutilation.

"Are we done here?" Father Gavra asked, clearly uncomfortable.

"Almost. May I see his hands?"

He nodded reluctantly and lowered the sheet another few inches. The monk's hands lay folded across his bare torso.

"There." Vivienne pointed. Both Nathaniel and the abbot leaned in closer. "What do you make of that?"

Across the fleshy pad of the thumb joint, several indentations were clearly visible.

"My God, they look like human teeth marks," Nathaniel said softly.

Father Gavra's face paled nearly to the color of the corpse. He looked on the verge of fainting. Vivienne raised the sheet so it covered the body again.

"Come, Father," she said quietly. "Let's step outside for some air."

The infirmary door led to a garden enclosed by a low stone wall. Dry stalks of lavender and other herbs she didn't recognize poked through the snow. They waited while the abbot took several deep breaths.

"I'm sorry to put you through that," Vivienne said. "But you see now that the men of Mara Vardac spoke truly. This is no ordinary wolf."

"By all the saints, I cannot believe it," Father Gavra said hoarsely. "And yet I must."

Vivienne scanned the rectangular garden. It took only a moment to spot the place where the monk had been attacked. The snow was trampled down and a fresh coating failed to obscure the pinkish tint where blood had been spilled.

"Were any traces of blood found inside?" she asked.

Father Gavra shook his head.

"So he was either chased out here or he went to meet someone," she said thoughtfully. "Had he been chased, he would have raised the alarm, so the latter seems more likely. I'd guess he was killed quickly. The wounds to his throat would have rendered him unable to cry out."

"That seems plausible," the abbot agreed. His voice was stronger, though his face was still ashen.

Vivienne hesitated. "I know you don't wish to consider the possibility, but—"

"This demon likely walks among us?" he interrupted, an edge of bitterness in his voice. "I would prefer not to, but I cannot reject it outright. The evidence certainly points to someone familiar with the routine here."

"Can you think of any monks who have behaved strangely, out of character in any way, these last months?"

He considered the question for a long moment. "None come to mind. But my duties here revolve around overseeing the monastery as a whole. Other than conducting the daily services, I don't deal with the brothers as closely as our senior monks."

"Who would that be?"

"Brother Constantin and Brother Florin." He frowned. "I must tell them everything. We will conduct an investigation, but quietly. You must understand that this is a place of strict routine. Our day is structured around the canonical hours. Some people believe the calling to God is a life of ease, but that is not so. There are nine services a day, corresponding to the life, death and resurrection of Christ our Savior. When the brothers are not at prayer, they are hard at work in the kitchens, stables and elsewhere."

"How many monks live here?"

"Twenty-seven. We used to have thirty, but a plague came at the end of the summer and claimed three lives. It was only thanks to Brother Adrian that the number was not greater. He quarantined the sick and risked himself caring for them." A look of deep sadness came into his eyes. "Brother Adrian had no enemies. Everyone liked him."

"Can we speak to the senior brothers? They might have seen something amiss."

"I'll arrange it. You might as well start with Brother Florin. He's the librarian. I think I already told you, Miss Lawrence spent most of her time with him."

He gave Vivienne and Nathaniel a firm look. "But I would ask you not to reveal anything about Mara Vardac until I can tell him myself. I will say only that you have come looking for your missing ward. Our brothers are country folk, steeped in the old peasant superstitions. I've already heard mutterings about a *pricolici* despite the vows of silence. If these rumors are confirmed, it would cause a panic."

Vivienne nodded her agreement. "Yes, the villagers are living under a cloud of mutual suspicion. The tavern was closed after several fights broke out."

Father Gavra sighed. "Such things bring out the best and the worst in men. And there is another consideration. If it is indeed one of the brothers, revealing that we are hunting him could bring more bloodshed. There is nothing so dangerous as a cornered beast." His gaze was curiously penetrating. "Do you have faith, Lady Cumberland?"

She hesitated for a moment, formulating an answer he could accept. "I believe there are forces for both good and evil in the world."

He nodded. "As do I. Perhaps you were sent here to kill this creature."

Yes, she thought — *if only I had the first bloody clue how to go about it.*

"Do you know any of the old lore about how one destroys a *pricolici*?"

"Only a few stories. None specified any particular method."

He barked a desolate laugh. "If my grandmother were still alive, I would ask her. But she has been gone many years now."

Vivienne shared a look with Nathaniel. "I've seen risen dead, what you call *nosferatu*. The head must be separated from the body with an iron blade. But *pricolici* are new to me."

The bells in the church tower began to toll. Father Gavra turned toward the refectory.

"The brothers are gathering for the midday meal. Come, I will introduce you as guests. No doubt rumors are swirling about you already."

They crossed to the refectory and entered through a side door. It was barely warmer inside than out. Again, Vivienne was struck by the harsh life here. With nine services a day, scheduled around the clock, the monks must hardly sleep at all. She followed Father Gavra to the dining hall, where all the brothers were gathered at long tables for a meal of vegetable stew.

They were a mix of young and old, all wearing black robes and hats. It was a somber scene, silent except for the scrape of spoons in wooden bowls. As the abbot gave a terse speech in Romanian, she scanned their faces. Most avoided eye contact, discomfited by the presence of a woman. A few gazed back with expressions that ranged from curious to tense and uncertain. The killing had clearly shaken them.

One of you is not what he seems, she thought. *But which?*

Father Gavra beckoned and a monk in his late fifties rose to his feet. He had watery brown eyes and a timid face. Thin shoulders hunched inside his robe as he set his bowl aside and came over to them.

"Brother Florin, would you escort our guests to the library?" the abbot asked in Magyar.

The monk nodded, casting a nervous smile at the visitors.

"We can dine together later," Father Gavra said, switching back to English. "But for now I will leave you in the good hands of Brother Florin while I attend to other matters."

The shadow in his eyes left no doubt as to what those other matters might be.

"Please follow," Brother Florin said in Magyar. His voice was soft and rusty as if he didn't use it often.

Father Gavra signaled to a monk with a thick black beard and broad shoulders. He must be the other senior official the abbot had mentioned.

Brother Florin walked in the opposite direction, Vivienne and Nathaniel trailing behind. She could feel the monks' stares and looked back once before they turned the corner. A young monk watched her with an intense expression, though he glanced away the instant their eyes met.

Goddess, she thought, *the sooner we get out of here, the better.*

CHAPTER 5

Unlike Father Gavra, the librarian spoke neither English nor German. Vivienne understood enough Magyar to follow his stammered explanation that Anne had asked about books on local folklore, claiming to be a collector of old stories just as she had at Mara Vardac. The monastery didn't have anything like that, he said, digging out the ones Anne had showed an interest in. Most of the works were religious texts, though there were a few histories in Latin and Greek.

Nathaniel had studied both languages at school and Vivienne was content to pass those to on him. She chose some old maps of the region and a book in Romanian on the history of Saint George's. They took chairs near the narrow window, which admitted enough daylight to make out the spidery lettering in the books. Brother Adrian busied himself at a desk copying a manuscript, but she sensed he was keeping a sharp eye on her and Nathaniel.

The books must be extremely old. Her dear friend and colleague Cyrus Ashdown would have been thrilled to spend an afternoon with these dusty volumes. Vivienne, on the other hand, wondered if it wasn't a waste of time. She couldn't shake the feeling that Anne was somewhere close by, in trouble and needing her help. All her instincts warned her that something was amiss — worse even than at Mara Vardac.

The hours passed and the light began to fade. She looked up as the door opened and Father Gavra entered. He smiled at Brother Florin. "Would you excuse us for a moment?"

The librarian laid down his pen and shuffled out.

"I told Brother Constantin all of it," the abbot said in a low voice. "He was naturally quite shocked. I asked if any of the brothers had behaved strangely in recent days, but he could think of no one in particular. I wish I'd known of the attacks on the village earlier. I'm afraid that if the trail did indeed lead here, it has gone cold now."

"So no one was missing last night around the time of Brother Adrian's death?" Vivienne asked.

"If they were, it wasn't noticed. I ordered all the rooms to be searched under the pretext that someone had stolen food from the kitchens, but nothing was found."

Vivienne suppressed her disappointment. "Will Brother Constantin keep it to himself?"

"I made him swear on a rosary. He understands the need for secrecy." Father Gavra glanced at the books. "It's nearly time for Vespers. I must lead the service. Have you found anything?"

"Only one reference by Pausanias," Nathaniel said, brandishing a thick volume in Greek. "He relates the story of a young athlete named Damarchus who ate human flesh and was transformed into a wolf for nine years for his sin. As long as he abstained from cannibalism, he could regain his form as a man. But if he ate human flesh as a wolf, he would be condemned to live as a beast forever."

"What did he choose?" Vivienne wondered aloud.

"The story doesn't say."

"It doesn't seem much use," Father Gavra said glumly.

"No, but it's all I found." Nathaniel shrugged. "I don't know what Miss Lawrence was after."

Vivienne reached up to return one of the books to its shelf. Her sleeve fell back, revealing the thick gold cuff around her wrist. She turned and noticed the abbot's gaze.

"That's an unusual piece," he said, peering at it with narrowed eyes. "A winged griffin?"

She pulled her sleeve down and smiled. "An old family heirloom."

"It has the look of antiquity." He paused. "What do you wish to do? The hour grows late for a return journey to Mara Vardac. You're welcome to spend the night in our guest quarters. The room is simple, but it has a hearth. You should be comfortable there."

"That's very kind," Vivienne said. "We accept, don't we, dear?"

Nathaniel took the hint. "Yes, thank you. I don't fancy riding back down that road in the dark and I doubt the horses do, either. Do you think we might have a quick look at the church first? The village priest said it was famous."

Father Gavra gave him a wan smile. "Of course. It is on the way. We have just enough daylight left to view the paintings."

"I was reading about the history of Saint George's," Vivienne remarked as they left the library, which occupied the north end of the refectory, and crossed the inner cloister. Two monks passed on their way to the kitchens, carrying buckets of water from the well. Others were tossing handfuls of grain to some scrawny chickens. "It's endured troubled times."

The abbot nodded. "Yes, the first buildings date back to 1589. The defensive wall was erected some twenty years later after incursions by the Ottomans and the Tatars. The Voivode prince who built Saint George's used it as a hiding place during his wars with the Wallachians." He stopped in front of the massive church. The exterior walls were covered with huge, vivid frescoes.

"That is the Hymn of the Dead," he said. "And the Ladder of John Climacus."

They paused to examine the second more closely. At the top, a host of saints and angels in red robes hovered above the rungs of a long ladder leading to heaven, their haloes painted in bright gold. Their outstretched hands assisted the righteous, while the poor sinners tumbled through gaps in the rungs where devils waited below to inflict torment. Some dangled precariously from the ladder halfway up, tempted by demons of worldly passions.

"Is that a monk?" Nathaniel asked, squinting at a figure being devoured by the devil.

"Indeed," the abbot said quietly. *"For our struggle is not against flesh and blood, but against the rulers of the present darkness, the hosts of wickedness in heavenly places."*

"Ephesians 6:12," Nathaniel murmured.

Vivienne glanced at him in surprise.

"Sunday school." He grinned. "I'm not a complete heathen."

Vivienne wondered what Anne had made of the image. She must have seen it. Did she suspect the *pricolici* was here? The explicit parallel with fallen monks could hardly have been lost on her. And it might explain why she said nothing of what had happened at Mara Vardac.

"Well, it's a remarkable work, the colors have hardly faded," Vivienne said as they continued on. "And the monastery's namesake, Saint George? There was little mention of his origins."

"For shame, Vivienne," Nathaniel said with mock severity. "Every child knows he slayed a dragon. That's how he came to be the patron saint of England."

"Ah yes, the old dragon legend," Father Gavra said dryly. "I suspect it was apocryphal. Saint George was a young soldier in the Roman army. When the Emperor Diocletian began his persecution of Christians, he refused to convert to the pagan gods and was martyred. The date of his execution, April 23, 303, is a very important holiday in our calendar. The people decorate their houses with greenery to celebrate the rite of spring."

"The Romans crucified him?" Nathaniel asked.

Father Gavra's lips thinned. "Decapitation. Would you excuse me for a moment?" He strode ahead to meet a tall, burly monk who'd just emerged from the refectory. Vivienne recognized him as the one Father Gavra had summoned in the dining hall.

Nathaniel shot her a look. "Ironic, don't you think?" he whispered, blue eyes gleaming.

They stopped to watch as the abbot made a sharp gesture as if in reprimand. The other monk glanced at them, open hostility in his face. He had the burning eyes of a zealot. Father Gavra beckoned them over.

"Lord and Lady Cumberland, this is Brother Constantin," he said, switching to German. "He is in charge of the novices."

The monk gave them a brief, sour nod.

"Have any arrived in the last few months?" Vivienne asked.

"Two," the abbot replied, looking pointedly at Brother Constantin. "They came at the end of the summer."

The monk turned his heated gaze on Vivienne. "Karol and Vasile. But they are both good boys from good families. Their training keeps them under my eye all the time. Most likely the trouble comes from a stranger." He eyed them hard as he said this, the implication being that they had something to do with it.

Father Gavra frowned. "That is certainly possible, but we must keep open minds on the matter. These people are here to help. Do you remember anything about the day the young English girl came?"

"I only saw a glimpse of her. She spent the afternoon in the library, then left."

Vivienne noticed that he didn't look at her as he spoke.

"Very well," the abbot said. "Come to me straight away if you remember anything else."

The monk gave a curt nod and strode away. Father Gavra

turned back to them with a sigh. "Brother Constantin can be rough around the edges, but he means well. He's just frightened. I trust him to keep quiet."

"With your leave, I'd like to search the forest around the monastery in the morning," Vivienne said. "It's probably hopeless after four weeks, but there could be some sign of Anne."

"You believe she was followed after she left?"

"If she was attacked not far down the road, she might have tried to run back to the gates. Or...." She trailed off. "I don't know what I expect to find, but I must try."

"There are paths through the forest," Father Gavra said. "We can gather some of the younger brothers to aid in the search tomorrow."

They walked to a small stone building near the infirmary and the abbot produced a ring of keys, unlocking the door and swinging it wide. "This is the guest house. I will have a meal brought to you. I'd thought we might dine together in the refectory, but perhaps it would be better if you eat in your room. I don't want to disrupt the routine any more than it has been already."

"Thank you," Nathaniel said. "You're most kind."

Father Gavra gave a wry smile. "I cannot say I'm glad for the circumstances that brought you here, but it's something of a relief to have someone with ... experience in these matters. It is all so very strange. I hope Brother Constantin is right. The thought that such an abomination might be under our very roof...." He detached the key from the ring, handing it to Nathaniel. "After the meal is brought, you may lock your door from the inside tonight. May blessed Saint George keep you until morning."

They bade him goodnight and surveyed the stark quarters. There were two single beds of straw thatch, each with a large crucifix looming down from the wall above, and a rickety table with a bowl for wash water. Nathaniel lost no time lighting a merry fire in the hearth. A few minutes later, a knock came on the door, and one of the monks silently handed him a tray with two bowls of vegetable soup and a hunk of brown bread. Once he'd retreated, Vivienne turned the key in the lock and set it on the table.

"Do you really believe Anne is out there somewhere?" Nathaniel asked, tearing off a bite of bread and dunking it in the soup.

"No, but it would be foolish not to make a search." She set her bowl aside and lit a cigarette. "The *pricolici* is here, Nathaniel. I'm sure of that."

"But if it looks like a man, how can we tell who it is?" He balanced the soup on his knees and held his hands to the fire, rubbing them briskly together. "I don't fancy staying here four more weeks until the beast shows itself again."

"The fact that Brother Adrian was killed precisely between the end of the Midnight Office and the start of Matins implies this person has some degree of control over the transformation. So far, the killings have all occurred during full moons. Perhaps that's when he's at the height of his powers and can't resist the bloodlust. But we don't know for a fact that he can't change between the lunar cycles as well." She scowled. "We know almost nothing. I wish we had Cyrus. He'd know every bit of lore there was."

"There must be a way to tell. We just haven't found it yet."

Vivienne drew deeply on the cigarette. "We're not dealing with something in the same class as undead ghouls. This is a living man. How he came to be a wolf ... who bloody knows? But assuming he is one of the monks, he looks entirely normal between cycles. And that bite mark implies that the change is not perfect."

They were quiet for a moment.

"Maybe we need to start with the last victim, Brother Adrian. The children were almost certainly chosen because they left the safety of the village. The *pricolici* couldn't have anticipated their dog would escape and that they would follow. He might have killed the woodcutter first, and that's what riled up the dog. But it seems clear he preyed on the man because he lived in isolation."

"That makes sense," Nathaniel agreed. "But you're right. Why Brother Adrian? He seems a much greater risk than the other victims."

"Precisely." Vivienne frowned. "The abbot said he was well-liked, selfless and devoted, but there was something about his face that bothered me. A kind of sensuous arrogance that seemed odd for a monk."

"The poor bugger was killed horribly," Nathaniel pointed out. "His final expression wouldn't be one of serenity."

"I suppose so. But why him in particular?"

"It could have been another crime of opportunity."

"Perhaps." She tossed the cigarette into the fire.

"And if we don't find any trace of her tomorrow?"

"Then we must return to Bucharest and send letters to Cyrus and Henry Sidgwick. Track down some of the S.P.R.'s foreign agents locally. Maybe Alec is back in England by now. At the least, Cassandane can come." She was Cyrus Ashdown's bonded, a veteran fighter of the undead. "If the pattern holds, we have nearly four weeks before the next killing. What we need most is information."

Vivienne was grateful to have Nathaniel, but she felt uneasy without Alec. They always hunted together. *Always.* And she couldn't help but wonder why, if werewolves were real, they had never encountered one before. Again, Vivienne felt a tickle of apprehension.

"It's awfully convenient the monks have taken vows of silence," she said with a scowl. "We must rely on the abbot to conduct the investigation."

Nathaniel stretched out on the straw bed. "My money's on

Brother Constantin. I think he was lying when he said he hardly talked to Anne."

"So do I. Though he also obviously dislikes women."

"I caught that too. Sad bugger." He unbuttoned his coat and laid a palm on his shirtfront. He had nice hands, strong and tan even in winter. "They could all use a good shag, I'd reckon."

Vivienne laughed. "Temptation in heavenly places," she said, thinking of the grim mural on the church. "Don't assume they're as godly as they pretend."

"You have a filthy mind." He looked at her with amusement. "And we can't discount Father Gavra himself. He seems a nice enough chap, but I don't suppose that means much."

"I haven't. But he's a prominent figure, it would be harder for him to disappear for hours without anyone noticing. The village is five miles away. That's a long walk."

Nathaniel gave a thin smile. "For a man. But what about for a wolf? They're at home in these mountains. If you didn't take the road but rather a direct line through the forest, it would be less than three miles. Enough to kill and return without being discovered, if you were lucky."

"Or an accomplice covered for you," she added.

"That, too." He gave a nervous laugh. "Perhaps all of them are werewolves."

Vivienne didn't smile. Her gaze went to the locked door. For a brief, unpleasant moment, she imagined it exploding into splinters. "Then we're in trouble, darling."

They got ready for bed in a subdued mood. Nathaniel kicked off his boots and curled up under the thin blanket. Vivienne blew out the candles, her mind still chewing over all they'd discovered that day. It struck her as unlikely that Brother Adrian could be brutally killed in the cloister without a single witness seeing or hearing anything. The *pricolici* would have had to transform shortly after the end of the Midnight Office, when the other monks had gone to snatch a few hours of sleep between devotions. Why hadn't Brother Adrian done the same? What led him into the infirmary garden in the small hours of the night?

Surely his killer would have been covered in blood, yet Father Gavra claimed none was found inside the monastery.

She smoked in the darkness, turning over different scenarios. The faint sound of voices singing in the church for Compline came and went. It would be a few hours yet until the next service. Vivienne fell into a light doze.

Years of practice gave her the ability to wake at a chosen time. Her eyes flew open a few minutes before the Midnight Office. Speculation was pointless. She needed to get a feel for what the monastery was like at the time Brother Adrian had been attacked. She thought of waking Nathaniel to tell him where she was going, but he'd insist on coming. She didn't anticipate danger, but she also didn't want to be caught creeping about and she was better off doing it alone.

Vivienne put her boots and cloak on in the dark. She groped for the key to the door, her breath catching at the loud click of the tumblers. Nathaniel muttered in his sleep but didn't wake.

She raised her hood and eased the door open.

CHAPTER 6

Vivienne slipped out of the room, locking the door behind her. The church steeple cast a long shadow across the cloister. In the moonlight, the fresco depicting the Ladder of John Climacus was a dark blur. She stood in the darkness at the edge of the guest house as the monks filed out of the refectory and into the church.

When the doors closed again she followed the wall around to the opposite side. Perhaps it was foolish, but Vivienne felt if she could just watch the midnight service unseen, her instinct might point her in the right direction. On the surface, the *pricolici* would look like the others. But she had long centuries of experience with the supernatural. Surely this man would be marked somehow by his curse.

From the low sound inside, the service was being conducted in the nave, which lay at the front of the church. She found a small door in the rear and slowly cracked it open. Hundreds of candles illuminated the interior. The inside was as richly adorned as the outside, with life-sized paintings of archangels standing watch beneath the high clerestory windows, surrounded by rows of other saints, martyrs and apostles.

The black-robed brothers all faced the pulpit at the far end, where Father Gavra stood with his head bowed to an open book as he led them in prayer. Vivienne took a deep breath and eased the door open, stepping quickly to the shadows of a rear transept. She could see no way to go further without being seen.

Then the monks began to sing a hymn. She listened as their voices harmonized, rising and falling. For a moment, she understood why they endured such a hard, cold existence. The flickering candles and gilded icons of the soaring nave made the monastery seem a holy place for the first time since she'd arrived there. And the singing…. It had such reverence and beauty.

The chanting faded and she turned to slip out again when she heard a single voice, muttering softly but fervently. It was coming through a narrow wooden door to her left that sat slightly ajar.

At the front of the church, Father Gavra began to speak the Latin liturgy.

Vivienne pushed the door open on silent hinges and entered a small side chapel. An old man with sallow, sunken cheeks and a long white beard knelt before the altar. He was praying with closed eyes, a crucifix clutched in one gnarled hand. His voice was hoarse, some old Magyar dialect. A first it seemed unintelligible, but as he repeated the same words over and over, she caught the gist.

"God preserve us from evil…. Saint George preserve us…. Christ have mercy on us…."

A sudden footfall made her turn. Brother Constantin stood behind her, his face dark with anger.

"What are you doing here?" he hissed.

Vivienne forced a smile. "I heard the singing. It woke me." She pointed to the old man. "Who is that?"

"Brother Nicolae," he growled. "He is old and confused. He often wanders off."

The name was familiar. "Isn't that the infirmarian who trained Brother Adrian?"

Constantin didn't reply, but she knew she was right. He studied her with an unreadable gaze.

"Please return to your room," he said in a calmer tone. "I must see him back to his bed. He will catch a chill."

Vivienne glanced at the old monk, who still muttered his prayers with eyes squeezed shut. Brother Constantin took a step past her, moving between them. He kept his right hand clenched in a fist, but she could see he was missing two fingers. Constantin noticed her gaze. His lips twisted and he raised his hand. For a moment, Vivienne thought he meant to strike her. But he only waggled the maimed fingers.

"I was a woodcutter in my youth, before God called me," he rasped. "Near twenty years ago now."

The wounds could have been that old. The skin had healed over completely, leaving two stumps just below the knuckle. But they didn't look like they'd been taken by an axe. The stumps were irregular, scarred.

"Please," Brother Constantin said in a softer tone, lowering his hand. "I must help Brother Nicolae."

"Of course," Vivienne said. "I didn't mean to intrude."

She walked away, turning back in time to see Constantin with his hand around Brother Nicolae's arm, lifting him to his feet, though he appeared to be treating the old man gently.

She didn't think Father Gavra saw her leave the way she came in, though he would certainly hear about it from Brother Constantin.

I wonder what that was all about, she thought as she returned to the guest house and let herself inside. The abbot did say the old man was growing daft, but he seemed afraid of something. Did he see his young assistant get attacked? But why would he keep silent?

Perhaps because he feared Brother Constantin.

Or someone else.

She spent an uneasy night, waking again when the brothers filed out for Matins.

This place is full of secrets, Vivienne thought grimly in the darkness.

But I'll ferret them out.

CHAPTER 7

T hey ate a breakfast of bland porridge in the refectory with the abbot, Brother Florin and Brother Constantin. Florin ate listlessly, hardly touching his bowl. Vivienne assumed Father Gavra had told him about the *pricolici*, for he seemed preoccupied with dark thoughts. Brother Constantin also said little, watching the other monks with a wary expression. He made no reference to their encounter the night before, though his hostility was unabated. She felt it every time he glanced her way. The unspoken accusation that she and Nathaniel were somehow responsible for Brother Adrian's death — or perhaps that fear they would discover who *was*.

Across the table, Father Gavra spoke quietly with Nathaniel, asking about his estates in Sussex and relating tales of his student days at Oxford. He was animated and seemed grateful to have someone to talk to. Not for the first time she wondered if the abbot was suited to his calling. He should be teaching at university, she thought, not languishing in this frigid backwater. But that was Father Gavra's choice. Perhaps he was fleeing his own demons.

Florin and Constantin ignored her and Vivienne took the

opportunity to covertly study the other monks, who sat together at long tables. She sensed tension in the stiff way they ate, not looking at each other, though the source was unclear. Elderly Brother Nicolae was not present.

After the bowls had been cleared away by beardless novices, Father Gavra invited her and Nathaniel to attend the morning service, called First Hour, corresponding to the time when Christ was brought before Pontius Pilate. They sat in the back of the church, Vivienne impatient for it to end.

When the liturgy was over, most of the brothers went off to perform their daily chores, but the abbot held a dozen back. They gathered at the main gate beneath the image of Saint George. It was a gloomy morning, the sky heavy and grey as if promising more snow by afternoon. At a gesture from the abbot, a young monk stepped forward.

"This is Brother Karol. He escorted Miss Lawrence to the road the afternoon she left."

Vivienne remembered the name from when they'd met Brother Constantin. He was one of the newest monks. The same who had stared at her in the refectory the day before. Brother Karol's dark eyes met hers for an instant, then flicked away. A film of sweat covered his brow despite the chill air. Father Gavra noticed and frowned.

"Are you feeling ill?" he asked. "If so, you can be excused—"

Karol shook his head, his jaw set. His vows of silence prevented him from replying, but he indicated through gestures that he wished to help in the search.

"Very well," Father Gavra said. He turned to Vivienne. "There are a few paths the brothers use to gather firewood. We can start there."

He organized the monks into pairs, accompanying Brother Karol himself. The temperature had risen, turning the snow to slush. Vivienne and Nathaniel chose a path leading northeast.

Dark firs closed in around them as they entered the woods, scanning the path for any sign of Anne.

"I snuck out last night," she admitted when they were out of earshot of the other searchers. "Took a look around."

Nathaniel arched an eyebrow. "Let me guess. The abbot was leading a Black Mass stark naked while the others bayed at the moon."

Vivienne smirked. "Now that would have been a spectacle. But I'm afraid it wasn't quite so exciting." She told him what she'd seen the night before. "The old monk, Brother Nicolae, didn't seem confused, just afraid of something."

"He probably heard about the *pricolici*," Nathaniel suggested. "In a place like this, I imagine it's hard to keep a secret for long."

"Maybe. Or the old infirmarian knows something." She stepped over a fallen log. "I'd give much to question him alone, but Constantin has his eye on us now. I'm sure he told the abbot I was in the church, though I haven't been reprimanded yet."

"Father Gavra never said we couldn't leave the room," Nathaniel pointed out.

"True, but he also didn't issue an invitation." She dodged as a fir bough nearly dumped melting snow on their heads. "Either way, I imagine we'll be heading back to Mara Vardac this afternoon. And frankly, I can't say I'll miss this place in the least."

"You don't think we'll find anything then."

"I don't know. But I do believe it would take more than a *pricolici* to best Anne Lawrence."

A squirrel scolded them from a branch above, grey tail lashing in annoyance. They passed paw prints in the snow that Nathaniel identified as a fox, but there was nothing to indicate a larger animal had passed through recently, and not a sign of Anne. Vivienne stamped her feet, shaking snow from her boots. The slush had seeped inside her woolen stockings. She fervently wished she was in sunbaked Marrakesh — or wherever Alec had gone.

She was about to suggest they head back when a faint yell

came through the woods. Vivienne shared a look with Nathaniel. Fear closed a fist around her heart as they both ran toward the source of the shouting. Her skirts were divided for riding, but they still slowed her down. She swore as Nathaniel sprinted ahead, his long legs devouring the rocky ground.

On either side, she could see the dark shapes of other searchers closing in. The shouts were coming from the direction of the monastery and sounded like Father Gavra. Vivienne splashed through a creek, the water soaking the hem of her dress. Through the lattice of leafless branches she could see two figures struggling at the base of the high wall. One was the abbot, the other Brother Karol. The younger monk's eyes were wild, his face twisted into a bestial snarl. He held a knife in one hand.

Karol slashed at Gavra, who raised his arm in a defensive gesture. The blade raked across his palm. A backhand blow knocked the abbot to his knees. Karol spun around, his head swinging from side to side like an animal at bay. The other monks slowed as they approached, fear and confusion on their faces. With a roar, Brother Karol ran straight for Vivienne and Nathaniel.

She was reaching for her knives when Nathaniel drew his pistol and fired off four shots in quick succession. One went over Karol's head, but the other three hit home. He jerked and tumbled to the ground, where he lay unmoving in the snow. Vivienne halted, watching him warily.

"I tried not to aim for the heart…." Nathaniel sounded shaken. "I've never shot a man before, Vivienne."

Karol's eyes were closed, but the lids fluttered as if he were dreaming.

"He's alive," she said. "We'd better tie him up before he wakes."

They went over to Father Gavra, who had been helped to his feet by the other monks. He winced in pain, staring at Brother Karol.

"Jesu Christo," he muttered. "He went mad."

"What happened?" Nathaniel asked. He still held the pistol in his hand, the barrel pointed down, but his gaze kept flicking to the prone figure of Brother Karol.

"We were walking along the wall when he suddenly tried make a run for it. I caught hold of his robe and he turned on me." Father Gavra shuddered. "His eyes looked strange. Too bright. He made a groaning sound and pulled the knife. It was all so fast...."

Brother Constantin bulled his way through the crowd, Florin trailing behind him. He glared down at Brother Karol, then at the abbot. When he saw all the blood, his face went pale.

"Karol attacked Father Gavra," Vivienne said. "Lord Cumberland shot him. He must be confined immediately before he tries to do more harm."

Constantin blinked and shared a look with Florin, who seemed shocked.

"We'll lock him up in the infirmary," he said.

Vivienne nodded. "I don't know the extent of his injuries, but I need to speak with him when he regains consciousness."

Brother Florin cleared his throat. "If he is the *pricolici*, perhaps it's better he does not wake up at all."

"What are you suggesting?" the abbot demanded.

Florin flushed but he seemed determined to speak his mind. "That we fire another bullet into his heart. What is the purpose of keeping this abomination alive? It tried to murder you! It killed Brother Adrian and those children."

"No one touches him until I find out what happened to Anne Lawrence," Vivienne said hotly.

Father Gavra stared at Florin until the librarian looked away. "Fetch some rope," he said wearily. "Brother Karol must be securely tied before you carry him to the infirmary."

"Do as he says," Constantin barked.

Six of the younger monks ran for the gate. Snow began to fall, fat, wet flakes that would accumulate quickly.

Nathaniel produced a pocket handkerchief and handed it to Father Gavra, who used it to bind up his hand.

"I must confess, I'm relieved it turned out to be one of the novices," the abbot said. "It troubled me to think the murderer could be someone I'd known for years." He stared at Karol. "I wonder how the poor boy became this foul thing."

"I intend to ask him that," Vivienne said. "But we must keep him alive until a doctor can be fetched. You need one yourself, Father."

"Brother Adrian had the skill to sew me up and keep evil humors from the wound," the abbot said. "But Brother Nicolae's hands are too unsteady."

"Come, Father," Brother Florin said. "We must get you inside." He glanced nervously at Karol. "You should rest and warm yourself by the fire."

"We'll stand guard over him until they return," Nathaniel said.

Gavra nodded and went off with Brother Florin. Karol lay on his back in the snow, his black robe spread around him.

"Do you think he panicked?" Nathaniel asked. "Tried to make a dash for it?"

"That's what it looks like," Vivienne replied. "You must ride back down to Mara Vardac. Fetch a proper doctor, and also the constable. We need to tell them what's happened."

"Aren't you coming?"

Vivienne stared at the high walls of Saint George's looming over the trees. "If Karol regains consciousness, I intend to question him. And if he *is* more than a man, I'm not confident the monks can manage him on their own."

Nathaniel frowned. "I don't like the idea of splitting up."

"Nor do I, but you promised to do as I say," she reminded him gently. "I don't see any other way."

He gave a reluctant nod. "It's still early. I should have no difficulty making it to Mara Vardac before nightfall."

"Be careful."

He gave her a sharp look. "You don't think the danger is passed?"

Vivienne met his eyes. "I'm not sure what to think. But did you see the other monks when Brother Florin called it a *pricolici*? There was no reaction. It's as though they already knew, or suspected."

They turned as a party returned from the monastery bearing a coil of thick rope. Nathaniel kept his pistol leveled at Brother Karol's forehead while they tied him up, but he didn't stir. Once he was trussed hand and foot, four of the novices carried him to the infirmary. Vivienne watched as he was tied to the bed. Brother Constantin offered to stand watch.

"Light a fire in the hearth," she said. "And cover him with a blanket. I don't want him freezing to death."

Constantin nodded curtly and it was done. When she felt satisfied Karol was secure, she asked if she might see Father Gavra. He was in his study, a fresh bandage covering the wound. He sipped from a cup of brandy.

"I blame myself," Father Gavra said dolefully. "Karol was the one who escorted Anne from the monastery. It was only his word that she left safely."

"I'll have the truth from him," Vivienne said. "In the meantime, Lord Cumberland has offered to ride down to Mara Vardac and get help."

Father Gavra frowned. "Don't you think you should go together? There's no need to stay, Lady Cumberland—"

She held his gaze. "Nathaniel can manage. I want to be here in case Karol wakes up."

The abbot seemed on the verge of another objection.

"Please, Father. He might know … what happened to Miss Lawrence."

He gave a slow nod. "Then you should leave soon, I think," he told Nathaniel. "The weather is taking a turn for the worse." He lifted the bottle of brandy and poured a measure into another cup. "Have this before you go out there. It'll keep you warm."

Nathaniel accepted gratefully, tossing it back. "I'd best be off." He glanced out the window at the falling snow. "It's a two-hour ride to Mara Vardac, longer in this weather."

"Travel safely," Father Gavra said. "The nearest doctor is in Satinari. Bring all the men you can."

Nathaniel nodded and Vivienne escorted him out to the stables. One of the young grooms saddled his horse and led it from the stall.

"Sure you won't come?" he asked, searching her eyes.

For a moment, she was sorely tempted. Something about what had happened didn't sit right. It was all too neat. But she wouldn't leave Karol, not when he might have the answers she needed.

Vivienne glanced at the infirmary. "I'll be fine. Frankly, I don't trust them. One of us needs to stay here or else Brother Karol might be conveniently dead by the time we return."

Nathaniel drew a deep breath. "Perhaps I should leave you the pistol."

"No, you take it. You're traveling alone. We don't know what's out there on the road."

She touched his hand and they briefly clasped fingers.

"Stay with Father Gavra," he advised. "I'll bring help by morning, if not sooner."

Vivienne walked him out to the main gate, where one of the brothers lifted the heavy crossbar and let him pass through. She watched his horse disappear down the road. Then Vivienne turned back toward the monastery, the snow thickening as she trudged to the infirmary.

CHAPTER 8

The wind picked up as soon as Nathaniel left the sheltered pass leading down from Saint George's. It drove the snow sideways, forcing him to lean low over the horse's neck. He rode as hard as he dared without wandering off the road into the trackless waste, or letting his poor horse step into a hidden hole and break a leg.

So he clung to his mount, whispering words of encouragement as they picked their way down the mountain. At last, Mara Vardac came into view, the dark humps of the houses looming through the heavy snow. Nathaniel galloped up to the palisade of sharpened stakes. A wagon blocked the gap and he called out until a group of men appeared, led by Andrei, the innkeeper's son.

"Let me in," Nathaniel croaked, his face so stiff and frozen he could hardly form the words. "I come from Saint George's with tidings about the *pricolici*."

That got them moving. Andrei and two others rolled the wagon out of the way and Nathaniel spurred his horse through the gap. He dismounted at the stables behind the inn. Master Korzha's son came trotting up.

"Go warm yourself by the fire," Andrei said. "I'll see to the horse."

Nathaniel nodded gratefully and handed over the reins. The animal whickered, glad to be home. He went to the back door and entered through the kitchens. The innkeeper's wife was kneading bread on the wooden table. Her eyes widened when she saw his half-frozen state.

"I must speak to your husband, mistress," Nathaniel said in German. "It's urgent. And fetch the mayor and the priest, as well."

She nodded once and hurried off, dusting flour from her hands. Nathaniel went through to the common room and stood by the fire. His fingers and toes were starting to tingle, which he took as a good sign. A moment later, the front door opened and Master Korzha came in with his son, Andrei. They were followed by Father Cernat and the mayor.

"Did you find Miss Lawrence?" the innkeeper asked.

"No, but we know who is behind the killings," Nathaniel replied grimly. "A monk named Brother Karol."

They all sat down at one of the scarred wooden tables and Nathaniel related their arrival at the abbey and the discovery that one of the monks had been savagely attacked inside the walls.

"The killer struck between the Midnight Office and Matins, when most of the monks were sleeping. He knew the monastery routine well."

"The *pricolici*?" the mayor asked.

Nathaniel nodded. "It happened on the night of the full moon. The monk's throat was torn out. The abbot thought it was an animal attack, but when we viewed the body, the marks of human teeth were clearly visible."

The men crossed themselves and muttered prayers against evil.

"This morning we organized a search of the forest. The abbot was attacked by the monk who accompanied him, a young fellow named Karol. He had a knife."

"What happened?" Father Cernat asked.

"I shot him, but he's not dead. They have him tied up in the infirmary." Nathaniel paused. "He needs medical attention. The abbot as well. Lady Cumberland stayed behind."

The mayor nodded uncertainly, though he seemed relieved that the ordeal was over. "We must ride for Satinari, but not until morning. The daylight is nearly gone and the snow too heavy."

Nathaniel accepted the truth of this. He'd barely made it down the mountain.

"Karol is tied up and locked inside the infirmary," he said with a sigh. "Let us hope that holds him for the night."

Mistress Elena brought out a simple meal and he related further details of what had happened. The sudden attack, and how Brother Karol had taken three bullets before he fell.

"You say the abbot's injuries aren't life-threatening?" Father Cernat asked.

Nathaniel shook his head. "It was a nasty slash, but not too serious. Thank God he's young and strong, else I fear that monk would have killed him."

The priest gave Nathaniel a strange look. "But he's old and blind, going on eighty now."

Nathaniel's eyes narrowed. "Father Gavra is no older than I am."

"Father Gavra?" The priest shook his head, bewildered. "No, no. The abbot of Saint George's is Father Nicolae. He's been there forever."

"But...." Nathaniel's thoughts raced. "How can that be? No one challenged him. Have you ever heard of a Brother Constantin?"

"No."

"He's supposedly one of the senior monks. What about Brother Florin?"

The priest paled beneath his thick red beard. "I do not know who these men are, but I fear they are not monks."

Nathaniel swore a bitter oath and leapt to his feet. "I must get back to Saint George's without delay. I need a fresh horse." His gaze swept the table. "Who will come with me?"

There was a terrible silence. Master Korzha muttered something more about the weather, refusing to meet his eye.

"Then I will go alone," Nathaniel said coldly.

"I will go," Father Cernat said, rising to his feet. He looked frightened but his voice was firm. "You should have a true man of God with you."

Nathaniel gave the priest a grateful nod.

"Get him a horse," Master Korzha muttered.

The innkeeper's son, Andrei, rose and slipped out the door.

"We'll ride for Satinari first thing tomorrow, Lord Cumberland," the mayor said weakly. "Fetch the constable. He'll know what to do—"

Nathaniel ignored him, tearing his greatcoat from the hook by the door. The wind knocked him back a step as he entered the dark lane. It was a foul night, the snow turning to sleet that slicked the ground in a thin layer of ice. He turned his collar up and strode to the stables. Andrei wasn't there, though he heard the horses snorting in their stalls. Nathaniel was looking around for a bridle and harness when he saw torches coming through the yard.

The sight of the dead children's father, Cristian, and five of his broad-shouldered cousins, all leading horses and carrying shotguns, was the sweetest thing Nathaniel had ever seen. Andrei strode along beside them. Without a word, he went into the stables and began to saddle three mounts.

A moment later, Father Cernat appeared from the door to the kitchen, the hood of his cassock drawn tight against the wind.

"Andrei says the Devil has come to Saint George's," Cristian said, a wild look in his eye. "But I will have justice for Marius and Daniela."

Father Cernat translated his words for Nathaniel, and the two men briefly clasped forearms.

The riders gathered more torches from the palisade and lit them against the darkness. With the children's father in the lead, they galloped back up the road toward the Monastery of Saint George.

CHAPTER 9

Vivienne watched Brother Karol mutter in his sleep. She'd taken a chair opposite his bed in the infirmary. He lay on his back, tied hand and foot. Sweat plastered his dark hair to his forehead.

She wondered if he could snap those ropes.

Now his head turned from side to side, his parched lips moving. Try as she might, Vivienne couldn't make out what he was saying. She rose and warily approached the bed. A few of the monks waited just outside the door, but Vivienne had asked them to leave her alone with him. Constantin had argued against it, but Father Gavra overruled him. She'd seen the look of fury on Constantin's face as she closed the door.

That was many hours ago. There had been no change in his deathlike slumber until now. Karol's eyes suddenly flew open and she jerked back, but they stared blankly at the ceiling.

"Brother Karol," she said quietly in Magyar. "Can you hear me?"

His head slowly turned in her direction.

"Did you kill the English girl? The one who came to see the library?"

He didn't answer, but his eyes filled with contempt.

"What are you?" she persisted. "Tell me and I might be able to help."

He turned his face to the wall. "You can't help me," he whispered.

"Are you innocent?"

There was no response.

"I know something is wrong here. Are there others who know too? Brother Nicolae, perhaps? I heard him praying in the chapel last night. He asked God to preserve him from evil."

Vivienne sat back down in the chair, studying the young monk's profile. The iron blade in her bodice was a reassuring weight. "I can protect you from the ones who would kill you. But you must tell me the truth."

Karol closed his eyes again and refused to say anything more.

After a while, Vivienne sighed and rose to her feet. She knocked on the door and it was opened by Brother Constantin.

"He's awake," she said.

Constantin nodded gruffly. He went inside and took the same chair against the wall Vivienne had occupied. He said nothing to the prisoner, but his gaze was like a thunderhead.

Vivienne returned to Father Gavra's study. He had a blanket across his shoulders and a fire roaring in the hearth. The brandy bottle was half-empty. He gave her a wan smile.

"How is your hand?" she asked.

He shrugged with one shoulder. "It pains me but the bleeding has stopped. Brother Constantin will lead the services for now." He paused. "Has Brother Karol said anything to you?"

Vivienne shook her head. "Not a word. I just left him."

"I hope Lord Cumberland manages to fetch a doctor soon." He sighed. "What will you do now?"

"It's my duty to stay and complete my investigation until it is resolved to my satisfaction," she said. "I hope you have no objections."

Father Gavra nodded. "Of course." He held up the bottle. "Won't you share a drink with me?"

"A small one."

He poured her a cup with his uninjured arm and handed it over. "Tell me something, Lady Cumberland."

Vivienne took a sip and inclined her head.

"Do you think Brother Karol is truly a *pricolici*? Or simply insane?"

"I don't know. If you believe the latter, you must discount what the villagers claimed to see in the woods when they found the children."

"Yes. But I did not see that myself. The more I consider it, the more it seems that the wounds to poor Brother Adrian could have been inflicted entirely by a man."

"They could have," Vivienne agreed.

"If he had a kind of madness, a bloodlust, perhaps he hoped joining the monastery would protect him."

"But it didn't."

"No. He managed to suppress it for a while, but eventually it became impossible to resist." He paused and studied the last half inch of brandy, his eyes glazed with tiredness. "Or perhaps Karol does have a wolf inside him. Marcus Aurelius said that nothing is evil which is according to nature. Do you think *pricolici* could be a natural occurrence? A mutation like those Mr. Darwin wrote about?"

"Brother Karol is the only one who can tell us how he came to be that way."

"What will become of him, Lady Cumberland? When the constable arrives from Satinari?"

Vivienne thought of the quote by the Reverend Baring-Gould.

He may still prowl in Abyssinian forests, range still over Asiatic steppes, and be found howling dismally in some padded room of a Hanwell or a Bedlam.

"I don't know. He'll be arrested and have a trial. We have no proof he did anything besides attack you just now. I'm not doubting his guilt, Father, but these questions will be asked." She smiled. "Unless he confesses, of course."

The abbot sighed. "I will have to address the brothers tomorrow, give them an explanation they can understand. This whole business has been awful. I have ordered them to stay in their rooms for now. I imagine you wish to rest as well. It's been a very long day for all of us."

Vivienne finished her brandy. She rose and started for the door, then turned back. "One thing puzzles me, Father. I've wondered how Karol managed to move about the monastery unseen on so many occasions. He must have snuck out on the night the children and woodcutter were killed and returned to his room without anyone noticing. The same for Brother Adrian."

She didn't include Anne on this gruesome list. Vivienne still believed her ward must be alive somewhere. Anything else was … unthinkable.

The abbot's eyes flickered with interest. "I'll confess, I've wondered the same myself. He must have had the Devil's own luck."

She smiled. "He must have. I might go ask Brother Florin if he has a copy of the monastery plans."

"And I will speak with Karol myself in the morning. Perhaps he'll be willing to make a confession to me, cleanse his conscience."

Vivienne bade Father Gavra goodnight and walked through the empty refectory. In fact, she had developed a suspicion about how Karol had moved around — assuming he was truly the *pricolici*.

The daylight faded as she made her way to the library. Brother Florin nodded at her from his place at the scriptorium, then continued copying a manuscript. Vivienne lit a candle and settled herself in the chair by the window, listening to his quill scratching away on the parchment.

"Do you know anything about secret passages?" she asked bluntly in Magyar.

Florin looked up at her, his watery eyes measuring. "As a matter of fact, yes. They were built during the reign of Prince Michael. None have been used in a very long time, of course."

"Might I see the original plans?"

"I'm afraid they were lost in a fire some years ago."

"Oh."

He laid his quill down. "But I could show you myself if you like."

Brother Florin led her through the refectory and down a flight of stairs to the kitchens, which smelled of onions.

"There is a false door here, you see?" He pressed a hidden lever at the rear of one of the pantries. The shelving swung open a few inches. A breath of cold, dank air brushed her skin. She held the candle high and peered inside.

"Where does it lead?"

"There are connecting passages throughout the abbey. I wouldn't recommend going far."

She glanced at him. "I won't, Brother Florin. Thank you."

"Perhaps I should accompany you?" he said diffidently. "I've done a bit of exploring before. I know some of the passages. They can be rather confusing."

Vivienne hesitated. "All right."

He gave her a sharp look. "Do you think Brother Karol came this way?"

"I suspect so," Vivienne admitted.

They entered a narrow space thick with dust and cobwebs. After several twists and turns, she saw the faint outlines of another door.

"Where does that one lead?" Vivienne asked.

"To the Chapter House, I think. It wouldn't be far from the brothers' sleeping cells."

"Are there any tunnels that pass beneath the outer wall?"

"I've wondered that, too." He shook his head. "But I do not know. I was afraid to go too far alone. It seemed easy to get lost."

They continued on for several minutes, sometimes turning sideways to squeeze through a tight spot. It was cold in the passages, yet she was forced to pause and wipe sweat from her brow. Vivienne tried to keep track of all the turnings, but her mind felt muddy. She'd hardly slept the night before.

"Perhaps we should return now?" Brother Florin asked behind her.

"Soon." She pressed on, eyes scanning the walls and floor for any signs of dried blood.

Something nagged at her. If Brother Karol had only come at the end of the summer, how had he known about the hidden passages? She supposed it was possible he'd discovered them on his own, but more likely someone told him. Except that Brother Florin said they were never used anymore.

Then the corridor widened and reached a dead end. A secret chamber, empty save for the scuff of footprints in the dust.

"I suspect this is the room where Prince Michael hid himself during the wars of the mid-seventeenth century," Brother Florin said behind her. "The monastery was besieged and sacked, though thank the Saints they didn't try to burn the church."

Vivienne raised the candle high. There was a tiny window high up in the wall that allowed some air and light, but no sign that the chamber had been used for nefarious purposes. She was about to concede defeat when she saw something glinting in the dust. Florin had turned back to peer into the passage. She strode forward and bent down to pick it up. When she stood, he was watching her with a strange expression.

"Did you find something?"

The thin gold chain dug into her palm as she closed her fist.

"No."

"I thought I saw you pick something up."

"Brother Florin, I'd like to go back now," she said evenly.

"Of course, of course." He turned toward the passageway. She saw his shoulders stiffen. The candle fell to the ground and rolled away, guttering out in the darkness of the passage.

"Forgive me," Florin mumbled, crouching down and groping for the candle. "I sometimes get the palsy in my hands."

She thought of his quill scratching against the parchment, hour after hour without pause.

Vivienne drew the iron blade from her bodice, her own candle casting a wavering pool of light.

"Brother Florin, I'd like you to turn around and face me now," she said firmly.

He half turned to her, but his features were cloaked in shadow.

"Is something the matter?"

The hair on her neck stood straight up. His voice was perfectly normal, but every instinct screamed at her that something fundamental was changing, slipping away....

Vivienne took a step back, putting more distance between them. "I have a knife and I won't hesitate to use it," she said coldly. "Now, I want you to go over to that window and stand with your back against the wall."

He raised his hands, which were not shaking at all.

"I think there's a misunderstanding, Lady Cumberland—"

"There's no misunderstanding. Go!"

He turned and walked past her. Every nerve ending tingled, but Florin did as she ordered.

"Now turn and look at me, please."

He spun around, his eyes throwing back the candlelight.

And Vivienne heard Father Gavra's voice.

"Lady Cumberland, are you in there? I see a light."

Candles were moving down the passage.

"Stay back," Vivienne warned in a loud voice, her eyes locked on Florin. "It's not safe. Get help, Father, quickly!"

Florin simply stood and watched her, his face blank as stone.

The footsteps halted and she heard a low argument in the passage. Then Father Gavra appeared, his face pale against his dark robes. Brother Constantin hovered behind him.

"You should have gone with Lord Cumberland," the abbot said, and his accent sounded different to her now. Softer. "I gave you a fair chance."

Vivienne exhaled softly. *So that's how it was. Well, so be it.*

She held up the gold chain, her own face grim. It had been a birthday present from Alec. "Where's Anne?"

"Safe."

Vivienne bit back a sob of fury. *"Liar."*

His brown eyes flashed with sudden anger. "I wouldn't lie about that."

"You lied about everything else!"

"Not everything. I did go to Oxford divinity school." He studied her. "Where's your bonded?"

The words gave her a chill.

"Go to hell."

He rubbed his eyes, and for a moment, she saw the weary young abbot, trying so hard to shepherd his flock through peril.

Vivienne heard more footsteps and backed deeper into the room, trying to keep them all in view. Constantin stepped aside and made room for Brother Karol. He looked entirely recovered, just another fresh-faced novice.

Father Gavra glanced at him.

"There are men coming up the road from Mara Vardac," Karol said. "With shotguns."

"Merde." A deep sigh. "Ah well, we tried, didn't we?"

Suddenly, Vivienne felt … strange. She reached for the wall, but it seemed too far away.

"Are you all *pricolici?*" Her tongue was thick and heavy.

Father Gavra ignored this question. He walked toward her and she shrank back, but he only slipped an arm around her waist, easing her down to the floor. Vivienne gave a slow blink and gazed at her hand. The knife was gone. She didn't even remember dropping it.

"Did he send you here?" Gavra demanded. "Where is he?"

She wordlessly shook her head. It was like a horrible dream.

"I put too much," he muttered.

"It's time we leave this place." Through the fog, she recognized the harsh voice of Constantin. "I told you we should have gone yesterday after—"

"Not now." The words were spoken quietly, but Constantin cut off.

Father Gavra seemed lost in thought. He had the look of a man who was calculating something. Then he gave a small, terrifying smile.

Vivienne slumped back. She felt pressure on her wrist, the one with the cuff, and she wanted to scream in revulsion, but her voice wouldn't come.

A whisper in her ear. "Tell your bonded D'Ange sends his regards."

CHAPTER 10

The wind moaned like a banshee as the party from Mara Vardac galloped up to the gates of Saint George's. They were locked tight.

"How will we pass through?" Father Cernat shouted.

"We must pray they aren't all *pricolici*," Nathaniel shouted back. "If the brothers know help has come…." He pulled out his revolver and fired two shots into the air.

They waited, huddled against the heavy buttress, and then torches appeared, moving across the cloister. He recognized Brother Grigori, the monk who had greeted them before, along with two others. Grigori lifted the heavy crossbar and the gates swung wide.

Nathaniel slid from the saddle, one hand gripping the reins in a frozen claw. Within the walls, the wind had died some and he could see unbroken snow covering the cloister except for the footprints of the men who had just let them in.

"Where are they?" he demanded.

The brothers glanced at each other but said nothing.

"Forget your blasted vows of silence," Nathaniel roared. "Where's my wife?"

One pointed back at the refectory.

"And Karol? The *pricolici?*" Cristian's eyes shone with fury.

"He was in the infirmary," Nathaniel replied. "Follow me!"

He swung back into the saddle and they galloped across the yard. The monastery was dark, with no sign of anyone about. Cristian burst through the infirmary door first, his cousins on his heels, all of them with shotguns ready in their hands, and Nathaniel heard a wordless shout of anger. He pushed inside. The room was empty, Brother Karol gone, his ropes frayed.

The father of the dead children muttered something in Magyar and then a shadow skittered through the torchlight at the edge of the room.

It was only a rat, but the men were wound tight as bowstrings.

Nathaniel heard the thunder of shotguns firing, the flashes blinding inside the chamber. He felt a sudden agony in his leg that knocked him back against the wall.

"Stop!" he shouted. "For God's sake, it was a bloody rat!"

The guns quieted, the stink of powder heavy in the air.

Nathaniel sank down against the wall, praying they hadn't come too late.

Gunshots shattered the haze. Then a long silence. She dreamt of Alec, dreamt he was trying to scream her name but no sound came out....

"*Vivienne!*"

Her eyes cracked open.

The voice was muffled by stone, but she recognized it now.

Nathaniel.

My dear Nathaniel.

"Vivienne!"

She pressed chilled fingers against the wall. Whatever was in the brandy seemed to be wearing off, though she still felt awful.

Her first effort was a sad croak. How dry her mouth was, like she'd been chewing cotton. Vivienne coughed and tried again.

"Nathaniel…. *Nathaniel!*"

This time he seemed to hear her.

"Where are you? I can't…." The rest was lost.

She gathered her strength and tried to stand. Failed. "There's a secret door in the pantry. It leads to a passage!"

A long pause. She'd almost given up hope when she caught a faint reply.

"I've been shot, darling, but I'll send someone straight over."

Long minutes passed and then she saw candles coming down the narrow passage. It was the innkeeper's son and Father Cernat. Andrei helped her to stand and they led her, stumbling, through endless twists and turns and finally out into the cold air of the cloister. The storm had eased and a few stars winked down as Vivienne emptied her stomach in the snow.

Father Cernat brought her a cup of water and she drank deeply.

"Did you pass anyone on the road?" she asked, feeling some strength return.

He shook his head. "And the gates were sealed behind us. No one has left."

Relief flooded her. "They must still be here then. We'll mount a search."

She felt like death warmed over, but it didn't stop her from enlisting Cristian and his brothers to comb every cell of the monastery, every outbuilding down to the chicken coops. But the men who had drugged her were gone without a trace.

Vivienne found Nathaniel in the infirmary. He lay on one of the beds, his leg resting on a pillow and a tightness around his eyes. They warmed with relief when she ran to him and took his hand.

"Who shot you?"

"It was an accident." He looked her over. "Thank God they didn't harm you. When I discovered the truth, I was so afraid, Vivienne."

She gave him a reassuring smile. "I'm fine. A little woozy, that's all."

And then she told him all that had happened in the secret chamber — or almost all.

"But why did Karol attack the false abbot if they were all *pricolici?*" he asked weakly.

She could see Nathaniel was exhausted and in a great deal of pain.

"I'm not sure yet. At first I thought he wanted us to leave, but then…." She trailed off.

The door opened and Father Cernat entered, a queer look on his face. "I just spoke to Father Nicolae."

"He's unharmed?"

"Perfectly so. And he denies knowing anything about the men you describe."

Vivienne felt a flash of rage and tried to bridle her temper. "Please explain to me how that can be possible. We were here for *two full days.*"

Cernat shrugged, though there was something in his eyes. "He did admit that the brothers buried in the cemetery were also killed by the *pricolici* some months ago." A cough. "Father Nicolae claims it was the man named Adrian."

She frowned. "The one lying dead in the infirmary?"

"That one, yes."

None of it made sense.

"What about the other monks? We have to question them—"

He shook his head. "They will not break their vows."

Vivienne swore softly. "I want to see Father Nicolae," she said. "Right now."

The old abbot was in his study, hands folded serenely, as if he had been waiting for her to come.

"May I sit?"

He made a small gesture at the chair.

Vivienne sank down, her back straight. "You know who they are." It was not a question.

"What is it you want?" he asked mildly.

"I want their names. Everything you know about them."

He leaned back with a sigh. "And if I told you? What would you do with the knowledge?"

"Find them."

He shook his head. "That would not be wise."

Vivienne wanted to seize him by his long white beard and shake him like a terrier with a rat. She clasped her hands to keep them from trembling. "Why not?" she asked tightly.

"Those men were not sent by the Devil." The abbot sighed. "Go back to London, Lady Cumberland."

"And the poor children's father?" she said with a scorn she could no longer conceal. "What will you tell him?"

"I've already spoken with him. He knows that justice has been done."

The abbot raised a finger and a brother appeared in the doorway.

"Please escort Lady Cumberland to the guest house," the abbot said. "Our interview is concluded."

Vivienne rose and strode to the door. She spun back and stared at him.

"If not by the Devil, then by whom, Father?"

He gave her only a gentle smile.

Vivienne refused to be packed off to the guest house, curling up in a chair in the infirmary as Nathaniel slipped into a fitful doze. When she heard his breath deepen to sleep, she finally broke down, sobbing as though her heart would break.

Alec, she thought. *Oh, Alec. What have I done?*

Outside, the blizzard was howling again.

PART II

"The Prince of Darkness is a gentleman."
  –*King Lear*

CHAPTER 11

Anne watched the light bleed from the sky. From atop the tower, she could see an expanse of pewter water on one side, dense old-growth forest on the other. Waves beat against a shingled beach far below. It was a spectacular view, framed by sheer white cliffs that looked as if they'd been sliced off with a sharp knife.

Anne barely noticed.

The sun slid below the horizon. Time slowed as the world teetered on the cusp between night and day.

Not long now, she thought.

The first stars appeared in the east. The wind picked up, skirling around the walls and dragging cold fingers through her hair. Anne stood immobile as a statue, her eyes fixed on the tiny stretch of road visible from the tower. It cut through the forest and was hidden by the trees except for a single bend a quarter mile away where the road topped a rise.

The dusk thickened. The moon began to rise. Anne watched, not daring to blink.

And then….

A mounted figure sped around the bend. It leaned low over

the horse, a dark cloak unfurling behind, there and gone in a heartbeat.

Anne stepped back from the waist-high crenellated wall and ran down a winding flight of stairs to the chamber below. It had a mullioned window with two missing panes. A moth-nibbled rug covered the floor. The western side of the ceiling leaked and she had dragged the bed to the opposite wall so it wouldn't drip on her when it rained.

A cloudy standing mirror caught the outlines of her reflection as she passed, a young woman with reddish-brown hair and hazel eyes that seemed to stare straight through you. A cameo with an ivory rose dangled from the velvet band around her neck. It was a delicate thing. Anne couldn't be certain what it was made of because if she touched the rose with the intention of removing it, she fell into a deep and dreamless sleep.

For the first two weeks of her captivity, she had learned this lesson again and again. She'd tried reciting *pi* to fifty places and allowing her hand to act of its own accord, creeping toward the talisman like a cat stalking a mouse. Tried loud singing and quiet meditation. Each time, she would wake in her bed with no memory of touching it and no idea how much time had passed.

Days, perhaps.

It irritated her that she woke in her bed rather than on the cold stone floor. It meant someone had put her there.

The man on horseback.

Without the wretched cameo, Anne would have torn the tower down to its foundations and strode off in search of the nearest train station, but the talisman blocked her power and left her weak as a mortal. Oh, she'd managed to push the heavy bed across the room so she wouldn't be rained on, but the task made her grunt and sweat.

Finally, Anne had conceded defeat and tried to climb to freedom. The tower was smooth stone, but the privy adjacent to her bedroom had a small window that led to a narrow ledge, which in turn followed the peak of a roof to a second square tower. Her captor was no fool, however, and exploration revealed that those windows were locked and shuttered from the inside.

Jumping was out of the question, she'd dash her brains out on the courtyard far below. So she'd torn up the old-fashioned gowns he left her and used the strips to make a rope, but it wasn't long enough. She'd still break both legs, maybe worse.

At last, Anne decided her only chance was to discover what her captor wanted and to outwit him. The problem was that he refused to show himself.

He came to the tower every day. She could hear his stealthy movements as he laid the dining table in the evening. Anne knew it was a *he* because she could smell traces of him when she entered the room afterwards — his starched linen shirt, the polished leather of his boots, and beneath that, a faint animal musk, not exactly unpleasant but not normal, either.

Pricolici.

Her own stupidity had delivered her into his hands like a motherless lamb. Just thinking about it made Anne want to murder someone, preferably *him*.

Tonight she aimed to seize her chance.

One more curve of the stairs and she stood before a wooden door so ancient it was nearly black. On the other side was a makeshift dining room, the last chamber she had access to — when her captor permitted it. It had a table and four chairs and a sideboard on which he would leave lit candles in the evening, though never on the dining table itself.

This told her something. He knew fire was anathema to her and kept it at a safe distance. It didn't matter because the talisman prevented her from touching the elements, but this indicated a certain level of courtesy. And he had yet to harm her in any way — besides holding her prisoner. Considering the brutality of the murders at Mara Vardac, Anne found this interesting.

The routine was thus: He would wait until she was in the

bedchamber. Then he would enter the dining room and lock the inner door to the tower, lay the table, unlock it again, and leave through the outer door.

It should have been a simple matter to catch him at it. To wait by the inner door until she heard the bolt slide open and then rush inside.

But he was always too fast.

By the time Anne threw the inner door open, the opposite door leading out of the tower would be closing, and by the time she reached *that* door, he would have bolted it again.

She'd tried two dozen times and been thwarted on every occasion.

It was frustrating, although the meals he left were excellent, if far too much for one person. Aromatic soups and stews, haunches of game and roasted vegetables. Once she'd determined the food wasn't laced with sedatives, Anne ate with relish. The thought crossed her mind that he might be fattening her up for the kill, but starving herself would make for a prolonged and far more unpleasant death — besides which, it seemed an awful lot of trouble for him to take over a single meal.

And so the hours passed, one merging seamlessly into the next. He always brought two buckets of clean water for bathing and drinking. Occasionally, he left her other things. One day, she'd found a chess set on the sideboard. She took it to her room and played both white and black, all the while plotting her revenge. She composed violent symphonies in her head. But she spent most of her time atop the tower, watching the light play on the water during the day and the slow movement of the heavens at night.

The evening before, he'd left her a novel. It was called *The Mysteries of Udolpho* and Anne threw it down in boredom after a quick perusal. The characters were always swooning, or being struck by terror and amazement. But if he was leaving her books and chess sets, he planned to keep her there for a long time.

It had already been at least a month by her reckoning. So Anne decided to force his hand.

Now she pressed her ear against the inner door to the dining chamber. For many long minutes, all was quiet. Then she heard the faint ring of footsteps ascending the tower. The bolt of the outer door slid open. She heard the previous evening's meal being cleared, and the clink of cutlery and dishes being laid out.

"Who are you?" Anne shouted through the door.

As usual, there was no response. He carried on setting the table as if he hadn't heard.

"Coward! Why am I here?"

He started whistling to himself, a jaunty little tune. She smelled the tantalizing aroma of a tomato bisque.

"You've left me no choice," she announced. "I'm throwing myself off the top of the tower. At least my death will be swift, you brute!"

Anne flew back up the circular stairs.

It had occurred to her that perhaps *The Mysteries of Udolpho* was a signal she was to play the maiden in distress, emotionally overwrought and suicidal. That dovetailed nicely with her own plans.

Anne hoped to hear the door open behind her, but all was quiet. Moments later she burst out onto the tower roof and clambered atop the wall. A hundred feet below, she could see a bit of the inner bailey and beyond that the precipitous drop to the cliffs and sea.

It was full dark now. The stars shone brightly and a bright three-quarter moon was rising over the forest.

It was bloody cold up there.

Anne shivered and rubbed her arms. She wore the only surviving gown, a velvet thing with puffy sleeves and a scandalous neckline. More than once, Anne had regretted shredding her entire wardrobe before calculating how much rope material she could get out of it.

She was just starting to think he'd called her bluff when a figure appeared in the doorway of the tower. Anne's eyes narrowed.

"You," she said.

Father Gavra.

They'd only spoken briefly when she arrived at Saint George's, but she recognized his face. He'd shaved the beard and his dark blond hair was tied back with a ribbon in a style that struck her as a century or so out of date. The black robe had been traded for a burgundy frock coat and snug trousers, well-cut but also long out of style.

"Come down from there," he snapped. Then, belatedly, "Please."

Anne didn't budge. "You're a Frenchman."

His accent was soft but unmistakable.

"I am," he agreed.

Anne studied him. He leaned against the doorframe in a relaxed manner, but his eyes were not warm.

"You have no right to do this," she said.

"I have every right."

The reply came swiftly and with heat. It gave Anne pause.

"Why?"

"You don't remember me."

"I've never met you before. At the monastery, yes, when you gave me drugged wine. But not before." She drew a breath. "If I've forgotten, please enlighten me."

"Oh no, it's not that easy, Miss Lawrence. I suggest you think harder on it."

"There's nothing to think about. I haven't a clue who you are or what grudge you hold against me."

He gave her an unreadable look. Then he crossed his arms and gazed up at the moon.

"Will you turn into a monster now? Go ahead." She filled her voice with scorn. "I'm not afraid of you."

He shrugged, anger fading to amusement. "Later, perhaps."

The wind gave a hard tug at her skirts like a mischievous child. Anne had a decent head for heights, but her skin prickled at the darkness yawning behind her.

His brow creased in a frown. "Come down, Miss Lawrence. This is a stupid, dangerous game you're playing."

"Then tell me what I've done."

His mouth set in a line. "No."

"You'll damn well tell me *something*," she burst out. "Where is this place?"

To her surprise, he answered freely.

"Le Côte d'Albâtre."

"The Alabaster Coast. That's Normandy, isn't it?"

He nodded.

She stared out at the dark water. The English Channel. Home was on the other side.

"Come down, Miss Lawrence. Your supper is getting cold."

She gave a bitter laugh. "Don't treat me like a child. What are you?"

Father Gavra — or whatever his real name was — arched an eyebrow. "Come down and I'll tell you."

Another sudden gust tore loose strands of hair from their pins and whipped them across her face. Anne inched backward until her heels were at the very edge of the wall. A muscle in his jaw tightened.

"Never mind about that," she said. "I want to know how long you intend you keep me here."

"I'm sure you do." His tone was casual, but his eyes were locked on her with an intensity he couldn't quite conceal. He was afraid of losing his prize.

"Tell me or I'll jump."

Another Gallic shrug. "It depends."

"On what?"

"I'm looking for something. When I find it…."

"You'll let me go?"

"Perhaps."

But she could see the lie in his eyes. He had no intention of ever letting her go.

She raised her hand to the cameo.

"No!" he cried.

Anne swayed, pretending to fall under the talisman's dark enchantment, though she'd been careful to keep her fingers a hair's breadth away from touching it. If he was too slow, she'd fall to her death. But he had to believe she was utterly helpless before he'd let his guard down. Whatever else he might be, Father Gavra wasn't stupid.

Her eyes slipped shut and her knees buckled. A hundred paces of open air rushed to meet her. Anne felt an instant of genuine terror and then hands closed around her waist. She found herself hauled over the wall to the safety of the tower.

She watched him through her lashes as he sank to one knee, breathing hard and muttering curses in French. He adjusted his grip so one hand cradled her back, the other the nape of her neck. Nothing about him signaled *man-wolf*. If anything, he looked like the type to sit around drinking cheap wine and plotting a revolution. Like an impoverished radical.

Or a priest.

Now his gaze rested on the ribbon around her throat, his hands warm against her bare skin. His lips parted slightly as though he meant to lean down and kiss her.

That's when Anne stabbed him with the sharpened stake she'd whittled from one leg of her bed and hidden in a slit of her bodice. It had taken her two weeks of hard labor. She drove it straight into his heart, where his frock coat had fallen open. He roared and dropped her. She skittered away, pressing her back against the wall. Blood pulsed from the wound, staining his snowy shirt black in the moonlight.

"*Merde!*"

Father Gavra threw his head back. The tendons his neck grew taut and his teeth clenched. Then he looked down at his chest, yanked out the stake with an expression of annoyance, and tossed it over the parapet.

"Don't do that again," he snarled.

Anne's own hands were shaking uncontrollably. She stared at him in disbelief as he removed his coat and unbuttoned his shirt. Blood slicked his chest, but when he blotted it with one sleeve, the skin beneath was smooth. He pressed his fingers against the spot, wincing a little.

"That's a neat trick, Father," she murmured.

He stood and stalked to the door, turning back with blazing eyes. Anne rose to her feet, feeling foolish and angry.

"I cook for you every day and this is the thanks I get?" He raised a hand to his forehead, leaving a streak of blood across his brow. "*Nom de dieu!* You are a little beast."

This hardly merited a response. Anne strode past him and started down the stairs. After a moment, he followed. She heard him sigh deeply. His moods seemed to change like the weather.

"Fair enough. You are unhappy. What else do you need? More books? I can get any ones you like."

She turned back just long enough to shoot him a poisonous look. He was frowning at the bed and the missing panes in the window.

"Is it warm enough? I'm sorry the roof leaks. This place is impossible to keep up."

"What do I need?" She pretended to mull it over as they took two more turnings and entered the lower chamber with the dining table. "You could let me go."

The reply was swift and brutal.

"No."

"Then bring me a violin. A decent one."

He nodded, his bloody shirt and hands ghastly in the light of the candles. She stared at the array of dishes with no appetite whatsoever. Her captor stalked to the outer door.

"Goodbye, Miss Lawrence."

The finality of his tone chilled her. As if he might keep her hidden away here forever and never speak to her again.

I must try to reach him. To make him see me as a real person.

"Wait," she cried.

He paused with his back to her, one hand resting on the door handle.

"I can't call you *Father* anymore. You're no monk. Will you tell me your name at least? Is it Gavra?"

He turned and regarded Anne for a long moment. His eyes were brown with a ring of gold around the iris. She remembered those eyes bearing down on her as she struggled through knee-deep snow, though he hadn't been a man then.

"It's Gabriel," he said, and shut the door behind him. The bolt shot home.

Anne sank into a chair, despair washing over her.

The name meant nothing.

CHAPTER 12

A nne watched the road again the next evening at sunset.
When Gabriel arrived, she ran down and gave a polite
knock. She was afraid he would return to ignoring her, but after
a moment the bolt slid back. He opened the door without a word
and continued laying the table.

Progress, she thought.

"Did you bring it?" she asked.

He pointed to the sideboard. A violin case sat there.

"*Merci*," she said.

"*De rien.*"

Anne opened the case and lifted the instrument from its
velvet lining, her eyes widening as she read the signature next to
the left f-hole: *Carlo Bergonzi*. One of the finest Italian luthiers of
the 1700s. She reverently traced the scroll with her fingertips.

"Do you like it?" He stood at the door, watching her.

"I…. Where did you get this? It's exquisite."

"I know people."

"Thank you." She gently returned it to the case. "I promise to
take excellent care of it."

He hesitated for a moment, then bowed and left without a

word, sliding the bolt shut after himself. Anne lifted it to her shoulder and drew the bow across the strings. It badly needed tuning, yet she could hear the glorious sound it would make.

She returned to the table and ate her supper, an airy soufflé and creamy potato soup with a sprig of fresh thyme, but her thoughts roamed elsewhere, piecing together the scant clues she had about his character. He knew how to cook. He could get his hands on a Bergonzi violin in a single day. He liked silly gothic novels.

He couldn't be killed, not by traditional methods at least.

When he'd bowed to her, for a fleeting instant he seemed familiar, but then it was gone.

She went upstairs and tuned the violin, then played for a few hours, wild gypsy tunes to suit her mood. When she finally returned the instrument to its case, her fingers were swollen and tender from lack of practice. Anne hadn't even wanted the violin. She only wanted to see if Gabriel would bring it to her. She wanted to make him to talk to her again.

Now she felt glad to have it. As much as she preferred solitude, the silence was starting to become oppressive.

She undressed and bathed with a bucket of cold water, shivering in the draft from the broken window. After she'd dried off, Anne combed her hair and wondered how had he come to be cursed, if it even *was* a curse. Were there others like him? Could he change at will? And how to reconcile the creature who had brutally murdered two children with the man whose only reaction when she stabbed him through the heart was to swear at her?

He seemed convinced they knew each other and that she'd done something to him, but he couldn't be more than thirty-five years old. Anne recalled her travels over the last two decades, the various mortals she'd encountered, and came up blank. She felt sure she'd remember Gabriel. He was pleasant enough to look at if not blindingly handsome, but he had a certain volatile energy that would have left an impression.

It couldn't be a case of mistaken identity. He knew she was a daēva and had taken precautions to contain her. He seemed to know *exactly* who she was. Anne frowned. Despite her diminutive size, she wasn't used to being the weaker party. Without the talisman, she could have bested five mortal men at once. But Gabriel had his own strange power and she was entirely at his mercy.

Anne crawled under the covers but sleep refused to come. Sometime after midnight she wandered back down to the dining room. The remains of the meal sat on the table, waiting for Gabriel to remove them. Her eye landed on *The Mysteries of Udolpho*. Anne opened it to a random passage.

"Emily gazed with melancholy awe upon the castle, which she understood to be Montoni's; for, though it was now lighted up by the setting sun, the gothic greatness of its features, and its mouldering walls of dark grey stone, rendered it a gloomy and sublime object."

Pure rubbish.

She dragged a chair into the yellow glow of a candle and turned back to chapter one.

The next night Anne waited atop the tower and watched the road. The Channel was rough and choppy, driven by a northerly wind with gusts of rain. When she saw the mounted figure race by, she went down to the inner door and waited until she heard the rattle of dishes from the previous night's supper being cleared. He was whistling a tune again — the same one she'd been playing on the violin.

He stayed to listen, she thought with a frisson of excitement.

"Gabriel?" she said through the door.

The whistling stopped.

"May we speak?"

There was a long silence. Then footsteps approached. The bolt slid open and he stood in the doorframe. He wore a grey woolen coat with a black velvet collar and deep cuffs. His beard was coming in again and he looked rough around the edges.

"What is it, Miss Lawrence?"

"I have a favor to ask."

"I know I need to fix the windowpanes—"

"No, it's something else. I need more dresses. The old ones got ruined."

The corner of his mouth quirked, as if he suspected just what she had done with them. Gabriel pointed to a trunk next to the door. "I brought you six, in various styles, with undergarments and two warm cloaks." His gaze roamed over her, but it was clinical rather than lecherous. "They should fit."

"Thank you." He started to turn away. "Also…."

"Yes?"

She pushed a tendril of rain-damp hair from her face and tried to look small and helpless. It was a look Anne had perfected over the years, to the chagrin all the men who'd underestimated her.

"I can't outrun you, not with this." She gestured to the rose cameo. "But if you're going to keep me here, you have to permit me some exercise. Just a short walk. I'll go mad. I… I can feel my body weakening." This was a lie but she uttered it with great sincerity.

He hesitated.

"Please. I'll wear chains on my legs if you insist. It doesn't have to be far."

"I'll think about it," he said.

Gabriel shut the door in her face and finished setting the table, then left and bolted her in.

Anne ate her solitary supper while the rain dripped outside. She dragged the trunk up to her room and examined the contents. Brocaded silks and duchesse satins and other frippery, all rumpled from being crushed inside the trunk. They smelled musty. Anne wrinkled her nose and carted the lot of it up to the top of the tower to air out.

She spent the evening playing her violin and finishing *The Mysteries of Udolpho*. Despite her initial reservations, Anne found herself drawn into the tale of Emily St. Aubert, a beautiful orphan who gets locked up at Castle Udolpho by the wicked Signor Montoni, an Italian brigand. Emily wept a bit too often for Anne's taste, but she enjoyed the supernatural goings-on and the doomed romance with the poor but dashing Valancourt.

Anne turned pages into the wee hours and slipped back down to the dining room when she was done to replace the book exactly where it had been on the sideboard, lying facedown at chapter two. For some reason, she didn't want Gabriel knowing she had devoured his ridiculous book.

The next morning, she was still lolling in bed when she heard sounds below.

Anne sat bolt upright. She rushed down the stairs in her cotton shift and found Gabriel sitting at the dining table. It was the first time he had ever come in full daylight.

"What are you doing here?" she blurted.

He glanced at *The Mysteries of Udolpho*. "It's bad for the spine to leave it open like that."

Gabriel untied the black ribbon from his hair. He picked up the book and slipped the ribbon between the pages.

Anne studied him for any sign of mockery and detected none. "Thank you. But I've lost interest in that one anyway." She paused. "Maybe you could bring another?"

His lips twitched. "Of course." He swept his arm toward the door. "Come on, then. Unless you've changed your mind?"

"No, I…. Let me just get dressed." Anne ran to the top of the tower and surveyed the gowns, which were all wet from the morning dew. She chose a blue one with a high neck and quickly changed, pulling her boots on and hurrying back down the stairs.

"These are the rules," he told her in a stern tone. "We walk within the walls for thirty minutes. If you try to run, or to hurt me, or to ask questions I don't wish to answer, it will be the last time you leave this tower."

Anne nodded. She had no intention of making a dash for it — not until she knew the grounds better.

Gabriel stood aside and let her go first. Her heart beat a little faster as she stepped through the forbidden door that was always barred to her. A second set of stairs wound down to the bottom of the tower and outside into a high-walled bailey. For the first time she saw the keep itself, which had been hidden by the curve of the tower.

It was not one of those fairytale concoctions of soaring spires and snapping pennants. The castle must have dated back to William the Conqueror, ancient unadorned stone meant to keep out invaders. Dead leaves piled in drifts against the outer wall. She saw no sign of servants or any other inhabitants.

They walked in silence, Gabriel's bootheels ringing on the stone. The rain had stopped, though the morning remained overcast. Anne had never seen him in daylight before. He looked tired, with dark circles beneath his eyes. They walked together through the bailey to an overgrown garden, still brown from winter.

"You eavesdropped," she ventured. "The other night. I heard you whistling *Zigeunerweisen*."

He glanced at her. "I was curious to know if you really played the violin or if you only intended to stab me with the bow."

Anne frowned. "What would be the point? You'd simply recover."

He said nothing to this. They walked another turn around the desolate garden. Anne pretended to be lost in thought but made sure to catalogue every detail. The main gates lay elsewhere but she could see a barred postern gate beyond the garden.

"Where do you go at night?" she asked. "Do you live in the castle?"

"It's mine," he replied, which was not exactly an answer.

Emboldened, Anne gave him a friendly smile. "How did you bring me here? Normandy is a long way from the Carpathians. The last thing I remember is falling in the snow and…." She cleared her throat. "You bounding toward me."

"We Traveled."

The way he said it conveyed that he did not mean by a coach and four. He meant by a portal through the Dominion.

He has access to powerful talismans and the ability to use them. Anne filed this away.

"What drug did you give me?" she asked.

A pause. "Laudanum."

She remembered raising the cup to her lips in Father Gavra's study. She'd come to the monastery half-frozen from the long walk from Mara Vardac and he'd been very polite and kind, offering her a bit of red wine to warm up. She hadn't wanted it, but it seemed rude to refuse. Two other monks had been present as well — Florin and Constantin — so afterwards, Anne hadn't been sure which of them had drugged her.

She'd gone to the library and begun reading the books and felt a lethargy come over her. Anne knew right away that they'd put something in her cup. So she'd sent Florin to fetch more books from the stacks and made a run for it, climbing the outer wall before the alarm was raised.

But he'd still caught her in the end.

They made another turn around the oval walkway in silence.

"What do you do all day?" she asked, hoping to prod him into conversation.

"Cook for you." His gaze fixed on the distant wall. "You think those dishes are simple?"

Anne's temper began to fray. "You make a joke of it, but it's not a joke to me," she said stiffly.

He muttered something inaudible in French.

"My brother will pay well for my safe return. Any amount you ask for."

He cast her a contemptuous look. "I'm not interested in money."

"Then what do you want?"

Gabriel's mouth set. "Justice."

"For what?" she demanded, exasperated.

He didn't reply.

Anne stopped walking, forcing him to halt. "Are you really a priest?"

"No, but I am a man of God." He said this in a low, serious tone and she thought he actually believed it.

"What's the difference?"

"I was never ordained, but I carry out His will all the same."

Not just a man-wolf, but a religious fanatic. Heaven help me.

"How did you know I would go to Saint George's? Were you expecting me?"

His face darkened. "Enough. I told you—"

Anne held up her hands. "All right. I'm sorry I broke your rules. Don't make me go back just yet. We'll talk of something else." He scowled and she touched his sleeve. "Please, it's been awfully lonely."

Another lie — Anne could happily go for weeks without hearing a human voice — but she sensed a crack in the façade.

"Your choice. Art? Philosophy? Music?"

Gabriel heaved a sigh. "Music, if you like. Tell me about the piece you played."

Anne smiled. *"Zigeunerweisen.* Lovely, isn't it? Composed by Pablo de Sarasate, a Spaniard. It's based on the rhythms of the czardas. Hungarian folk dances. They start off slow and get faster and faster…."

They took four more turns around the oval path. The sun broke through the clouds, drying the stones under their feet, and when Anne kept her word, Gabriel seemed to relax a bit. He had a fondness for the romantic composers — Chopin, Schumann, Liszt — but disliked opera, which surprised her given his propensity for melodrama.

"We should get back," he said at last.

Her steps slowed as they approached the tower. She felt a sudden dread of entering and Gabriel seemed to sense it. He turned to her, his voice softer than she'd ever heard it.

"We can walk again tomorrow if you wish."

She looked at him, trying to hold her claustrophobia in check. "Yes, thank you."

He escorted her to the dining room and saw her through the inner door.

"I'll return later with your supper."

Anne nodded. The bolt slid home.

While she ate, Gabriel went up to her bedchamber with tools and panes of glass and repaired the window and the leaky roof. Anne tested the outer door, but he'd locked it with a key. When he left, she found another novel on the sideboard.

The Castle of Otranto.

Anne licked gravy from her fingers and opened to page one. By the third paragraph, a servant was foaming at the mouth. By the fourth, Princess Hippolita had fallen into a swoon because her son, the unfortunate Conrad, had just been crushed to death by an enormous helmet with black plumage. All on the morning of Conrad's wedding to the beautiful Isabella.

Anne was enthralled.

But even as she read by candlelight late into the night, her mind kept returning to that postern gate beyond the garden.

Over the next week, Gabriel walked with her every morning, rain or shine. They talked about meaningless things and she refrained from pressing him about the nature of his grudge. The excursions lasted an hour or so and then she would return to her tower. It was the most time she'd spent with another person in years.

Gabriel never let her out of his sight, not for an instant. That was as she expected.

But on one particularly fine morning, Anne decided to test his new goodwill.

"Gabriel," she said cheerfully. "Can't we walk outside the walls today? The bailey is so small. We just go round and round like rats on a wheel. I'm sure the view from the cliffs is beautiful."

His eyes narrowed. "So you can push me over?"

She laughed as if he'd made a jest, though the thought had crossed her mind.

"Not at the edge. I just want to see the water."

"You can see it from the tower."

She adopted a hurt expression. "Never mind."

He was quiet for a while. Then he said, "There's a path that goes down to the shore. It's steep."

She gave a careless shrug, though the victory was sweet. "I don't mind."

He led her to the postern gate and opened it with a large key. The ground on the other side sloped down to a switchback trail cut into the side of the cliff. Gabriel gestured for her to go first and they picked their way down to the shingled beach.

She could see why he'd permitted it; the shore was nothing more than a narrow crescent that would be fully submerged at high tide. But her heart lifted at being *somewhere* besides the garden and the tower. Gabriel sat down on a boulder as she ran to the edge of the water and let it lap at her boots. Colonies of grey and white kittiwakes nested in the crags of the cliffs. A cormorant flew low over the water, dark and serpentine. Anne loosened the pins in her hair and let the wind take it.

"When you came to the monastery, you said you were a student of folklore," Gabriel asked behind her. "Was that true?"

Anne didn't turn. "Yes."

"What kind?"

"Any kind."

But this was another lie. There were certain stories she chased, seeking their source. Hoping they might hold a grain of truth. It was the driving force of her life. Not even Vivienne and Alec knew that, though she wondered if they suspected.

"You came to hunt the *pricolici*, no?"

Anne glanced over her shoulder. "And I found him."

"What other stories do you like?"

"Hmmm. Fairies. Witches. Kelpies and bugbears. They're real, you know."

"You're teasing me."

"Not in the least."

"Have you seen such things?"

He sounded genuinely interested.

The wind stung her cheeks as she rounded on him. "Why do you care?"

"I'm only asking."

"Well, don't," she snapped, more harshly than she'd intended. "Nothing personal, remember? *Your* rules."

A black cloud extinguished the sun. A spattering of rain hit her face. Gabriel's brows lowered and he looked on the verge of saying something more when the skies opened. They ran for the path, instantly soaked, and made their way up the slippery cliff face in foul humor.

Anne slammed the inner door shut before he could lock her in.

CHAPTER 13

B y sunset, Anne was full of remorse.
She'd gained a toehold, only to squander it with a childish outburst.

So when Gabriel returned with supper, she apologized and asked if he would stay to eat with her. He looked surprised at the invitation — and not exactly eager.

"Just for a few minutes," she coaxed.

He looked out the window and she had the distinct impression he was gauging the light outside. Rain swept the tower in grey curtains.

A dark and stormy night….

"For a little while," Gabriel agreed.

They sat down across from each other. Anne ladled turtle soup into a bowl. He looked even more like a scholar in the candlelight, more like the gentle Father Gavra she remembered, even though she knew he was no such thing.

An awkward silence descended. It was one thing to be escorted on a walk outside, another to have an intimate dinner as friends might. Gabriel seemed all too conscious of this, sitting stiffly, his hands folded in his lap as he watched her eat.

"It's very good, thank you," she said.

"*De rien.*"

He met her eyes briefly, then looked away.

She spooned the rich broth into her mouth, trying not to slurp although it was very hot.

"Oh." Relief flashed across his face as remembered something, reaching into a coat pocket. "I have something for you."

Anne accepted the slim volume, peering at the cover. "*Frankenstein, or The Modern Prometheus* by Mary Shelley."

Gabriel smiled like a satisfied cat. "Open it and read the inscription."

She did so. "*To Lord Byron, from the author.*" Anne raised an eyebrow. "You stole this, didn't you?"

He waved the accusation away. "I don't steal. I bought it. A very special edition. You know that Byron proposed the story-telling contest that inspired the story?"

"No, I didn't." She leaned her elbows on the table. "Tell me."

He poured a glass of wine but didn't touch it, just twirled the stem in his fingers. "Mary was seventeen when she began having an affair with the poet Percy Bysshe Shelley. He married her two years later, after his first wife killed herself."

"It sounds just like—" *One of your novels*, she'd been about to say, but that would mean admitting she'd read them. "Go on."

"Later, they spent a summer at Lake Geneva with Byron. The weather was miserable so they passed the time inventing ghost stories. Mary had a dream about a poor monster, disowned by its creator and doomed to wander in search of a mate, not realizing it was the only one of its kind." The candlelight burnished his irises to a rich gold. "Tragic, no?"

"Terribly."

Another silence descended.

"I have a game," Anne said.

He leaned back, waiting.

"Not stories. This game is about answering questions truly. One each."

Gabriel considered this. "Maybe. But don't ask what I intend to do with you."

"Why not?" she demanded.

That sudden heat returned. "Because you won't like the answer."

Anne felt a jolt of dread. "Just tell me what I've done. What crime I've committed."

"Your brother stole something from me, something priceless. So I'm taking something from him."

"This is about *Alec*?" Her fists balled. "Then why don't you damn well lock *him* up? Women aren't chattel, you know. You can't just use us to pay debts."

He rose and stalked to the window, throwing his hands up. "That's not what I meant. You don't understand anything."

She studied the taut line of his shoulders. "What did he steal from you?"

Gabriel turned, his face blazing.

"Never mind, don't speak of it." She gave him a level look. "No need to have a tantrum. I'll ask something else."

"Like what?" he snapped.

"Were you born with the ability to change into an animal?"

He blinked in surprise. "The answer is no." He drew a deep breath. "Now it's my turn."

"Fair enough."

"Why do you hunt the old stories? You weren't honest before."

Anne met his gaze. "Because sometimes they're true."

"Which ones?"

"Not the bugbears, I'll admit. But the stories about *nosferatu*, risen dead that drain the life from their victims. Wights and ghouls."

"Are they all so ugly?"

"No. I've seen other things, too, enchanting things. Once I saw a mermaid in the Zambezi River with hair of black kelp and a smile like the sunrise."

His gaze narrowed. "But that's not what you're really looking for, is it?"

"You've asked four questions now."

"You never answered the first one," he shot back.

"I did."

Gabriel scowled.

"It's just not *all* of the answer. But you won't get the rest until you tell me things I want to know."

He turned back to the window, his voice sulky now. "I'm not playing if you cheat."

"Very well." She ran her fingers down the spine of the book he'd given her, tracing the letters stamped in gold leaf. "Here's one for free. I don't believe in the Devil, nor some almighty God either. I suppose you think I'll burn in Hell for that."

He snorted. "You're hardly the first atheist I've met."

"Well, good for you, Gabriel," Anne said dryly. "But I think I have more experience than you do in these matters, and what mortals call the *supernatural* is in fact part of the natural world. It simply exists in a dimension that's rarely seen because they cannot open their minds to it." She thought of Mara Vardac. "Until it comes and steals their children from their beds at night. So I follow the stories where they lead me and I kill the monsters." She touched the corner of her eye. "Because I know how to see them for what they are."

Gabriel was quiet for a long moment. "It is evil men who make this evil world," he said in a low voice.

"You've read Saint Augustine."

"Every word. He was a true sage."

"He had some interesting ideas, I'll grant you. But I don't believe evil is the result of man's original sin. It's a matter of choice."

"And you think I'm evil?"

Anne said nothing.

"Yet you're not afraid."

"If you wanted me dead, I would be. That much is clear. But I'm of more value to you alive. It's the only reason I'm sitting here."

"*Nom de dieu!*" Gabriel pushed off the windowsill and spun around. "You're trying to make me feel *guilty*." He stabbed a finger at her. "I'm the wronged party here."

"No," Anne said patiently. "You already feel guilty. That's why you cook these elaborate meals and bring me priceless books and violins. All of it is unnecessary. You could simply give me a crust of bread and a cup of water and be done with it. But it assuages your conscience to think you're treating me like royalty."

He stared at her, then laughed and shook his head.

"And since you're atoning for your sins, you can give me a tour of the house now."

"What?"

"I'm not tired and I don't want to go up there yet." She glanced at the inner door to the tower. "So you'll have to drag me, screaming and wailing, up the staircase. I'll likely end up with bruises. Or you can just show me around. One more hour."

He blew out a breath. "Thirty minutes."

"Done."

Anne smiled.

Full dark had fallen outside. Gabriel lifted the candle and followed her to the stairs. This time, when they reached the bottom of the tower, he unlocked another door. It led to a large, gloomy gallery festooned with cobwebs.

"You see?" he said with a curt gesture. "Nothing of interest."

Anne strode past him and examined the row of portraits on the walls, all of unsmiling aristocrats with stiff collars and bad wigs. "Is this your family?"

He laughed. "I don't come from money."

"But you own this place now."

He shrugged.

"What happened to the people who lived here?"

He drew a slow finger across his throat.

"You murdered them?"

He shot her an affronted look. "No! Don't you know your history?"

"Ah. Executed in the Revolution?" she guessed.

"They deserved it."

"That's rather callous, don't you think?"

His face darkened. "If you'd seen the way the peasants lived back then, you wouldn't feel sorry for them."

"It was a hundred years ago." She cast him a shrewd look. "A bit before your time, wasn't it, Gabriel?"

He cleared his throat. "The name of the house is Chateau de Saint-Évreux. It sat empty for a long time. I bought it cheap, but I never came here much."

"Until now."

"Yes. Can we go back now?"

"No."

Gabriel sighed but followed as she walked to the end of the gallery and up a wide staircase. They drifted through the keep like ghosts, passing through rooms with furniture covered in sheets and more cobwebs dangling from the chandeliers. There were creaky suits of armor and all sorts of nasty medieval weapons hanging in brackets on the walls, which she pointedly ignored.

She knew he was watching her closely.

"It's getting late," he said.

"Just one more." She darted ahead before he could seize her arm and pushed open a door on the uppermost floor. Anne made a sound of delight.

"The music room!"

She whisked the sheets off, admiring the pianoforte and harp, which stood a full foot taller than her. The western wall facing the sea had beautiful stained glass windows, though most were broken. Gabriel set the candle atop the piano and danced his fingers across the keys, wincing slightly at the off-kilter notes.

"Do you play?" she asked.

In answer, he launched into the first chords of Schumann's Toccata in C Major, a notoriously difficult piece.

"Show-off," Anne muttered, shards of glass crunching beneath her feet as she crossed to the windows.

"They must have been broken by one of the storms that blow in from the Channel," Gabriel said, his feet working the pedals, fingers flying as the octaves gained speed.

"Lucky thing you have shutters." She grinned at him. "You're a good cook, but a poor housekeeper.... Damn!" She pressed her hand to her mouth. The music cut off and Gabriel was suddenly at her side.

"Let me see it," he demanded.

She held out her palm. Blood flowed freely from a long gash.

"Make a fist," he ordered. "I'll bind it up."

"You could use that." She pointed to one of the dust coverings. "I'll wash it out when we get back."

Gabriel hurried over to the sheet puddled at the base of the harp. The moment his back was turned, Anne slipped the catch to the shutters, taking care to keep them closed. She spun back just as he was rising. He tore a strip from the sheet and bent over her hand with an intent, focused expression.

He was always like that, she realized. Whatever Gabriel did, whether it was laying the table or buckling his boot or listening to her talk, he gave the task his full attention. It was a quality very few people had.

"There. I have a clean dish towel in the kitchen. You might need stitches—"

"It's fine. I'll heal."

He nodded. Anne prayed he wouldn't look over at the hook to the shutters, now dangling loose.

"I suppose we'd better get back," he said.

They returned to the tower and Gabriel hovered in the doorway, asking if she needed anything else. He obviously had little use for first aid, and seemed to feel bad that he didn't have any iodine or bandages. Anne gave him a cheerful smile.

"I'm fine, really. Thank you for the tour, Gabriel. Goodnight."

She derived great satisfaction from closing the door in his face.

She went up to her room and played the violin for a spell. Then she waited.

When the moon was setting and she estimated the hour to be after three, she pulled her boots back on. The music room was no accidental discovery. It was the very room in the adjacent tower that had thwarted her once before.

But not tonight.

Gabriel had never come to check on her after dinner, not once. In fact, after seeing the rest of Chateau de Saint-Évreux, she felt sure he went someplace else. Who could live in that dismal, drafty old castle? He always arrived on horseback.

Yes, she thought, he must go elsewhere to do … whatever it is he does.

She didn't like to dwell on what that might be.

Anne went into the privy, opened the window, and hoisted a leg over the sill.

CHAPTER 14

T he rain had stopped, but the peak of the roof between the two towers was still slippery. Anne crept along it with care, conscious of the long drop to either side. It was very dark and she couldn't see a glimmer of light in any direction. She tried to remember what towns might be found along the Alabaster Coast. Once Gabriel discovered her gone, he would pursue her relentlessly, she had no doubts about that. He was a man who took things personally. A man with an explosive temper.

And he might be able to hunt by scent.

The laudanum had left her memory fuzzy around the edges. Anne remembered little about the night he'd tracked her in the snow, only his glowing eyes and the lonely whistle of the train. In some ways this was worse because her imagination conjured up all sorts of visions of the beast that lived inside him.

But fear made a person careless, and Anne took pride in being precise and logical, so she put the thought from her mind and focused on reaching the second tower without falling.

Somewhere nearby an owl screeched, startling her. She clung to the roofline until her heart slowed, then resumed crawling, knees straddling the slate tiles. At last, she reached the second tower. She stood and inched her way along a narrow ledge to the window, fumbling with the shutters until she found the one she'd left unlatched. They opened outward so there was a terrifying moment where she hung, feet dangling over a hundred feet of open air. Then a toe found the sill and she swung inside, dropping silently to the carpet.

Anne stood there for a full minute, listening to the sounds of the house. The rustle of mice nesting in musty goosedown mattresses. The creaks of loose boards settling. Nothing else, though Gabriel's familiar scent lingered in the room like a specter.

She retraced their steps from the evening before, navigating by the faint starlight coming through the windows. She found the gallery of dead nobles and followed it to the end where it flowed into a grand entrance hall with two large doors. Anne laid her palm on the heavy oak and took a deep breath.

It swung open.

He hadn't bothered to lock it.

Why?

Because he never expected her to get this far. Well, he'd be in for a rude surprise.

Anne stepped into the night.

A low fog hovered above the ground, swirling around her legs as she ran across the inner bailey. Now for the curtain wall. This presented a minor obstacle. She wasn't as strong or fast with the talisman around her neck, but she could still climb like a monkey and this wall was in far worse condition than the tower, with cracks that had gone unrepaired for decades. Anne removed her boots and hooked her fingers into crevices in the stone, scaling it with grim determination. Descending the other side proved trickier, but she managed it with a few scrapes, dropping to the soft ground from six paces up.

Ragged shreds of cloud raced overhead, the moon appearing and vanishing. She followed the wall, staying in the shadows, until she stumbled across the road. Anne set off at a brisk walk, still recovering her strength. The road wound through the woods, hard-packed earth with deep ruts from the carts and carriages that had once come to Chateau de Saint-Évreux.

She'd gone about a half a mile when she thought she heard the faint thunder of hooves. She hurried to the shelter of the woods where the firs grew thickly together and crouched down. Rain dripped from the branches of the trees. Two screech owls called to each other in the night, thin, unearthly cries that reminded her of the train whistle. Night insects chirped in the carpet of dead leaves.

Anne heard no more hoofbeats, but she decided the road was too exposed and set off into the forest. It was old growth, untouched by an axe for generations. This made for easier travel since the dense canopy of hardwoods kept the undergrowth sparse. After several minutes, she saw an unbroken stretch of darkness ahead. Anne's steps slowed as she approached a high brick wall.

The whole estate was enclosed.

She gazed up at it, gathering courage. Her legs ached from running and climbing, and her arms hung at her sides like dead weights. The adrenaline burst of escaping the tower was ebbing, but she had to scale the wall. There was no going back now.

Suddenly, Anne realized that the nocturnal sounds of the forest had ceased, leaving a pocket of perfect silence. Her scalp prickled as she slowly turned around.

Nothing....

Her eyes strained to see into the darkness. Mist swirled around her bare feet, lapping at the wall like a white sea.

There.

At the edge of an open meadow about sixty feet away, a humped shadow. It might have been a boulder, except for the two gleaming pinpricks of silver. Even from a distance, she felt its gaze fixed on her.

Coppery fear flooded her mouth. She spun and ran at an angle away from the meadow into a denser thicket, frantically seeking a hiding place. Thorns dragged at her gown and rocks bit her bare feet. The blood thudded in her ears as she mentally cursed the talisman around her neck. Freed, she would have been swifter than a gazelle. But this was like running in a suit of armor.

A twig snapped behind her. Anne stumbled and fell headlong down a steep slope into the shallows of a creek. She rolled to her back in the chill water as a massive weight crushed her into the streambed. She felt a thick ruff of fur between in her fingers and then teeth pressed against her throat, claws digging into her skin. The same animal musk she'd smelled before filled her nose, but a hundred times more potent.

"Stop, Gabriel," Anne whispered hoarsely, unable to draw breath. "Please … don't.…"

And then she heard his voice, hard and commanding.

"*Donné! Au pied!*"

The beast on top of her emitted a deep growl. Anne felt the vibrations of it rumble through her ribcage, where the massive chest pressed against her.

"*Donné!*"

The weight lifted. Anne drew a ragged breath as something huge slunk off into the trees. She sat up and examined the claw marks on her arm in a daze.

"*Nom de dieu.*" Gabriel crouched beside her, fully human but with leaves in his hair and streaks of dirt across his bare chest. She expected one of his titanic furies, but he looked … frightened. He cupped her face and she saw only concern in his eyes.

"Where are you hurt?"

She blinked and looked down. A shaft of moonlight fell across a pale hip and muscled thigh.

Oh God, he's naked.

"I've had worse," she managed. "A thousand times worse." She held up her arm. "Just scratches, see?" But they were deep and rivulets of blood ran down, dripping from her elbow.

Gabriel cursed roundly and slid his arms beneath her back, lifting her as easily as a child. Anne opened her mouth to object, but she felt suddenly very tired. Her dress was soaking wet. A shiver wracked her body.

Without another word, he started to run through the forest. She laid her head on his shoulder and watched the crescent moon overhead through drowsy eyes. It followed them all the way back to Chateau de Saint-Évreux.

She expected to be returned to her prison, but Gabriel entered the main keep and kicked open a door on the third floor. The master bedroom, judging by the palatial size of the four-poster bed. Anne was too exhausted to care as he eased her onto the coverlet.

"Drink this." He pressed a cup to her lips.

She weakly tried to push it away. "No laudanum."

"It's not, I swear. Just brandy, to help you sleep."

Anne sniffed it, then took a small sip. Warmth spread through her frozen limbs.

"The sheets are clean. But I must dress your wounds." His voice was both rough and oddly gentle. "Trust me, you don't want to be awake for it. Once more."

He raised the cup to her lips again and Anne swallowed a mouthful, then turned her head away, nestling her cheek into the pillow. A pile of books sat on the bedside table. She read the titles with bleary eyes.

On Grace and Free Will, by Saint Augustine.

A battered copy of *The Koran* in Arabic.

And *Tales of the Grotesque and Arabesque*, by Edgar Allen Poe.

Gabriel sat on the edge of the bed, fussing with a needle and thread. She smelled the sharp tang of spirits. Anne reached up and patted his cheek, the brandy smoothing away the pain in her arm. Her thoughts felt pleasantly slow. "You're a peculiar man,

Gabriel." She smiled. "I should have known it wasn't you. It had silver eyes and yours are gold."

He frowned down at her. "Just sleep, Anne."

As consciousness fled, she realized it was the first time he'd ever used her Christian name.

Anne woke to bright sunlight spilling through the windows. For a moment, she had no idea where she was. Then she saw Gabriel sitting in a chair, looking haggard but more like himself. All traces of mud were gone. His hair was tied back in a black ribbon. He wore a blue frock coat and snug trousers and looked every inch the dapper country gentleman — had the year been 1760.

"That was a very stupid thing you did," he growled as their eyes met.

"Good morning to you, too," Anne retorted, sitting up against the headboard. Her arm was bandaged from wrist to shoulder with what looked like one of Gabriel's old shirts. She felt woozy and hot. "Don't pretend you wouldn't have done the same if you were in my place."

He leapt to his feet. "That doesn't make it any less foolish!"

"How was I to know you had some vicious ... *pet* ... roaming the grounds? You never tell me anything. If you'd warned me, I might—" She bit her lip. There was no point in being nice to him anymore. He'd never let her out of his sight again. Anne looked down at the frilly nightgown and her fury redoubled. "And you undressed me."

He threw his hands up. "You were soaked to the bone! Believe me, it was no great thrill."

They glared at each other for a long moment.

"What was that?" she demanded. "Not a wolf or a dog. It felt like a bloody rhinoceros with teeth."

Gabriel didn't reply.

"It has to do with what you are, doesn't it?" She studied him. "What was done to you, Gabriel?"

"Nothing was *done* to me. And I'm not a monster, whatever you might think."

Her lip curled. "No? You killed those children in Mara Vardac."

Gabriel stiffened, but the fight seemed to leave him. "That wasn't me," he muttered.

"Who then?"

He sank back into the chair and laid his head in his hands. "I made a terrible mistake, Anne. I trusted someone I shouldn't have. His name was Adrian." Gabriel looked up at her with reddened eyes. "He paid for it. I tore his throat out myself, just as he did to the children."

Anne stared at him until he turned away. "Let me go," she said quietly. "I won't tell anyone where this place is. You have my word. But you've no right to keep me here any longer."

"I can't."

"No, you *won't*. There's a difference."

"You don't understand."

"Then help me to understand!"

"I never wanted you, Anne." Gabriel sounded weary. "You shouldn't have come to Saint George's." He stood and walked to the door. "But now it's too late. I have to finish it. I *have* to."

Anne prided herself on self-control, but his blind stubbornness shattered her calm into a thousand sharp pieces. Her hands trembled with rage.

"I was wrong," she shouted at him. "There is a Hell. And you're the Devil!"

Gabriel stared at her for a long moment. "You can stay in my bedroom until you're well. Mr. Poe claims the death of a beautiful woman is, unquestionably, the most poetical topic in the world." He gave Anne a vicious, wounded look. "But then you'd do me no good at all."

"My brother will come for me," she spat. "He'll find me if it takes him a thousand years."

Gabriel smiled bleakly. "I'm counting on it."

The door slammed shut.

CHAPTER 15

Alec Lawrence sat on the flagstone veranda of the Hotel Santa Catalina, his cane propped against a wicker lounge chair and a cup of tea steaming at his elbow. The waves of the Atlantic broke on a white sand beach in the distance. Beyond, he could see the dark peaks of volcanic islands and the triangular sails of yachts racing across the bay.

Another day in paradise.

The weather on Gran Canaria was hard to argue with. The temperature perpetually hovered in the mid-seventies and a gentle sea breeze nudged pillowy clouds along the horizon. Alec had tossed his coat aside and opened his collar, revealing a tan throat that made a pleasant change from his usual pastiness. He wished he could roll up his shirtsleeves too, but the gold cuff circling his wrist would draw unwanted attention.

Ah, well. He could live with that.

Alec took a sip of tea and basked like a cat.

The Hotel Santa Catalina specialized in catering to wealthy Britons fleeing the cold and damp of winter. The staff did a smashing teatime, with cakes and sandwiches and Darjeeling with fresh cream. Alec took a lemon cake from a tray and sighed happily. He'd only intended to stay for a week or so, but he kept finding excuses to prolong his holiday.

He knew he should send a cable to Vivienne. Every day, he resolved to do it. And every day, he somehow forgot until it was too late.

I needed some time away, he thought. *I bloody earned it.*

Alec smiled as a white-jacketed waiter refilled his cup and brought a fresh platter of sandwiches and pastries.

Three more days, he vowed. *Then I'll go back to London.*

Just the thought made him vaguely depressed. Alec ate several custard tarts.

At least he might catch a glimpse of Anne. Such sightings were rare, he thought with wry tenderness, but she always came home for her birthday. No doubt she'd be haring off for some-place else within a matter of days. Sometimes he envied her complete freedom.

Alec's routine was to wake early while the other guests were still sleeping off the previous night's revelry and go swimming in the sea. Then he'd walk into town and prowl through the Mercado de Vegueta, stopping for lunch at one of the little open-air cafes along the corniche. A siesta followed, after which he'd claim a chair on the veranda and mingle with the other guests, most of them Brits and Continentals. Then came dinner — a sumptuous black-tie affair — after which he'd retire to his rooms and sit on the balcony, watching the stars wheel across the sky.

Alec closed his eyes, listening to soft buzz of conversation. He liked being anonymous, one of the holiday-making herd. He'd never indulged in anything resembling a *vacation* before, certainly not without Vivienne. They spent all their time hunting the endless tide of creatures that tore through the veil of the Dominion and made mischief in the world of the living. Things had gotten a bit better since they managed to close the last of the Greater Gates, but then they'd been called in on the case in New York last year.

What an utter nightmare *that* turned out to be.

Alec brushed crumbs from his hands and pushed away the plate before he polished off the whole thing. He resolved to insist on a holiday once a year — alone. As much as he missed Viv, it was healthy to take time apart and only distance would accomplish that.

The bond between them was much more than a physical connection. She lived in his head, just as he lived in hers. They couldn't read each other's thoughts — thank God — but raw emotions leaked through.

But when he got far enough away from her, Vivienne became a whisper instead of a shout. He could still vaguely sense her presence, and could have found her anywhere in the world simply by following the magnetic tug of the bond, but her emotions were no longer tangled up with his.

It felt ... strange.

Alec picked up a copy of the local newspaper, *El Liberal*. The biggest news was the opening of a new theater called the Teatro Pérez Galdós. The rest of the front page was devoted to a bitter rivalry with the newspaper on Tenerife, which he read with amused interest until a feminine voice broke in.

"Why, hello again, Mr. Lawrence!"

He squinted up into the light. A blonde woman with lightly sunburnt cheeks gazed down at him, her lips curved in a smile. Alec stood and bowed from the waist, leaning on the handle of his cane.

"Miss Carlisle."

She beamed at him with a set of perfect white teeth. *American* teeth. Miss Carlisle wore a sleeveless gown with tiny lace gloves that were pointless and, Alec thought, extremely erotic. She had warm brown eyes and a lanky, athletic grace.

"Mrs. Mackenzie," he said to the older woman with tightly curled hair and a steely gaze who stood at Miss Carlisle's side. "What a pleasure."

Miss Carlisle was heiress to an oil fortune and Mrs. Mackenzie was her chaperone. Alec had been seated across from them at dinner the night before. When her minder retired to the powder room, Miss Carlisle confided that she'd been sent off to Europe after a minor scandal with a suitor. In contrast to the stiff English girls, she was funny and forthright with a twangy drawl he found appealing.

"Won't you join me?" he asked, sweeping his hat from an adjacent chair. "They've just served tea. I was a selfish pig and ate all the custard tarts, but there are still scones and watercress sandwiches."

Miss Carlisle inclined her head and sank into the chair, crossing her ankles demurely though her smile held a hint of the devil. Mrs. Mackenzie's lips tightened — her single task was to keep Miss Carlisle out of trouble and Alec Lawrence looked like trouble — but then her eye lighted on the tray of pastries and she softened a little.

"I suppose I could use some sustenance," she muttered, settling into the chair to Alec's left. She snagged a pastry and fanned herself with the other hand. "This tropical heat is exhausting."

Alec exchanged a deadpan look with Miss Carlisle, whose eyes twinkled.

"It's the humidity," she said. "I don't suppose you've ever been to the great state of Texas?"

"I haven't had the pleasure."

"Well, it's awful hot, but more like a desert, you see. Poor Mrs. Mackenzie isn't used to the wet." She licked her lips as she said this, reaching for a watercress sandwich.

"Well, I'd trade with you in a heartbeat. London is a dreary place. Lord Byron said the English winter ends in July and recommences in August."

Miss Carlisle pulled a face. "I wouldn't like that. Though I'm looking forward to seeing Buckingham Palace." She looked at Mrs. Mackenzie. "We're planning a tour of England in April."

Alec stared out to sea. He had a brief flash of a ghoul dressed as a second butler tottering toward Queen Victoria's bedchamber. He'd been pursuing the thing when it got inside the palace through a side door. Alec had raced down the corridor and beheaded it moments before it reached the Queen, prompting a scandal that led to the creation of Scotland Yard's Dominion Branch.

"Mr. Lawrence?"

"Sorry." Alec turned back to her. "Wool-gathering. What did you say?"

Miss Carlisle eyed his cup of tea. "All your countrymen are having gin and tonic," she said with a teasing smile. "Tell me you're not one of those temperance sorts who preach against the evils of liquor."

Alec sipped his tea and set it back into the saucer. "I'm afraid so, Miss Carlisle. I never drink spirits."

She looked genuinely bewildered. "Whyever not?"

Alec sighed as he pondered a semi-truthful reply. "Because they make me feel warm and fuzzy."

"And what's wrong with that?" she demanded with a laugh.

"Nothing. I just prefer to keep my wits about me."

"Well, I think it's admirable," Mrs. Mackenzie put in. "Drunkenness is unbecoming. The male species is idiotic enough without the assistance of alcohol."

"Now, Mrs. Mackenzie," Miss Carlisle chided.

"She's perfectly right," Alec said. *"Bacchus hath drowned more men than Neptune."*

Mrs. Mackenzie shot him the first approving look he'd ever gotten from her. "Now that's clever! I have to admit, you Englishmen have a way with words."

Miss Carlisle studied him with a speculative gaze. "Are you

really from England, Mr. Lawrence? You don't sound like it. Your accent, I mean."

Alec was used to this, but he played along. "What do I sound like?"

"I don't know. French, maybe. Or Spanish." She frowned. "Though neither is quite right. You sound like … like you grew up speaking another language but moved to England when you were a boy. I can hear traces of your mother tongue. Something softer."

Alec made a noncommittal noise. She was dancing around the edges of the truth. He had indeed grown up speaking another language, but it was not French or Spanish or anything she would recognize. It was a language long dead, known only to a handful of scholars.

Miss Carlisle wouldn't be put off. "Tell me, Mr. Lawrence, don't be coy. Coy men are even more irritating than drunk ones."

"You read me like an open book," he said with a shrug. "I was born in Portugal. My family moved to London when I was six. My father's a banker. But my mother always spoke Portuguese to me."

Mrs. Mackenzie gaze him an appraising look. "Say something."

Alec raised an eyebrow.

"In Portuguese." She made a shooing motion. "Well, go ahead."

Alec sighed. He had a sudden feeling of uneasiness and wished they'd leave him alone.

"*O amor é uma amizade que pega fogo.*"

"Which means?"

"Love is friendship set on fire."

Alec knew this would provoke her. Mrs. Mackenzie scowled, though Miss Carlisle looked pleased.

"Come." The older woman tried to stand and found herself impeded by the large quantity of cakes she'd consumed. "We're due for a game of croquet on the lawn with the Davises."

"Must we?" Miss Carlisle pouted.

The tone brooked no argument. "Yes, we must. It'll do you good to spend some time with girls your own age." Mrs. Mackenzie cast Alec a narrow look. "Good afternoon, Mr. Lawrence."

"Good afternoon." He held out a hand and levered her from the chair.

"Perhaps we can play a game of whist after dinner," Miss Carlisle said hopefully.

"I'm not very good at cards."

She lowered her voice to a murmur. "I'll teach you."

Her gaze promised to teach him any number of things. Thankfully, Mrs. Mackenzie was busy adjusting her skirts and failed to notice.

Alec opened his mouth to utter a flirty reply when a sudden burst of emotion shot through the bond. His bad knee jerked, knocking the teapot from the tray. It shattered on the flagstones, spewing a puddle of lukewarm tea. The ladies jumped back. Miss Carlisle exclaimed something, but Alec barely heard a word. His heart raced, his tongue suddenly dry.

The fear that gripped him was not his own.

Vivienne.

"What's the matter?" Miss Carlisle asked, her brow creased with concern. "Are you all right?"

Alec murmured some excuse. The intensity was fading, but it didn't matter. Something dire had happened and he needed to get back to London as fast as possible.

"I do apologize," he said, pulling himself together enough to smile reassuringly, though he wanted nothing more than to run straight to the nearest ferry. "I think I'd best lie down. The heat. Perhaps we'll see each other at dinner."

Before she could reply, he gripped the silver falcon capping his cane and strode through the French doors into the cavernous lobby. Well-dressed guests gathered in a ragged line at the front desk, stacks of steamer trunks off to the side. A bellhop cast him a quick curious glance as he crossed the thick maroon carpet to the lift and waited impatiently while the arrow crept toward the lobby level.

The door opened on polished wood and mirrors. Alec told the short, moustachioed operator his floor and the lift began to ascend. He glanced at himself in the mirror, searching for some sign of the inner turmoil that raged just below the surface, yet he was neatly combed and pressed as usual. Brown hair and eyes, slender build, every inch the English gentleman. What a farce.

Vivienne.

Damnit.

She was fine. Of course she was fine.

The elevator reached the top floor and the door opened. Alec stepped out. He hurried down the deserted corridor, fumbling in his pocket for the room key. Number 513. Behind him, he heard the door close and the whir of the cable as the elevator began to descend.

He was a few feet away from the door to his room when he felt it, like a hard punch to the gut.

Not the bond this time.

No, this was different.

The sensation made his skin crawl.

Something dangerous.

Part of him was less worried about *what* the hell it was and more about *why* he'd suddenly developed this sixth sense. He'd never had it before.

Not until their last case.

But that was a topic to be mulled over later.

Alec stopped walking and drew a slow breath through his nose. He flicked the hidden catch on his cane and the sheath fell away, revealing an iron rapier inside. Alec crept forward until he stood before the door to his room. The sensation lessened.

That came as a surprise.

He'd expected whatever it was to be waiting inside.

Moving silently on the balls of his feet, Alec approached the room next door, number 511. The feeling intensified, rolling over him in a dark tide.

He hesitated. A ghoul?

Only one way to find out.

Alec took a deep breath and slid into the Nexus, the place where all things were one, the source of elemental magic. He could hear the overlapping thump of two hearts beating beyond the door. Both male — he detected a whiff of testosterone.

Alec's shoulder slammed into the door. It flew off the hinges with a mighty splintering of wood.

The room beyond was a mirror image of his own. It had a generous sitting area with a blue silk couch and two matching armchairs. The décor was Old World, the furniture heavily carved and embroidered. Dark landscapes hung on the walls. One side had doors leading to the terrace, which were closed and shuttered. The other opened to a bedroom and bathroom. Those doors were also closed. The only sound was a ceiling fan whirring overhead.

A young man in a bowler hat sat in one of the armchairs beneath a dramatic painting of a ship wrecked on a reef, storm clouds lit from beneath by a jagged bolt of lightning. He was smoking a cigarette and playing solitaire on a glass table. He looked up in almost comical surprise as the door sailed across the room. Alec was on him in an instant, seizing the lapels of his coat and hurling him against the far wall. He struck it hard and slid to ground, stunned.

Alec stepped over him and kicked open the door to the bathroom. The second man was waiting inside. He was a giant, easily six and half feet tall, with huge, wild eyes and very pale skin. He stood in front of the claw-footed bathtub with a crossbow pointed at the door. In the heightened clarity of the Nexus, Alec saw his hand shaking, smelled the waves of fear rolling off him.

Before the door had rebounded, the giant released the trigger. Alec whipped his head to the side. The bolt sped past his face and buried itself in the wall beyond. The giant tossed the crossbow aside and pulled out a hunting knife. Despite the fact that he towered over Alec and had at least a hundred pounds on him, he had the look of a cornered animal.

Which meant only one thing: He knew Alec was a daēva.

The giant's lips drew back from his teeth. He was girding himself to attack. Before he could move, Alec darted forward and knocked the knife from his hand, but the man was quicker than he expected, kicking Alec in his bad knee with a size fourteen boot. White agony exploded through the joint, along with fury.

They knew his weaknesses, too.

Alec heard the other man moving in the sitting room and decided it was time to end this charade. He reached for earth power, intending to crack some bones ... and hit a wall. The Nexus popped like a soap bubble.

His power had just been blocked, trapped in the bond.

What the hell was Vivienne doing?

Alec flailed against the barrier, knowing it would do no good. If Vivienne were here, he'd scream at her to release him, but she wasn't and he couldn't worry about that now. He swept his sword in a deadly arc, slashing the giant's throat from ear to ear. Blood sheeted down his body as he toppled. Alec spun around and limped into the sitting area, his knee still screaming. The second man was backing toward the balcony. Judging by the look in his eyes, he knew exactly what was coming for him.

"What are you?" Alec asked softly.

The man didn't reply. He was a few years younger than his companion, mid-twenties, with dark hair and smooth cheeks. Decently dressed, neither rich nor poor. He looked like the fresh-faced students Alec would see streaming out of the buildings at University College in London. Yet Alec could sense the danger in him.

"I'll spare your life if you tell me who sent you."

Five stories below, the distant thunder of carriage wheels rattled along the seaside corniche.

The man smiled grimly. "Go to hell, daēva," he said in a thick French accent.

"Why are you here? What do you want from me?"

The man's eyes hardened. He turned and ran for the balcony. Alec lurched forward. His fingers brushed the man's coat as he smashed through the shutters and vaulted over the wrought iron railing. Alec leaned out over the balcony in time to see him hit the street just ahead of a carriage. The horses whinnied, rearing up in their traces and nearly overturning the carriage as they danced to the side.

Alec cursed in Old Persian, the native tongue that still emerged in times of intense fear or frustration.

There'd been no hesitation. Whoever they were, these men had iron discipline and their instructions clearly included not being taken alive.

Alec went back inside. The giant lay dead on the black and white bathroom tiles amid a lake of blood, his eyes staring blankly at the ceiling. Alec swore again, mainly at himself. He'd meant to keep at least one of them alive for questioning. He rummaged through the man's clothes, finding only a wad of banknotes and a ticket stub from the ferry.

He quickly searched the other rooms. There was nothing — not a single personal item. The men must have been staying elsewhere and using this room only for surveillance. Alec hurried out, retrieving the sheath to his cane from the corridor. Happily, it was still empty. He stopped in his own room just long enough to wash the blood from his hands and toss his belongings into a valise, then took the stairs down as fast as his bed leg would allow.

He estimated six minutes had passed since the second man went over the balcony.

Alec slowed to a walk once he reached the red-carpeted lobby. The Hotel Santa Catalina had just opened two months before and it still looked pristine, a luxe playground of crystal chandeliers, marble floors and Greco-Roman statues in niches. The hotel manager was trying to calm a hysterical woman dripping with jewels, leaving a junior clerk to handle the front desk. The people milling around had all gone outside to gawk and the lobby was almost empty. Alec stepped up to the gleaming desk.

"What happened?" he asked.

"A terrible accident, señor," the clerk said. He looked shaken and he kept glancing through the plate glass windows at the crowd gathered outside. "May I assist you with anything?"

"I heard a disturbance in Room 511. It sounded like a violent argument. Who's staying there?"

The clerk frowned. "You must be mistaken, señor. That room is currently unoccupied."

"I'm certain I heard something. Would you mind double-checking?"

The clerk opened the large guest book and ran his finger down the page, then spun it around it to face Alec. "Empty, you see?" He swallowed. "But you ought to tell the police. They'll be here any minute." He lowered his voice. "Someone fell."

"My God," Alec said. "That's terrible."

The clerk glanced at his suitcase.

"Checking out, Señor Lawrence?"

"Yes. And I'm in a bit of a hurry."

A flicker of suspicion crossed the clerk's face as Alec settled the bill — he was starting to put two and two together — but the manager was still trying to soothe the loudly sobbing woman and he had been trained to treat guests with the utmost courtesy and delicacy.

Alec slid a folded five-pound note across the counter.

"Thank you for your help, I'd best go see if the police have arrived."

The clerk nodded and he limped across the lobby and down the front steps. Alec pushed his way through the crowd gathered in the street, ignoring the offended murmurs. The man lay on the paving stones, his head twisted at an impossible angle. It was clear he was dead. No one had approached the body.

"He jumped," someone said in the hushed voice of tragedy. "From the fifth floor. I saw it. Threw himself straight over the rail like the Devil himself was on his heels."

It was only a matter of time before they found the second body. They might think the two men fought, that one killed the other and then leapt to his death. It would all be quite neat except for the fact that Alec had stepped in the blood and tracked it into his own room. He'd been so preoccupied by the loss of his power, he hadn't noticed until it was too late.

I need to get the hell out of here, Alec thought, crouching down and rifling through the man's pockets.

Mutters of disapproval erupted.

"Hey there!" someone called out. "What are you doing?"

Alec ignored them. The pockets were empty save for a cigarette case with a strange symbol engraved on the lid. It looked vaguely familiar, though Alec couldn't quite place where he'd seen it before. He thrust it into his own pocket.

"You've got blood on you, Mr. Lawrence."

He looked up into the eyes of Miss Carlisle. They no longer danced with mischief. Now they were filled with confusion. Alec followed her gaze to his coat sleeve. The fabric was dark enough that it hadn't been visible in the lobby, but beneath the bright sun a stain was visible. He touched it and his fingers came away red.

"You're hurt," she said softly.

Alec said nothing. It wasn't his. She bit her lip.

"Did you see it happen? Mrs. Mackenzie and I were on the lawn. I heard a scream…."

Alec glanced over her shoulder. The elevator operator stood with the hotel manager in front of the pink façade. They were looking at him and whispering together, no doubt about the fact that he rode up to the top floor just minutes before the victim plunged to his death.

"Farewell, Miss Carlisle," Alec said. He rose and kissed her hand. "It was truly a pleasure to make your acquaintance."

She gave him a look that was both fearful and intrigued, and seemed about to say something more when Mrs. Mackenzie came charging out of the hotel. She bulled through the crowd and seized Miss Carlisle's arm, pulling her away from the body.

"It's no fit sight for a young girl," she exclaimed with a shudder. "What sort of hotel is this? I'll have nightmares for the rest of my life! And where are the authorities? Are they planning to leave this poor creature to rot in the sun like a stray dog—"

Right on cue, Alec heard the shrill blast of a police whistle.

He grabbed his valise and limped away as fast as he dared into the tangle of streets off the corniche. As he turned the corner several policemen hurried past. He averted his face and stared into a shop window. As soon as they were gone, he started running for the pier where the passenger ferries to Cadiz departed. Date palms and red hibiscus trees lined the main thoroughfares, but Alec avoided the busiest routes, taking a path through the steep, narrow alleyways he'd spent weeks exploring.

He reached the terminal just as one of the ferries took on the last passengers.

Would Miss Carlisle tell them about the blood? Perhaps not, but it didn't really matter. The police would be on the fifth floor by now.

His knee throbbed like a rotten tooth as he staggered the last quarter mile to the pier, where a nearly full ferry sat at anchor. Alec bought a third-class ticket and went aboard. It was crowded with tourists just like himself, half of them red from the sun, hot and tired and with the glum look that signaled the end of a holiday. The berths were below and there was a scrum around the cramped staircases leading to the lower decks. Alec found a place at the bow and propped his elbows on the rail.

Some enemy he'd forgotten about — or wasn't aware of in the first place? It was more than possible. One didn't live as long as Alec Lawrence had without leaving a trail of stepped-on toes.

He watched grey gulls float on the air currents. Any minute, he expected to hear a police whistle. The ferry was the first place they'd look. Then he felt a vibration through the soles of his shoes as the great steam engine fired up. A ripple of excitement moved through the passengers. The crew tossed the mooring lines to the pier, where a handful of locals waved goodbyes. The ship chugged out of the harbor and met the swells of the Atlantic. Somewhere to the east lay the coast of Morocco, though it was too far to see. In two days, he'd be in Cadiz. With any luck, the Spanish police wouldn't be waiting for him.

Alec's gaze turned northwest, following the pull of the bond. His fingers tightened around the silver falcon head of his cane.

He wouldn't be returning to London until he found Vivienne and he knew she wasn't there.

She was somewhere much farther away.

If it meant diving over the rail of the ferry and swimming, Alec would do it in a heartbeat, but for now…. At least he was moving in the right direction.

CHAPTER 16

For two days, the snowfall didn't cease. It blanketed Saint George's monastery in a shroud of white, leaving the party from Mara Vardac stranded within the high walls.

Father Cernat cared for Nathaniel himself, setting the broken bone and brewing poultices from the herbs in the infirmary to dull the pain and stave off infection. But they both knew his skills were not enough.

"Lord Cumberland needs a hospital," the priest whispered to Vivienne, who kept a vigil at his bedside. "He's strong, but…." The look in his eyes made her afraid.

She made sure the fire stayed lit and replaced Nathaniel's blankets when he pushed them to the floor, burning with fever. When she did find snatches of sleep, she suffered from nightmares, though she never remembered them — only woke with a scream trapped in her throat.

The children's father, Cristian, came to check on Nathaniel's condition each morning. No one knew who had fired the shot, but Vivienne could see he felt terrible. Yet when she asked him what Father Nicolae had told him, he refused to speak of it.

Vivienne demanded another audience with the abbot. This was denied.

And so she sat in the infirmary, listening to the monk's voices rise and fall in the church, listening to the wind blow along the ramparts, and burning with a desperate need to find Alec. To see his face, touch his hand.

Just once more before she lost him forever.

And then, on the third day, dawn broke with clear skies and the reinforcements from Satinari finally arrived. A doctor, the constable, and a dozen other men, including the mayor of Mara Vardac and the innkeeper, Master Korzha.

"The pass is open?" she asked, having thrown her cloak on and run out to the gates to meet them.

Master Kozha nodded from his horse. "The snow is deep but the wind scoured it from the road." Relief showed on his face. "We came in time then."

Vivienne didn't reply. She hurried back to the infirmary while a group of monks saw to the new arrivals. Nathaniel's eyes were open, though his handsome face was ghostly and tight with pain. She eased herself down to the edge of the bed and took his hand.

"Vivienne," he murmured.

She helped him drink some water. "The doctor is here, my dear. He'll see to you."

He gave a small nod. "Tell me again what happened. It's all a fog...."

"Gavra was no abbot. I still don't understand, Nathaniel, but he has Anne. Florin and Constantin were his conspirators." She drew a breath. "He claimed Anne is still alive."

"Thank God," he muttered weakly.

"They escaped, I've no idea how." Vivienne paused. There was much Nathaniel didn't know about her. She would tell him all of it someday, but not now.

Yet she could make a beginning. "I have what's called a bond with Alec Lawrence. The cuffs we wear ... they're not simply a symbol. They have power, Nathaniel. Magic. Do you understand?"

"No, but that's all right." He searched her face. "Go to him. I'll return to England as soon as I can. The doctor's here now."

A tear ran down her cheek. "Thank you," she whispered.

Vivienne kissed Nathaniel softly on the mouth. He gripped her hand.

She gave the constable her statement, impatient to leave. And then she was striding for the stables, calling for her horse.

Vivienne galloped down to Mara Vardac, stopping only to pay Mistress Korzha for the mount and take the carvings of Innunu and Kavi, She of the Nine Flails who meted out vengeance. The rest of the luggage she abandoned.

From Satinari, Vivienne caught a train heading east. She followed the bond where it led her, not eating or sleeping, through a succession of villages and towns and cities, hardly aware of where she was, only where she *needed* to go.

With each hour, Alec drew closer.

Vivienne understood he was doing the same thing she was, and it lent her strength.

And then, after three days of hard travel, she found herself in a tiny train station somewhere in the mountains of Switzerland. Her hands shook as she heard a whistle shriek in the distance, saw a puff of smoke, and a minute later the train pulled in and she was running like a madwoman down the platform, searching the faces of the passengers as they stepped off.

And here came Alec, levering down the steps with his cane, his face pale and drawn. Vivienne barreled into him, her cheek pressing against his coat collar, and he held her for a long moment as she sobbed uncontrollably.

"I found you, Viv, don't worry," he whispered into her hair. "What's happened?"

She pulled away, trying to steady herself. Alec looked

shocked. She knew he'd never seen her like this before. Not once, in all their long years together.

"Is it Cyrus? Cassandane?"

Tears streamed down her cheeks as she held up her naked wrist. "A man took it … not even a man. *Something*…." She was nearly incoherent. "He gave me a message."

Alec stilled.

"He said to tell you D'Ange sends his regards." Her voice broke again. "Who *is* he, Alec?"

They caught a night train to Munich.

Vivienne fell asleep with her head on Alec's shoulder. He listened to her soft breathing, felt her heart beat in rhythm with his own.

He knew she hadn't rested in many days, so he hadn't told her all of it. She wouldn't have absorbed much anyway. Alec had simply said it was a man he'd hoped might be dead and that they needed to go to Cyrus Ashdown right away. She had nodded, compliant in a very un-Vivienne way. And then she had slept like a child in his arms, rousing only to change trains or eat the awful food he'd bought in the stations.

Alec couldn't think beyond getting to Ingress Abbey.

Please, God, let Cyrus still have it.

Alec understood now why he had suddenly lost control of his power. It was a queer side effect of the cuffs that the bond remained until the gold band touched the skin of another mortal, but if Vivienne wasn't actually wearing hers, the daēva's ability to use the Nexus would be trapped inside it.

But Alec didn't give a damn about that. What terrified him was that if their bond snapped, Vivienne would age and die, and he didn't know if it would be gradual or all at once. Would all that borrowed time suddenly catch up with her?

He rested his cheek against her forehead and watched his reflection in the dark forest speeding past the train window.

If he hadn't left her alone, this would never have happened.

Now, four trains later, they were finally pulling into Greenhithe Station in the tiny English village of Dartford. Alec roused her and hired a cart to take them to Ingress Abbey. An enormous neo-Gothic manor on the banks of the Thames, it had been a convent before King Henry seized it to fund his ruinous wars with France.

Vivienne seemed to revive as they rattled down the long driveway. She sat up straight, her hands tightly folded in her lap.

Cyrus's bonded daēva, Cassandane, must have seen them coming through a window. She threw the front door open and enclosed them both in a bear hug. A tall, broad-shouldered woman who kept her hair cropped short and preferred men's clothing, she was one of their dearest friends — and half of the only other bonded pair remaining in the world.

"No Anne?" she asked with an edge of worry … though not too much. It *was* Anne, after all.

Vivienne shook her head. "Inside. We'll tell you all of it."

They found Cyrus in his library, warming his slippered feet by a coal stove. Threads of silver wound through his hair and he looked much older than Vivienne, a man in his middle fifties. This was because he'd lost his bond with Cassandane for a period a long time ago, aging in the interim until they finally found each other again.

Cyrus had penetrating eyes, a patrician nose and thin, harsh lips, but they formed a smile at the sight of his visitors. He rarely, if ever, left Ingress Abbey anymore.

Alec strode across the room, his heart beating fast.

"Do you still have it? The rose cross?"

Cyrus raised shaggy brows. He gave a slow nod.

Alec fell into an armchair. "Thank Christ." He leaned over and handed Cyrus the cigarette case. "This was in the pocket of a man who followed me to Gran Canaria. Ring any bells?"

Cyrus took the case and examined it. "Oh, dear," he murmured.

"Out with it," Vivienne snapped, her old fire returning. "What does the symbol mean? Who is he?"

Cyrus met her eyes. "The Archangel Gabriel. The messenger of God."

She stared blankly. "Who the *hell* are you talking about?"

Alec answered. "His name is Gabriel D'Ange."

Vivienne sank down in a chair next to Alec. "Father Gavra," she said softly.

"That's what he called himself?" Cyrus asked. "It's Gabriel in Romanian."

"Give me that." Cyrus handed her the case. She glanced at it, then took one of the cigarettes inside and lit it, her jaw tight. "Well, he has Anne." She held up her wrist, pulling back the sleeve of her gown. "And my cuff. So let's have the whole story and see if we can find a way out of this mess."

Cassandane drew a sharp breath. Cyrus made a noise of sympathy.

"I'm so sorry," he said gently.

Vivienne glowered.

Alec leaned back, stretching his achy leg. "It was a long time ago. I'd been hearing rumors of an angel of death, a vigilante who preyed on men of power who had escaped punishment due to their money or influence. He left dozens of bodies across Europe, all drained to husks."

"A necromancer?" Cassandane asked.

"Clearly, but not the usual. This one had particular tastes. His own brand of rough justice."

"I do vaguely remember that," Vivienne said with a frown.

"They were bad men, his victims?" Cassandane gave Alec a funny look.

"Yes."

"I would've let him have his fun," she muttered.

"He was an *Antimagus,* Cass," Alec replied with a touch of asperity. "Our sworn enemies, remember?"

She grunted and poured a glass of *palinka,* the nasty home-made moonshine she drank like water.

"The trail led to Strasbourg, then part of the Holy Roman Empire," Alec continued. "The year was 1614, I believe." He looked at Cyrus, who nodded. "The man we sought had a strong interest in Christian mysticism. He would carve a symbol into the withered flesh. The sign of the Archangel Gabriel."

Vivienne raised an eyebrow.

"I started asking discreet questions. They led me to the Society of Unknown Philosophers and eventually to two men. Johann Constantin Andreae and Gabriel D'Ange. They were both members and practitioners of natural magic."

"Natural magic?" Cassandane frowned. "I don't know that."

Cyrus removed his spectacles and started cleaning the lenses on one sleeve. "Heinrich Cornelius Agrippa coined the term in his 1526 *De vanitate.* It encompasses arts such as alchemy and astrology as opposed to ceremonial magic, in particular goety and theurgy, which deals with the summoning of spirits. White versus black magic, if you will."

Alec cleared his throat. "Andreae and D'Ange were also key figures in an even more elite and secretive organization called the Rosicrucian Order. The Order was said to consist of no more than eight members, all sworn bachelors and devout Christians. On the surface, it seemed benevolent. Charity for the poor, that sort of thing.

"I came to suspect the Order was more than they claimed, but I couldn't prove anything. And I didn't want to act unless I was sure. So I befriended D'Ange. I gave him the impression I might be a suitable candidate. And I finagled an invitation to his house."

Despite the years, Alec still remembered that night. The smell of beeswax candles, the dusty bottle of wine they'd shared. D'Ange's quiet intensity as he spoke of his new Order.

"He was called away during dinner and I took the opportunity to look around. I found a hidden door that led to a small chapel. It had a stained glass window depicting the Archangel Gabriel." Alec's voice hardened. "I knew then it was him. The altar had a bible and a Rosicrucian cross. I wanted to unnerve him, to goad him into making a mistake. So I took the cross."

"What happened to D'Ange?' Vivienne asked.

"He left Strasbourg that same night, I don't know why. And you returned. We went to Athens to find the Greater Gate there. I never saw him again. But shortly after, the Order published several manifestos." Alec looked at Cyrus, who had an encyclopedic memory for such things.

The old magus nodded. "*Fama Fraternitatis*, published in1614 in Kassel, Germany. It was followed by *Confessio Fraternitatis* and then *The Chymical Wedding of Christian Rosenkreutz* in 1616. The last was quite different from the first two."

"How so?" Vivienne asked.

"It was more ... I don't know, more *personal*. Poetical, if you will. Andreae was the anonymous editor. It related a dream by Rosenkreutz, the supposed founder of the Order."

"Supposed?"

"We believe he was a legend," Alec said. "A phantom. That the real founder was Gabriel D'Ange." Alec sighed. "I never crossed paths with D'Ange again and the Order went underground after that."

"And the cross you stole?"

"I gave it to Cyrus when I saw him a few years later." Alec smiled faintly. "He'd just fled Prague after being tossed out a third-floor window by Protestant rebels."

Cassandane gave a snort, eyeing her bonded with amusement. "The Second Defenestration. I told you to leave them alone."

"Where was I while you were in Strasbourg?" Vivienne asked.

"You'd gone into the Dominion to hunt necromancers."

"Oh, *right*." She tossed the cigarette into the stove. "May I see this cross?"

"It's in the strong room," Cyrus said.

They followed him to a chamber with an ironbound door and waited while Cyrus produced a set of enormous keys.

"He's like a squirrel hoarding acorns," Vivienne murmured. "Magus, I always wondered if you had the Grail itself stashed away in here."

Cyrus didn't smile.

The room beyond was cavernous. Alec's gaze took in an extravagant clutter of objects ranging from rusty swords to musical instruments from a bygone age, and a thousand other things, all stowed with care on wide floor-to-ceiling shelves.

Cyrus went directly to a glass cabinet and took out a cedarwood box. He eased the lid open.

Vivienne squinted. "I thought at least it would be a fancy one," she said with a note of surprise. "It's not even gold."

The cross was the size of her palm, plain wood, with a rose carved in the center.

She held it up to the candlelight. "What does it signify?"

"There are various interpretations," Cyrus replied. "The blood of Christ and the power of redemption. Christ's mother, Mary, who was always closely associated with the rose. But it can also symbolize the union of opposites and the dualism in nature. D'Ange adopted the symbol, but the rose cross is much older than his Order, most likely dating back to the first century." He paused. "This one could be that old."

Vivienne shook her head and handed the cross back to Cyrus, who tucked it into the velvet lining. "Gabriel D'Ange," she said softly. "I thought he might be a werewolf, but it never occurred to me that he wasn't even the bloody abbot of Saint George's. He knew so much about the monastery's history, the paintings, all of it. He struck me as a genuine man of God."

"He *was*," Alec said quietly. "Or claimed to be."

"The question is, what is he now?" Cyrus wondered with a troubled frown.

"I never saw him change," Vivienne said. "But one of the others, yes. I think he was about to when D'Ange came."

"And he has Anne." Alec pressed a hand to his forehead, feeling a stab of guilt. He'd been so preoccupied with Vivienne, he'd hardly given a thought to his own sister.

"Did she know about any of this?" Cassandane asked.

Alec shook his head. "She'd only stopped to see me in Strasbourg for a single night. I didn't tell her why I was there."

As usual, Vivienne spoke the words no one else wanted to.

"Will D'Ange hurt her?"

Alec let out a long breath. "I don't know. He's a strange man."

"I don't think he will," Cyrus said firmly. "Not without a reason. He always had a rigid sort of honor, if that makes sense."

"Nothing makes sense," Vivienne muttered. "Why now, after all this time?"

None of them had an answer for that.

CHAPTER 17

"I'm so sorry," Vivienne said quietly, after Cyrus and Cassandane had gone off to bed and they sat alone in the library. "It's my fault. I should have gone with Nathaniel—"

"Hush. It's not your fault. If it's anyone's fault, it's mine."

"What if—"

"D'Ange uses the cuff?" Alec said icily. "I don't know, Vivienne. I suppose we'll deal with that if it happens."

The light from the coal stove played across her high, regal forehead and generous mouth. Cassandane had given her a pair of trousers and a man's shirt. Vivienne was tall but more slender and it seemed to swallow her up.

She was silent for a long moment. "Do you ever.... Ever wish you hadn't—"

Alec rose and knelt beside her chair. He took her hand. "Vivienne," he said, his voice suddenly hoarse. "I don't regret a single moment of the lifetimes I've had with you. And if he bonded me right now, it would still be worth it."

She looked into his eyes and let out a soft breath. Then she reached for him. Alec pulled away.

Vivienne was on her third glass of *palinka*.

"I'll make us some tea," he said.

She laughed. "Tea? But that might sober me up."

Alec stuck the bottle under his arm and stood. "I'll be back."

She sighed and lifted the walking stick. "Don't you want your cane?"

Alec smiled. "I'll need both hands for the tray."

Vivienne leaned it against her chair and returned to staring out the windows at the unkempt garden beyond.

As Alec walked down to the kitchens, he thought again of Gabriel D'Ange. They hadn't known each other long. He remembered only a man with polished manners and a humble air that concealed the monster beneath.

Alec puttered around the large kitchen, gathering the tea things. With his power trapped in the cuff, he had no fear of fire. It was strange to light the stove like a mortal, to bring the kettle to a boil himself, with no urge to seize the wild power of the flames and try to work them.

He didn't know why daēvas couldn't touch fire. Only that if he did, he would die.

He threw a handful of leaves into the teapot and filled it with steaming water. Then he added a saucer of cream, six sugar cubes and two chipped porcelain cups.

The wind howled along the slate roof as he made his way back to the library. Through the darkened windows, he could see the shapes of the trees swaying outside.

Vivienne is hanging by a thread, he thought. I'll have to hide the *palinka* until we return to London.

She never, ever drank to excess, in part because she knew he despised the feeling of drunkenness, and he couldn't really blame her for it now. He was almost tempted himself. But he didn't want her that way, even if—

Alec was three paces down the hall when he was slammed with the skin-crawling sensation of something from the Dominion. He halted, head cocked. The house was quiet, the low wind the only sound.

Alec set the tea tray on the floor. One of the cups gently rattled against its saucer. He let out a slow breath and stood.

The corridor was dark with doors all the way down. Around the far corner, he could see a glint of light from the library. Alec started toward it, eyes flicking to either side, alert for any sign of movement. Most of the doors were closed, but a few stood open an inch or two, revealing a crack of darkness beyond.

Something was here, among them. The only question was whether he could find it before—

A shadow slithered out of the doorway on the left just ahead. It gave off cold waves of *wrongness*. The reek of the Dominion grew overwhelming. Alec caught a sudden flash of movement. Startled, he staggered back through the opposite door, tripping over something that crashed to the floor with a clatter like old bones. A quick look confirmed that the obstacle was exactly that, one of Cyrus's bizarre skeletons. He collected anything outre — mermaids, giants, two-headed unicorns — and refused to listen when Alec told him they were fakes, glued together by charlatans.

Alec hopped over the bones, putting as much distance as possible between himself and the door. Moonlight spilled through the window, illuminating a diamond-patterned carpet and more strange outlines strung together with wire and wax. His gaze swept the room, searching for anything he could use as a weapon, but a creak snapped his attention back to the solid black rectangle that led into the hall.

Very slowly, a face moved into the moonlight. It had gleaming white skin and onyx eyes with no pupils.

A girl.

She'd been no more than twelve when the wight took her. She must have been pretty, with a perfect little bud of a mouth and wavy golden hair. Now the hair was dirty and snarled, and the mouth curled in a smile too old and cunning for the rest of her features.

"Daēva," it hissed, holding out a hand tipped with black talons.

So it could talk. Not all of them did.

"Go back where you came from." Alec's throat felt too dry. He hated wights, especially the children.

She tilted her head and took a step forward.

Alec snatched up one of the skeletons and hurled it at her. She dropped to a crouch, tapping her nails on the floor. *Rat-a-tat.*

Rat-a-tat.

Wights weren't especially strong, but they were bloody *quick.* If those nails opened an arterial vein, death would come swiftly.

Alec grabbed a standing lamp and used it to fend her off, steer her away from the doorway.

She feinted, but he saw it coming and swung, knocking her away.

She was back on her feet in an instant. Lunging, batting the lamp aside....

Another shadowy figure loomed in the doorway. He saw a flash of steel.... And Vivienne's sword neatly claimed the wight's head.

She rushed to Alec's side, her face hard and sober. "Did it hurt you?"

He shook his head. "A few scratches, nothing more."

Distant shouts drew them to the strong room.

Cassandane stood over two more dead wights. The heavy door had been smashed in, and Cyrus crouched among the mess inside. Half the glass cabinets were broken and his precious collection had been strewn across the floor.

Alec bit down and tasted blood. "The cross?" he asked tightly.

Cyrus scanned the wreckage, his face bleak. Then he frowned. "No, it's there...."

He pointed. The cedarwood box lay on the floor. Alec picked it up and opened it. The rose cross still nestled in its velvet lining.

"We must have scared him off," Cassandane said.

Cyrus was muttering to himself.

"Is anything else missing?" Vivienne asked.

He shook his head. "I've no idea. I'll have to check everything against my records."

"You can't stay here," she said gently. "This old heap. Just the two of you. It's not safe."

Cyrus rounded on her, his usually mild face ablaze with fury. "I'm not going anywhere until I know what's been taken. Perhaps he wasn't after the rose cross after all. I have all sort of things in here...." He trailed off, crawling over to a set of reed pipes and clutching them to his chest like an infant.

Vivienne shared a look with Alec. "We have to tell Sidgwick and Blackwood what's happened. Launch a full inquiry. I want every resource they have bent on finding him. And if D'Ange wants to trade...." She glanced at the cedarwood box. "He seems to know where to find us."

"First thing in the morning," Alec agreed. He no longer sensed any danger within the walls of Ingress Abbey.

"I'll take care of him," Cassandane said, her eyes on Cyrus. "You go. Cable if anything happens."

"Still think D'Ange is a *harmless* necromancer?" Alec snapped.

Cassandane gave him a level look. "I never said he was."

He immediately felt stupid. "I'm sorry, Cass."

She patted his arm. "Go get some sleep. I'll keep a watch."

"There's another dead wight in the room with the skeletons," Alec said, his gaze turning to the pair that lay headless in the hall. A man and woman. Likely the poor girl's parents.

Cassandane gave a nod. "I'll burn them all in the garden."

He trudged upstairs with Vivienne. She paused before going to her own room.

"I saw the tea tray in the corridor," she said softly. "The cups were all upright, neat as a pin."

Alec tensed, but he couldn't lie to her. Not his own bonded. "I sensed the wight, Viv. Before I saw it. Almost like a bad smell. It was the same in Gran Canaria with the men D'Ange sent … though not exactly. The reek of the Dominion wasn't present. Only that they posed a threat."

Her eyes narrowed. "Do you think it's because of what happened in New York?"

"I think so."

She thought for a moment, then nodded. "Well, that's good. It's useful."

Alec forced a smile. "Yes. Goodnight, Vivienne."

PART III

"Those who dream by day are cognizant of many things which escape those who dream only by night."
—Edgar Allen Poe

CHAPTER 18

In the blustery gloom of March, Anne's fever turned into a wracking cough. Gabriel spent the days in an armchair reading as she recuperated, though they rarely spoke. He brought her broths and tea and slowly nursed her back to health. Sometimes, she heard him playing the pianoforte in the music room, dark, funereal pieces that suited both their moods.

When Anne grew stronger, she began to take little walks around the castle. She found open rifled-through trunks full of elegant gowns and realized she'd been wearing the clothes of a dead woman, but this seemed appropriate. Part of her had died the night he caught her and she roamed the halls in a melancholy daze.

Gabriel never suggested she return to her tower, nor did he lock her in. But he never left the castle during the day anymore, and after the sun set.... Well, she knew where he went now.

Where he slept — if he did at all — she had no idea.

One afternoon, when rain slicked the windows and fog from the Channel pressed thickly against the glass, Gabriel came in with the chess set in his hands. It was the same one he'd given her in the first days of her captivity.

Anne was sitting up in bed, reading *The Fall of the House of Usher*. She glanced at him and deliberately laid the book face-down on her lap.

"I thought you might want to play."

She knew he'd never apologize. Nor would she. But holding a grudge required too much energy.

"All right," Anne said.

He pulled two chairs up to the window and laid the board. They played three bloody, drawn-out games. Anne won two.

"Not bad," she said, leaning back. "But your schemes are too elaborate. They tend to go wrong."

"Not always."

"You should read Gioachino Greco's masterwork on the subject. You might learn something."

"Pah. The Calabrian? I met him once. He wasn't that good."

Anne laughed.

They played often after that and the brittle tension between them eased, though Anne thought often about the creature that attacked her. Gabriel had claimed he wasn't born with the ability to change his form. She wondered if she could learn how to do it herself. The idea was intriguing. If she could change her form.... Well, that would alter the equation between them.

And so the days passed. There was always work to be done; hauling water from the well, chopping firewood to cook with. Gabriel taught her to split logs with an axe, and she taught him to read the movements of the stars. They spent the afternoons walking in companionable silence along the shore at low tide, studying the things the sea tossed up on the shingle. One day they they found a barrel of salt cod, which Gabriel thought disgusting. On another, the remains of a huge fish from the deep that he insisted was a sea monster, though Anne suspected it was simply an overlarge basking shark.

She dug through the library and found some thick tomes on

physics and mathematics in French, which she laboriously struggled through, asking Gabriel to translate when she encountered unfamiliar words.

He pulled the sheets off the furniture in some of the second-floor rooms and beat the dust from the carpets. And Chateau de Saint-Évreux no longer seemed quite as gloomy as it once had.

They were in the thick of battle at the chessboard one day, Anne down a knight and both rooks, when Gabriel said, "You still don't remember where we met."

She grew very still. "I told you I don't."

He watched her closely, his expression unreadable. "The Opera House in Strasbourg. You were wearing a black silk dress with lace sleeves." He swallowed. "And your hair was lifted off your neck in a chignon. I thought you had a very fine neck."

She frowned. "Don't you hate opera?"

"I only said that hoping it might make you remember. Actually, I adore it."

Anne frowned. "Strasbourg…."

"*L'Orfeo* was playing."

It was the music that finally unlocked her memory.

A brief vignette only. She'd been with Alec. He'd introduced her a to man in the next box. She hadn't paid much attention when he bent over her hand to kiss it. She'd clean forgotten the name and hardly recalled the face — only the back of his head and the black ribbon in his blond hair. Anne had left Strasbourg the next day. But yes…. Perhaps.

"It was such a long time ago," she whispered, her unfocused gaze roaming the board. "Nearly three hundred years."

As far as Anne knew, only two things that passed for mortal lived that long. Daēvas and….

Anne's hand flew to her mouth. "You're a necromancer."

Well, of course he was. How could she not have guessed it before?

"I don't deny it." Gabriel seemed unflustered. "But I prey on the wicked. And I always behead the ghouls I bring through."

"Define *wicked*."

"Slavers. Men who profit from the misery of others. Child killers."

"Like you."

"*No.*" He leaned forward. "You must listen without judgment if you wish to know the truth."

Anne crossed her arms. "Go on, then."

"Your brother stole a holy relic from me, blessed by the Virgin Mother herself. It's priceless. Just after we met, I was called away on urgent business. One of my Order had been murdered by another necromancer. When I returned, the cross was gone, and so were you and Alec Lawrence. He used a different name back then, but it was him."

Anne knew nothing of this. "Why would he do such a thing?"

"To teach me a lesson. To bait me. I don't know!" He threw his hands up. "The years passed. I was preoccupied by other things, other wars, but I never forgot." Gabriel's jaw tensed. "So imagine my surprise when you arrived at Saint George's. I saw you crossing the cloister and knew you instantly."

Anne wasn't sure if she should be flattered or disturbed. "You remembered me?"

"It was your ears."

She flushed. Anne paid little attention to her appearance beyond trying to stay clean, but she'd always been self-conscious of the way they stuck out.

"I'm teasing," he added in a gentler tone. "It was the way you carried herself. Like no one else existed. You're not an easily forgettable woman."

She held his gaze. "Why were *you* there?"

"I was hunting the man who killed those children, just as you were." He picked up one of her captured rooks and turned it over in his fingers. "When I saw you again ... it was as though no time had passed at all. My temper flared. I assumed you had known what your brother did. That he must have sent you there."

"But why? For what purpose?"

"I don't know," he muttered darkly. "But it couldn't be a coincidence."

"Why not? You're paranoid, Gabriel."

"Perhaps." He leaned toward her. "And perhaps that's why I'm still alive."

"Go on."

"I pretended to be the abbot only so I had a plausible excuse to speak with you. To try to discover what you wanted. All the other brothers had taken vows of silence."

"And what happened to the man you impersonated? Did you kill him too?"

Gabriel laughed richly. "Father Nicolae is an old friend. He'd permitted me to stay at the monastery while I sought Adrian. You were not brought to me right away, don't you remember? It was a simple matter to quickly discuss the matter with him. Explain who you were. He gave me permission to use his study."

"I told you—"

"You *lied* to me. I could … smell it. You said you were there only to look at the old books, the frescoes."

Anne had to concede he was right. She had lied. Because she'd suspected the *pricolici* might be one of the brothers. The abbot, even. "So you drugged me. Brought me here."

"I had no choice. I would never have harmed you, please believe that."

Anne let out a long sigh. She did believe him. "And the *pricolici*?"

"It took me months to track him to Romania." Gabriel's face hardened. "But I did, Anne. And I put him down. What he did was … it was my fault." He sighed. "Adrian was a brother of my Order. The stain of those children's deaths is forever on my soul."

Anne frowned. "When did you catch him?"

"A month after you came, on the night of the full moon. He had preyed on the monks at the monastery once before. It's what drew me to Romania in the first place. He must have grown hungry again." Gabriel gave an evil smile. "He did not know I was there waiting for him."

Something about his story troubled her. She thought of the man on horseback, riding hard down the road at sunset. "But how did you hunt him and still come to the castle each day?"

"I Traveled. I don't like opening gateways in my own home, but there's a pond in the forest. I would leave my horse there, grazing, and then return to Saint George's."

Anne was stunned. The Dominion was a dangerous place. If the creatures that guarded the underworld had found him…. Well, they misliked necromancers. "You took that risk?"

Gabriel shrugged as if it was nothing. "I wouldn't entrust your care to another, Anne."

Her lips tightened. "You should have just let me go."

"I couldn't. Not until I knew where your brother was. In truth, I almost hoped he would come after you."

"Because you're an obsessive!"

He flushed. "Maybe I am. A little bit."

"So what if Alec had come? What then? Would he be dead now?"

Gabriel looked affronted. "I'm not a savage. I only want what's mine. But not to kill him. That was never my intention."

He gazed at her without guile, though Anne sensed *something*.

"And he never came?"

"No."

Anne felt a small pang, though she wasn't surprised. She disappeared too often for Alec to worry overly about her. It was her own fault.

"Well, you netted the wrong fish, Gabriel. So what now?" She waved a hand around the room. "I live here for another three hundred years?"

"No." He spoke it softly, almost with regret. "I'll contact your brother and trade you for the cross. Then you can leave Chateau de Saint-Évreux. Fair enough?"

"Yes." She paused. "When?"

"Soon." Gabriel gestured at the board. "It's your move, Anne."

CHAPTER 19

*O*nce upon a time, there was a prison fortress called Gorgon-e
Gaz on the shore of the Salenian Sea. It was where the Empire
kept the Old Ones. The daēvas who couldn't be trusted to fight as slaves.

A place of unimaginable suffering.

*Until a mortal woman named Tijah came along with a daēva
named Achaemenes and five daēva children seeking to liberate their
parents.*

A heroic battle ensued.

*The undead Druj came in a numberless horde to defend the fortress,
driven by Antimagi clad in human skins, black lightning lancing from
their fingertips. But the children summoned a great wave and drowned
their enemies in the deep waters.*

*When it was over, Tijah lay dying. Achaemenes bonded her to save
her life, though she despised him for it at the time.*

*And Gorgon-e Gaz was broken in half, the sea washing through its
ruins.*

*One of the little daēva girls who had fought the necromancers, who
herself had worn the cuff of a slave, crawled inside. Her name was Anu.*

"Father?" she called out. "Mother?"

Years later, when the little girl grew up, it was not the dark or the chill or the screams of the wounded and dying she remembered most clearly.

It always was the smell.

Anne's eyes opened.

She stared into the darkness, the dream fading, though her skin still crawled with nameless dread. She rolled over in Gabriel's bed and rested her cheek on one hand.

He was a necromancer.

An Antimagus.

She forced herself to picture it. He would have talismanic chains hidden somewhere. An iron collar, linked to a bracelet. And through this barbaric talisman, he would drain the life from his victims to stay young himself.

Anne had been raised and bred to fight his kind. Necromancers triggered an instinctive revulsion in her very marrow.

Then why do I still like him?

What the bloody hell is wrong with me?

Anne had little use for mortals. Half of them would try to burn her if they knew what she was, and the other half would run screaming. Their lives were flyspecks against the backdrop of her own existence, so she'd never seen the point in getting close to one.

But Gabriel was different. He'd always shown her kindness, even when she threw it back in his face. He was tempestuous but not cruel. And he would never die.

Can I judge him fairly without knowing more? He hints at things....
The Order he spoke of.

What if we aren't enemies after all?

And then: *Alec.*

Once, Anne had worshipped the ground he walked on, but she came to realize that although he loved her, he would always belong wholly to Vivienne. Their relationship was platonic but passionate in a way she'd never understood. Anne's bond had been a shackle. Theirs was a sacred union. One soul in two bodies.

She sometimes wondered what that must be like, yet she learned to embrace her solitude. The freedom to go where she liked, when she liked, until the craving for company drove her back home. This had happened less frequently of late.

She couldn't deny a certain wordless longing for … something more.

Now that Gabriel had promised to let her go, she wondered if she would miss him. Anne thought she might.

It was confusing.

She rolled over and tried to sleep, but the first rosy fingers of dawn were painting the sky before she fell into a fitful rest.

This time, she didn't dream.

***

Anne was withdrawn the following day, which Gabriel interpreted as anger. As was his way, he brought a peace offering.

"A telescope?" She turned it over in her hands. It was made of brass and quite heavy.

"I found it up in one of the turrets. It uses glass lenses—"

"To refract and magnify light. Alec has one, though it produces chromatic aberration." Gabriel looked blank. "It's a sort of prism effect."

"Shall we test it out?"

"Where?"

"I was thinking the tower might be the best place."

Anne hadn't been there in ages. Gabriel had brought all her things to his room. But she wasn't about to let him know how much she still disliked that tower.

"All right." She paused. "Did you send the letter?"

"I'll have to ride into town. Tomorrow, I promise."

She bit her tongue. For all the fuss he'd kicked up about his precious relic, he didn't seem in any great hurry to get it back.

Anne followed him up the narrow, winding staircase. Her chest tightened when they passed through the chamber where she'd slept. It looked even smaller than when she was confined there. Her first month at Chateau de Saint-Évreux had consisted of long intervals of boredom punctuated by fear, both that her faceless captor wouldn't return — and that he would.

Only when she stepped into the fresh air of the roof did Anne relax.

She watched Gabriel set up the tripod on the parapet, cursing softly as he wrestled with the brass fittings. His coat strained against the lines of his back and she reflected that one hard push would send him toppling him over the edge. Had he forgotten that the last time they stood on this tower together she'd stabbed him in the heart?

No. Gabriel never forgot anything.

Then he turned, his brown eyes bright, and bent his knee in a courtly gesture.

"Ladies first."

Anne leaned into the eyepiece, adjusting the focus ring. The magnification was roughly twenty times. She swept it through an arc of velvet sky, finding Mars and Jupiter.

Like her brother, Anne had a keen mind for the natural sciences. It was the one thing they shared that Vivienne had little interest in. The last century had seen spectacular advances — steam-driven ships and locomotives, Pasteur's work on germ theory, the genius of Faraday, Edison and Tesla. She devoured all of it, conceding that some mortals at least used their brief time on this earth wisely.

But Anne didn't miss the feverish pace of London, the new electric lights and chattering crowds. No, like Alec, she preferred the wild places. And out here, in the middle of nowhere, the sky seemed alive with light, just as it must have been for the astronomers of old.

"What's your position on Galileo?"

Gabriel was taking a turn at the eyepiece. "Hmmm?"

"The Church burned him as a heretic for daring to say the earth orbited the sun." Her tone was cool. "It's one of the reasons I don't care for organized religion."

Gabriel straightened and regarded her for a long moment, choosing his words carefully. "I used to be a true believer. Not the kind who burned women as witches, or old astronomers for star-gazing, but I was a zealot in what I thought was the one true faith. I fought in the Crusades, all the way to Jerusalem."

He sighed. "It changed me, Anne. The mindless slaughter on both sides, the atrocities perpetrated in the name of God. I was left … deeply disillusioned." Gabriel braced his palms on the parapet, gazing at the water.

"Afterward, I spent many years traveling the world, seeking out the great sages. Seeking order and meaning in the chaos of existence. Seeking the *truth*. I studied the teachings of Thābit ibn Qurra and the Pagan prophet Trismegistus, lived among the Sufi mystics in India. When I had absorbed all I could, I founded my own Order. The Order of the Rose Cross. Beholden to no authority but my own and God's."

"And what does it do, this Order of yours?"

"Carry out His will on earth."

"That's a broad mandate," she said dryly. "And I suppose you interpret this divine will?"

The hint of a smile touched his lips. "I believe in a just, loving God who is perfectly good and forgiving. But not all men walk the right path. That's why He needs ones like me."

"Interesting. And what of non-believers? Apostates? Do you *correct* them as well?"

"I have no interest in that. God gave us the freedom to choose.

I'm talking about those who commit irredeemable harm against their fellow human beings."

"Well, that's reassuring." She leaned into the eyepiece, studying the constellations. "What day is it, Gabriel?"

"The sixteenth of March. Why?"

"Tomorrow is my birthday," she said with some surprise.

Time seemed to stand still at Chateau de Saint-Évreux. There were no clocks, no calendars. Gabriel lulled her with food and books, games and music. They both wore the clothes of people a century dead.

No, Anne thought, time hadn't stopped. It actually ran *backward* in this place.

But two full months had passed in the real world.

She always spent her birthday with Alec and Vivienne. Some years it was the only time she saw them, but she made sure to come home for the occasion. Anne felt a twinge of sadness. They must be out of their minds with worry by now.

"How do you celebrate it?" he asked her, his face intent.

She shrugged. "Cake. Sometimes the theater and a late supper at the Savoy. Dancing."

"Do you still count the years?"

She smiled. "No. Not for a very long time."

"Nor do I."

Anne rubbed her arms, pretending to be chilled. "Let's go down, Gabriel. I'm tired."

"Of course." He packed up the telescope and tucked it beneath his arm. "I'll ride into town and post the letter tomorrow…. It will be your present."

Anne forced a smile and nodded.

Gabriel was absent for most of the next day. She sat at the window, sketching the dark clouds that mounded on the horizon and the seabirds flying ahead of the coming storm. She wondered what he'd written in his message. Knowing Gabriel, it would be full of purple prose and dire threats. She just hoped Alec had kept the damned cross. Where she'd be if he hadn't…. Anne put the thought from her mind.

At sunset, Gabriel returned in a fine humor. She heard him whistling in the kitchen and much banging of pots. He stuck his head in her open door two hours later and crooked a finger.

Anne raised her brows.

"Come," he said. "I have something for you."

She set her charcoals aside and followed him down the main staircase, along the gallery of dead nobles who stared down their aristocratic noses at the interlopers, and into a cavernous space that had been the ballroom. The gilt ceiling dripped in places with rainwater, and the inlaid parquet floor was a ruin, but Gabriel had draped the walls with sweet-smelling spruce branches that gave it a festive air. A four-tiered cake with pink rosettes sat on a long table to the side.

She looked at him. "You didn't have to—"

"Hush. Eat your cake."

So she sat down and had two pieces. It was a light sponge layered with sticky raspberry filling and Anne thought she'd never had better. She leaned back and rested her hands on her stomach with a contented sigh. "You're making me fat." She glanced at him. "When I first came, I wondered if you planned to devour me."

"*Nom de dieu.* Really?"

"It crossed my mind. All that rich food."

He seemed amused. "Like Little Red Riding Hood. But since you speak of fairytales, I have a better one." He reached beneath the table and gave her a parcel wrapped in brown paper and twine. "Happy birthday, Anne."

She unwrapped the parcel and laughed. "You're impossible."

La Belle et La Bête. Anne opened the cover. It was a large edition, with lavish illustrations. Beauty playing a harp at the castle as the Beast looks on in a red cloak. The single red rose, thoughtlessly plucked from his garden. Her vain, greedy sisters. And at last, Beauty kneeling before the poor dying Beast.

She glanced up at Gabriel. He looked oddly subdued. "Do you like it?"

"Of course I do."

"It's still early." His gaze swept the ballroom. "Would you take a turn around the floor with me, Anne? I haven't danced in a long time."

Her throat went a little dry. Gabriel had never behaved inappropriately in any way. He hadn't laid a single hand on her since he carried her back from the forest that night. She had no doubt that when he asked for a dance, that's all he intended.

And she wanted to, but….

"On one condition."

His eyes warned her to honor the boundaries he'd set. "What is it?"

"That you tell me the story of how you came to be … what you are."

He seemed relieved. "That I can give you."

Gabriel held out a hand. Anne took it. His fingers were strong and warm.

"What shall we do for music?" she asked.

"I'll hum something. Do you like to waltz?"

She nodded. So he rested a hand on her waist, feather-light, and hummed the opening bars of some old melody as he swept her onto the floor. The water dripped on their heads when they passed beneath the leaks and Gabriel kept her always at the precise distance of a proper waltz, but Anne was very conscious of his palm cupping the small of her back and his smell, clean and male but with that elusive trace of something … feral.

Anne was no stranger to men. She'd had her share of mortal lovers, though none she permitted herself to become entangled with. That would be worse than foolish. To watch them age and die as she lived on…. No, such self-inflicted suffering was not Anne's cup of tea. But she'd missed the nearness to another body. The exchange of heat and energy. And Gabriel…. Well, he was slender and firm, with a quick, graceful step. A terrible candidate in every other way, but still.

Too soon, he stepped away from her and bowed.

"Thank you, Anne," he said solemnly. "I've missed dancing."

His cheeks were flushed and she could almost, *almost* see the boy he had been a long time ago.

"I'll keep my promise now. But you'll have to listen while I wash up. I left a mess in the kitchen and I hate waking up to dirty dishes." He pulled a face. "It makes me *triste*."

This mundane admission made her smile.

Anne carried the plates and Gabriel carried the mauled remains of the cake. She'd never ventured into the kitchen before. Unlike the rest of the house, it had no coating of ancient grime. He clearly kept it spic-and-span – when he wasn't baking elaborate cakes. Now the counters were dusted with flour and eggshells, piles of batter-smeared mixing bowls and wooden spoons.

"Can I help?"

He waved the offer away and rolled up his shirtsleeves. "It's your birthday. Eat some more cake. If you don't, I'll have it for breakfast and my teeth will fall out."

So Anne sat down at the scarred wooden table and watched him fill a bucket with soapy water.

"Are you ready?" He glanced over his shoulder, a gleam in his eye.

Anne's breath caught. "Yes."

Gabriel's voice lowered to a melodramatic whisper. "Then I shall tell you the tale of the Beast of Gévaudan."

CHAPTER 20

"First you must understand that there are different kinds of magic," Gabriel said. "The magic of the Dominion that summons revenants and wights and things of darkness. We call this necromancy. Then there is natural magic. Bending the elements to your will. As a daēva, you already know that. But there is other esoteric knowledge that can be learned if one is patient and devoted."

"Such as how to change one's form?" Anne asked.

Gabriel dried a plate and slid his hands back into the soapy water. It was strangely erotic to watch him wash dishes. The muscles in his forearms flexed as he moved the sponge in lazy circles across the plate.

"*Oui.*"

"So there's truth to the *pricolici* legends?" she asked, looking resolutely at the cake.

"I think so, yes. There have always been men who ran with wolves, who gave themselves over to the wild and the savage." He rinsed a knife. "But that is something you are born with, not from God or the Devil. What I am is not *pricolici.*" He glanced at her. "Hand me that bowl, would you?"

Anne did.

"It was the year of our Lord 1764. I was living in the Marg-
eride Mountains at a remote manor house. The Duzakh was
tearing itself apart in a bloody civil war and I thought it wise to
retreat to the countryside while they destroyed themselves. I had
long stood against them. One in particular, a necromancer
named Jorin Bekker, was hunting the followers of my Order,
slaughtering them where he found them. So when the killings
began, I thought it might be him."

"But it wasn't?"

"Witnesses reported seeing a fearsome creature with huge
jaws, much larger than a wolf. A man-eater. The attacks multi-
plied, claiming dozens of lives. You cannot imagine the terror of
the peasants. They eked out a pitiful existence grazing their live-
stock in the forest, and these solitary adults and children were
the main targets. Finally, the King put a bounty on its head and
sent men to hunt the Beast of Gévaudan, as it came to be known."

Gabriel shook his head. "They tried everything. Bloodhounds,
parties of soldiers with muskets combing the woods, professional
wolf-hunters who knew the art of stealth. But the Beast was
cunning. He outwitted them all and they could not catch him.
The captains blamed the peasants, and each other. A fiasco. Then
one of them managed to shoot a large wolf. He claimed it was the
Beast. They stuffed it and sent it back to Versailles." Gabriel
snorted. "Louis displayed it in his court for his nobles to shudder
at."

"But it wasn't," she breathed from the edge of her chair.

Gabriel refused to take the bait. "Some weeks passed. I went
out walking one day, deep in the woods."

"You weren't afraid?"

He shrugged. "I thought the reports of its size were probably
exaggerated, and I am not exactly helpless. There had been no
attacks near my home for a long time. It was a fine spring day,
the sun bright and warm. Then I noticed the birds had stopped

singing. It was so quiet I could hear only the beat of my own heart." The sponge paused and his gaze grew distant. "But I felt something watching me. You know that sensation? The cold prickle at the base of the neck? Yes, that is what I felt that day."

Anne swallowed. She knew it well.

"The Beast was on me before I could blink. Never have I seen anything move so quickly. It caught me by the throat and would have destroyed me in another instant."

"But…. I thought you couldn't be killed."

He gave her a grim smile. "Anything can be killed, Anne. Not to give you ideas but, yes, if my throat had been torn open, my lifeblood emptied upon the earth and my flesh partially eaten, I think that would do the trick." Gabriel resumed washing. "Luckily, I was quick, too. The moment I heard the birdsong cease, I readied myself. I always carried my necromantic chains because of Bekker. As those huge jaws closed around my neck, I snapped the collar shut around *his*. It was all I could think to do at the time. I had no ulterior motives. Only to save my own life.

"How he howled in fury! He knew he belonged to me now." Gabriel drew a deep breath. "I had never used the chains on an animal before, and the Beast was no normal creature. The torrent of him nearly knocked me off my feet. Hunger and fear, but also…. How to explain? I could smell each pine needle and the musk of the stag that had passed a day before. The muscles in my thighs quivered with the urge to bunch, to spring, to run as fast as the wind. I tasted my own blood on his tongue and it was sweet as nectar.

"His bones held the echoes of an ancient magic, the magic of that unseen world you spoke of, Anne, and I realized I could not kill him. He was a man-eater, but there was no evil in him. He did only what his instincts demanded. So I used my will to calm him, to slow his great heart and show him I meant no harm. Then I led him back to my house and gave him a brace of rabbits."

Anne nodded slowly. "I'm glad you didn't kill him. He was unique in the world."

"That's what I thought, too. But the Beast had a mate. She came to the walls of my manor and howled. The servants were terrified, but I ordered them not to report it."

"Poor thing," Anne muttered.

"I know." He looked sad. "I tried to catch her, but she ran away. After a while, she stopped coming."

"And you kept him in chains?" She frowned.

"Only for a little while. I became…. A bit obsessed. It was a novelty when I thought there were no novel experiences left to be had."

Anne nodded. She understood this too.

"We fed together and slept together and ran together in the forest. After a while, he followed me even without the chains." He dried a plate and looked at her. "I never drained him of life, not a drop. I hid him and protected him. Eventually, I knew I needed a better place to keep him, one with high walls and space for him to roam. I found this old ruin and bought it on the spot."

Gabriel looked pensive. "Fate placed him in my path that day, Anne. I believe that. He became my teacher in ways long forgotten by men. And over many, many years, I learned to use his magic to transform myself. It takes great mental concentration. My first efforts were … clumsy." He laughed. "I looked like a mangy dog. But I got better at it with practice."

"And now you can transform at will."

"*Oui.*" He dried the last bowl and set it aside, turning to rest against the counter.

She hesitated. "What do you become?"

"You don't remember?" He gave a slight smile. "Then I will show you sometime, if you wish. But not tonight."

"Why not?"

Gabriel laughed. "Because I am tired from baking birthday cakes."

"But it can be taught?" she persisted.

He gave her a shrewd look. "You wish to learn?"

"I'm only asking." She kept her voice light, although Anne was profoundly intrigued by his story.

"It can." Gabriel's face darkened. "I taught three others of my Order. Men whom I trusted with my life. One of them was Adrian. After what he did at Mara Vardac, I vowed never to teach another. I thought I knew all there was to know about the transformation, but I was wrong. The magic is old and powerful. It can be darker than I imagined."

"In what way?"

"The beast you become is a reflection of the man inside, but more so. Like the telescope, it magnifies your soul. And Adrian's was … unfit." He tossed the dish towel aside. "There. I've bared my heart to you, Anne. Very few people know that story. *Very few.* Now you tell me why you hunt the old stories."

She tensed. "I already told you—"

He made a sharp gesture. "No. You could do anything with your life, be anyone. But you chose this. I want to know why." His voice softened. "I won't judge you for it, I swear."

She almost told him. He had given of himself, something of value, and wanted her to give in return. Gabriel was not the sort of man to accept copper when the debt was in gold. But she'd never confessed her reasons to another living soul, not even her brother, and the thought of doing so filled her with a strange shame.

"Because they fascinate me," she said with a smile. "Did I tell about the time I was caught in a hail of toads? I was in Northumbria, looking into reports of a bogle, when a great dark cloud came and disgorged hundreds of little things that looked like hazelnuts…."

Gabriel listened to her ramble for a minute or two with mounting scorn. Then he turned without a word and stalked out the door. Anne hardened her heart against a pang of regret. She'd be leaving this place soon anyway.

"Let them eat cake," she murmured, sticking a finger into one of the rosettes and licking the frosting off.

It tasted like ashes.

CHAPTER 21

Dinner the next night was of exceptionally poor quality.

A dry meatloaf with too much salt and a single half-cooked potato, cold, with a fork sticking out of it. Gabriel dropped the plate in front of her and sank into a chair at the head of the formal dining table, six seats down, a goblet of wine in his fist and a glower on his face.

"*Bon appétit*," he said.

Anne smiled and lifted the fork, gamely taking a bite from the potato and crunching it between her teeth. "Delicious. You've outdone yourself, Gabriel."

He brooded and watched her eat. One taste of the meatloaf sent Anne groping for the water pitcher, but she refused to be cowed by his sulking.

Some perverse part of her kept trying to draw him into conversation. To make him erupt, as he so clearly wanted to do. But he seemed to have the same idea, responding in monosyllables yet refusing to be drawn into one of his towering furies — just to spite her, Anne thought sourly.

She was tired of pretending they were friends. Tired of his constant company. She wanted to be alone again. To have her power back! Sweet and compliant had gotten her nowhere. It was time for new measures.

Two months she'd been his captive. It was only Gabriel's word that he'd even posted the letter. What if he hadn't?

Anne expected him to shun her at dinner, and thus had brought *La Belle et La Bête* to peruse while she ate. Now she leafed through the book, pretending to be absorbed in the pictures.

"So you're an Antimagus. Have you drained many people?" she asked, slicing off a bit of meatloaf and chewing with her mouth open.

His eyes flicked up from the goblet. "What do you think?"

"How many?"

He made an impatient gesture. "Too many to count."

"How charming. And you call yourself a man of God. I think all this moralizing is just a convenient way for you to stay alive without suffering any guilt."

He scowled at her. "You are a savage, Anne, with no appreciation for anything that truly matters." He leapt to his feet and snatched the book away, flicking a bit of potato from its pages. "I think I am Beauty and you are the Beast!"

"I prefer the beast to the man," she said with contempt. "At least the beast is honest." Anne shoved her plate away.

Gabriel's eyes flared, the pupils dilating. He gripped the table.

"You're a rank hypocrite. I've told you everything you asked, but you withhold yourself. Tell me what you're looking for! It's not werewolves and goblins."

She kept a sullen silence.

"Perhaps I'll tell *you*, then." He leaned forward and something in his face made her go cold. "We're more alike than you care to admit. I know where you come from. What was done to you. The same was done to me. A man named Balthazar bought me for the price of four pigs when I was nine years old and delivered me to the tender mercies of Neblis."

The name struck Anne like a slap to the face.

Neblis.

The daēva queen from Bactria who raised an army of Druj and necromancers and marched to war against the Empire, until the young conqueror Alexander drove her back. Her name was forgotten now, erased from the collective memory of a more civilized age. But a handful still remembered and Anne was one of them. Some of her army had laid siege to….

She could hardly make the words come, terrified of his answer. But she had to know.

"Were you at Gorgon-e Gaz?"

Gabriel shook his head. "No, though I heard what happened there. I had already fled, a deserter."

Anne felt the blood rush back to her hands. She knit them together under the table.

Gabriel's voice was quiet and deadly. "So you see, I know exactly how daēvas were trained. How they were punished for disobedience. I *remember*. Yes, I've killed people. Did the men who abused you deserve to live? There's no justice in the world except what we make ourselves. You of all people should know that." He studied her. "I think maybe you're looking for someone in particular. Someone who wronged you—"

"No." Anne met his eyes. "It's not that. I… I'm looking for my own kind." A tear ran down her cheek and she brushed it away impatiently. "I only know two others. Alec and Cassandane. They're both bonded. The rest…. They vanished after the war. I don't know if…." Her throat caught and she took a sip of water. "If any are still alive. The tales would be distorted, of course. They might be called wizards or fairies or djinni. But if there *are* free daēvas in the world, I would like to meet them. That's all."

Gabriel looked puzzled. "Why couldn't you tell me this?"

"Because…." She sighed. "Oh, I don't know. It just sounds so … pathetic."

"No." He took a handkerchief from his pocket and gave it to her. "Not pathetic at all. Just lonely."

She shot him a look. "That's a synonym for pathetic."

"Then I am pathetic, too."

"It's not the same. You have your Order of the Rose Cross. Others like you."

Gabriel gave her a cheeky smile. "There's no one like me."

Anne laughed and wiped her nose. "That's undeniably true."

They were silent for a moment.

"What if you never had to feel lonely again?" he asked.

Her heart beat painfully, still raw and tight. "What do you mean?"

"I'm sorry we came to know each other this way. More than you can imagine. I…. I've wrestled with it for days. Weeks." Gabriel always seemed so certain of himself. He lived in a world of moral absolutes — as he chose to interpret them. But now he sounded tentative. "I tried to avoid you, Anne, but you made that impossible. And, well…. I've come to care for you, and I think perhaps you for me."

"Perhaps I have," she conceded.

"When I told you the story of the Beast and you asked if the ability could be taught…." He picked at the pearl buttons on his waistcoat. "It would take years. But if we were bonded—"

Her chair scraped back. "You'd make me your slave," Anne snarled, knowing it was unfair but too shocked and furious to restrain herself.

She'd lost her temper more times in the last week than she had in the last century.

"No!" Gabriel was vehement. "Never. If you wanted to leave me, I wouldn't stop you. But you would have all my gifts." His voice lowered to a seductive purr. "I know you want to. I could see it in your face last night. You wondered what you might become. What it would feel like to have claws and fangs, a tail to lash when you get angry at me—"

"And what would you get out of it?" she demanded.

"Life without death," he said simply. "You call me a parasite.

Then help me stop killing, Anne."

"Oh, no. Don't you dare put that on me."

He crossed his arms, hurt in his eyes. "Would it truly be so bad? You like my cooking." He glanced at the meatloaf. "Most of the time. You could come and go as you wished. I have my own life, you know. I won't interfere in yours."

"You make it sound so simple."

"Because it is."

"Was this your plan all along? Coax me into bonding you?"

"Absolutely not."

"Yet you happen to have a set of cuffs." Her eyes narrowed. "Where did you get them?"

"An old woman at the bazaar in Kabul," he replied smoothly. "She had no idea what they were, of course. I bought them decades ago. A curiosity. I suppose they belonged to a pair of Immortals."

She shook her head. "I do care for you, Gabriel. Against my better judgment."

An eyebrow rose.

"But when I was freed, I swore never to allow myself to be bonded again. You must understand that."

"I do. And I don't expect you to make up your mind on the spot. Just think about it, Anne. That's all I ask of you."

"I don't have to. The answer is no."

"We'll see."

His calm was maddening.

"All right, Gabriel. If I were to agree, there would have to absolute trust between us, yes?"

"Of course."

"So prove it to me now." Anne raised a hand to her throat. She could sense the rose cameo dangling from her neck, inches away. "Take this off."

He hesitated.

"You see. You don't trust me."

"And if you try to kill me again? You know all my secrets now." His eyes darkened. "This time you might succeed."

"I won't. I promise."

A slow cannonade of thunder rattled the windows. Gabriel rose.

"Don't break my heart by lying, Anne," he said softly. "Just ... don't."

La Belle et La Bête.

She lay in bed, the book open across her chest.

In the story, only true love could reverse the spell.

But what if Beauty didn't *want* to reverse the spell?

What if she wished she were the Beast?

If you bonded me, you'd have all of my gifts.

Oh, Gabriel did know her. Too bloody well. He knew exactly what to promise that might tempt her.

But no. She'd be mad to even consider it.

Anne climbed out of bed and paced to the window, peering into the night. The Beast of Gévaudan was out there somewhere. It had been a shadowy presence the night she encountered it in the forest, but she suddenly wanted to see it, this creature of ancient magic and dark appetites. To look it in the face, or at least catch a glimpse.

Gabriel's bedroom looked out over both the bailey and the woods beyond the wall. She sat in a chair by the window, her eyes growing heavy but determined to wait. The hours passed. And then, just before dawn, Anne saw something moving through the trees. She sat up, instantly alert. It slunk through the dappled shadows, moving low to the ground, lithe and sleek. Then it passed beneath a huge oak and disappeared for a moment. Anne held her breath. A few seconds later, Gabriel emerged, walking upright and clad only in moonlight.

He strode through the postern gate and drew up a bucket of water from the well, dousing it over his head. Then he rolled his shoulders and tipped his head back, arms raised to squeeze the water from his hair.

Their eyes met.

Anne pulled back from the window. Had he truly seen her? It was only for the briefest instant. She couldn't be sure.

But she raced to the bed and leapt under the covers.

She heard the massive front door open and soft footsteps climbing the stairs. They padded down the corridor and paused for a brief moment in front of her bedroom, then continued on. A door closed softly somewhere in the house.

She sat up and threw the covers off.

Oh, what the hell.

Anne went to her door and opened it. She smoothed her nightgown and dragged fingers through her hair. Then she started down the corridor, reservations crumbling to dust. At the same instant, Gabriel appeared from the other direction. He'd yanked on a pair of trousers and a linen shirt, open at the throat, and by God, he looked good.

"Anne," he breathed, eyes widening.

"I was just—"

He took a step towards her when they both heard the sound of hooves on the road.

Gabriel frowned. "Excuse me, Anne. I… I'm sorry." He spun on his heel and hurried down the stairs. He seemed annoyed, but not surprised or alarmed.

He was expecting someone.

Anne slipped after him.

The rider must have already reached the front door, for she heard it open and the murmur of voices. She crept as close as she dared, but they'd gone into the library and closed the door. Like all the doors at Chateau de Saint-Évreux, it was thick and nearly impervious to eavesdropping.

Still, Anne did her best.

She seemed to have missed some crucial part of the conversation though, because most of what she heard made little sense, as well as being conducted in French, which she was rusty at. Gabriel seemed enraged at the rider, his voice a harsh staccato. From what she gathered, the man had done something Gabriel did not approve of. She heard the word *fantôme* several times, which she thought meant a wight or a ghoul. Also *Duzakh*, and *Bekker*. To her intense frustration, the rest of it was inaudible.

When she heard footsteps approach, Anne darted for the stairs, just rounding the first curve as the door opened. She crept back to her bedroom. Gabriel did not return to her, though she heard him pacing downstairs long after the rider had departed.

A soft knock roused her late the next morning. Gabriel stood in the doorway, dressed more formally than usual, in a dark coat with silver buttons and polished boots. He clearly hadn't slept and violet shadows smudged his eyes.

"I must leave you, Anne. For a few days only."

"Where are you going?"

"London. The Duzakh is gathering and I must deal with them. You have free rein here. There's food in the kitchens. For God's sake, just stay within the castle walls. Will you promise me that?"

"And if you don't return?"

"I will. And then…. We can talk more."

Once she would have rejoiced at being left alone. She might have made another run for the wall, Beast or not. Now she felt only dread. She knew enough about the Duzakh to understand that Gabriel was walking into a viper's nest.

"Who was that last night?"

"A man named Constantin. One of my brothers in the Order." His jaw tightened. "He stepped over the line about a certain matter I set him to attend to, but I'll sort things out myself."

"Be careful," she said, touching his cheek.

He closed his eyes for a moment, leaning into her fingers.

But he made no promises he couldn't keep.

Anne watched through the window as Gabriel galloped off on his horse, bent low over its neck.

She spent the day reading but found it hard to focus. Dinnertime came and went. Anne had little appetite. They didn't spend all their time together, but she always heard him somewhere in the house, playing his pianoforte or rattling around in the kitchen. The silence was oppressive.

Finally, she succumbed to curiosity — and perhaps a desire to feel his presence — and sought out the room Gabriel slept in. It wasn't hard to find. It was the only one with fresh linens, a room far less grand than the one she'd taken over. Anne sat down on the rumpled bed and looked around. One of his shirts was thrown over a chair. She saw a brush and polish for his boots, a razor and small shaving mirror. And a book, with one of his black ribbons carefully holding a place.

Anne picked it up. *The Chymical Wedding of Christian Rosenkreutz.*

The publisher's watermark was a cross with a rose at the center. Printed in 1616, two years after they'd first met.

She lay back on Gabriel's pillow and started to read. The story was divided into seven days and read like a fever dream, steeped in romance and mystical allegory. It told of a Bride and Groom, and the narrator's arduous journey to a castle for their wedding. He endured captivity and any number of strange experiences, but the tone of it was joyous and full of wonder.

Anne read it straight through without stopping, a shaft of sunlight creeping across the room as the hours passed. At last she closed the book, the smell of him on her skin, and let out a soft breath.

No author was named, but she knew who'd written it.

A beautiful, demented fantasy, she thought.

Just like Gabriel.

CHAPTER 22

C ount Balthazar Jozsef Habsburg-Koháry climbed the steps of the townhouse on Portland Place and rapped the knocker once. The middle-aged woman who opened it cast a professional eye over his elegant Chesterfield coat and silver-tipped walking stick. She gave him a warm smile.

"Do come in, sir."

She ushered him into a parlor festooned with maroon velvet drapes. Balthazar removed his hat, which was duly placed on a rack.

"Your coat, sir?" she asked.

"Thank you, I'll keep it," he replied courteously.

She didn't seem sure what to make of this. Balthazar forged ahead.

"My name is Count Koháry," he said with a bow. "I am seeking companionship this evening. A gentleman friend gave me this address."

At the mention of a title, the madam's smile widened. "A foreign noble," she murmured. "How exciting. Where are you from, milord?"

When pressed, Balthazar claimed to be a distant cousin of the

Hungarian princes who were booted out in 1858. In fact, he lacked a single drop of royal blood, but he was rich as sin and most people seemed to take his word for it.

"Buda-Pesth," he replied.

"Please, have a seat." She gestured at a sofa. "Do you have any particular preferences, milord?"

"It makes no difference," he replied honestly.

The madam retreated to a back room and returned with a lovely young girl of perhaps twenty, dark of hair and with a creamy English complexion. She wore a thin robe that barely concealed the outlines of her firm body.

"This is Lucy. She'll be happy to accommodate you, Count Koháry."

The girl smiled at him and took his hand, leading him up a rickety flight of stairs to a small room on the third floor. A threadbare carpet covered the floor. A bed stood against one wall, the sheets hastily straightened from the exertions of the previous client. She let her robe slip from her shoulders and raised a hand to unbutton his shirt. Balthazar gently caught her wrist.

"I prefer to remain clothed," he said.

She arched an eyebrow. "Whatever milord prefers."

"Come, sit on my lap, Lucy." Balthazar drew her down to the bed and began stroking her thighs, easing them open. He took his time about it, nuzzling her neck a bit, trying not to rush although he ached with a different need. The least he could do was make the experience an enjoyable one. By the time he slid a warm hand between her legs, she gave a cry of genuine pleasure.

"Now there's a good girl," he murmured.

As one finger slipped inside her, his other hand lifted a pendant from his own neck and laid it around hers. His hand moved with calculated precision and it didn't take long to bring her to climax. Balthazar gave a little shiver as life poured through the *ouroboros* dangling from the chain, poured from *her* into *him*.

When her tremors had subsided, she touched the pendant, a serpent eating its own tail. It was cunningly wrought, with life-like scales and glittering emerald eyes.

"What's this?" she asked, curious.

"Just a fetish of mine." He lifted her hair and returned the talisman to his coat pocket.

The girl looked at him, wide-eyed and adorably disheveled. "Now it's your turn, milord."

He eased her from his lap and stood. "That's all I wanted."

She gave a disbelieving laugh. "What, milord?"

Balthazar dropped a thick wad of banknotes on the table. "A tip," he said, unable to meet her gaze.

The girl seemed astonished at her good fortune. Balthazar picked up the robe and hung it over her shoulders. Yet when she looked away, he couldn't resist studying her with a guilty eye. Did she always have that faint line next to her mouth?

He never knew how much he'd taken from them, if was an hour, a day or a year.

But at least he tried to make it worth their while.

"Well, you're certainly one of a kind," she joked as he strode to the door. "I ought to pay you."

Balthazar gave her a weak smile.

He wished he could say he had standards. That he would never despoil a virgin or pay a woman for sex when in fact he was stealing her life force.

But he couldn't.

Balthazar would take what he could get when felt himself starting to weaken.

Not weaken. *Die*.

She stuck her head out the door as he walked down the stairs. "Come back anytime, my name's Lucy, don't forget!"

The madam looked surprised to see him leaving so soon, but when he gave her an even larger wad of money, her face grew calculating.

"Won't you stay for a while, Count Koháry? I can arrange a late supper." She gave him a coquettish grin. "I have other girls, too, even prettier than Lucy. You haven't seen half of 'em."

"I must decline your kind offer," Balthazar said, taking his hat from the hook and setting it on his head. "But thank you." He gave her a bow and headed down the front stairs with a new bounce in his step.

Balthazar would never return. His only ironclad rule was that he never stole from the same woman twice.

Sometimes a single encounter sustained him for months. Other times, he felt himself weakening after only a week or two. Was it because he'd taken more from the first one? Again, who knew.

But he would feel a lethargy come over him when he waited too long. The exhaustion of a drawn-out illness. Once he had waited to see what would happen next. It wasn't encouraging. The aging rapidly accelerated.

Only then had he fully grasped the predicament he was in for all eternity.

Balthazar strolled around the corner where his manservant Lucas Devereaux waited with a carriage. He sat back as they rattled off, his eyes half-closed, walking stick resting across his knees. Luckily, he liked women in all shapes, colors and sizes. There were far worse ways to earn one's immortality.

Lucas drove them straight to Balthazar's townhouse in Mayfair. He'd only returned to London so he could sell it and leave as soon as possible for his estate in Basque Country. There were people who might be looking for him and he had no burning desire to encounter them again. The Lady Vivienne, in particular. But he couldn't resist squeezing in one last liaison.

It was past midnight by the time Lucas delivered him at the front door and went off to stable the horses. Balthazar unlocked it and entered the dark house. He kept no other servants when he came to town. The fewer who saw his face, the better. The housekeeper and cook only knew that they had a foreign employer who traveled a great deal and demanded the utmost privacy when he was in London. They kept the house ready for him, and the cook came in the early mornings and made food that she left for Lucas to heat up. It was an odd arrangement, but he paid them well and they seemed to expect eccentricity from a Hungarian count.

Balthazar climbed the stairs and headed for the study, thinking he'd have a brandy before going to bed.

Gabriel D'Ange was sitting in his favorite chair by the fire.

"*Bon soir,*" he said cheerfully.

Balthazar froze for a moment, then strode to the sideboard and poured himself a drink.

"You could have asked for an appointment."

"I happened to be in the neighborhood."

"And what is the nature of this impromptu call?" Balthazar inquired with a thin smile, his mind racing. A visit from Gabriel D'Ange was not something one generally hoped for. "I don't mean to be rude, but it's rather late."

"Straight to the point? All right, then. Bekker's in town."

Balthazar stilled.

"Are you sure?"

Gabriel tossed something on the table. Balthazar picked it up. It was heavy card stock, dark blue with gilt lettering. An invitation to a masked party at the Picatrix Club the following night. Gentleman only.

"He's calling the Duzakh together again."

Balthazar fingered the invitation, then dropped it back on the table.

"Why are you telling me this?"

Gabriel laughed. "Let's not play games. I know you had a hand in the civil war. Whispering in this ear and then that one, intercepting some letters, forging others. Pushing those *fils de putes* into devouring each other."

"And what if I did?"

"Your protégé. Lucas Devereaux. Didn't Bekker kill his family?"

Balthazar's jaw worked. "You know he did."

"So we both have reason to hate him." Gabriel stretched his boots toward the fire. "I plan to attend. I have a few men, but I could always use another."

"Sorry, I'm busy that night."

Gabriel turned cold eyes on him. "Yes, you've always been a mercenary, haven't you?" The tone was withering. "Loyal to none but yourself. But some of us have a higher purpose."

Balthazar drained his glass. "Are you still calling yourself an archangel, Gabriel?"

"Not anymore. I've mellowed."

Somehow Balthazar doubted this.

"A temporary alliance only," Gabriel persisted. "I've had … setbacks lately. The Order's numbers have been winnowed."

Balthazar picked up the invitation again, studying it. There was no name specified, which didn't surprise him. The Duazkh were nothing if not paranoid about their true identities.

"How did *you* manage to get one? Doesn't Bekker loathe you?"

"I put out the word that I had something of great value." Gabriel reached into his pocket and withdrew a leather glove. He put it on, then reached into a different pocket with the gloved hand and drew out a thick gold cuff. It glowed in the firelight. "A peace offering."

Balthazar covered his shock. Such talismans were rare indeed. "Where did you get that?"

"It was Vivienne Cumberland's. You know her?"

"By reputation only," Balthazar lied. "Did you … harm her for it?"

"No." Gabriel returned the cuff to his pocket.

A strange wave of relief passed through Balthazar. "What do you plan to do?"

Gabriel shrugged. "None of them trust each other. They'll be ready to bolt at the slightest provocation. We go in and liven things up a little. Once it all goes to *merde*, it will be a free-for-all. I'll improvise something nasty for Bekker, never fear." He stood. "Bring your man Lucas. I hear he's a brawler."

Lucas. He should have returned by now.

"Where is he?" Balthazar demanded coldly.

"He'll be along soon, I'm sure."

"If your men laid a hand on him—"

Gabriel walked to the door, his dark coat blending with the shadows. "It's time to choose sides, old friend. Keep the invitation in case you decide to cancel your plans. I have another." He paused, his voice soft. "It was good to see you again. You're not an easy man to find, Balthazar. No, not easy at all."

When he was gone, Balthazar raised an unsteady hand to his forehead. Gabriel was telling him he could track him down anywhere, anytime.

Not for the first time, Balthazar wished he'd never passed through that flyspeck village in Gaul.

A minute later, Lucas burst into the room, his clothes disheveled though he appeared unhurt.

"Fucking bastard," he muttered. "I saw him leave. Two of them held me at gunpoint in the stables."

Balthazar set his empty glass down, his good mood utterly soured. He handed Lucas the invitation. Lucas's eyes narrowed as he scanned it. He knew who owned the Picatrix Club.

Jorin Bekker. The worst of the Duzakh by far, and that was saying something.

Officially, Bekker was a Belgian national, a wealthy merchant with business interests in the Congo and elsewhere, but that was simply a matter of convenience. Bekker's allegiance was entirely to the gold he'd amassed in the slave trade and other vile endeavors. Balthazar knew he was the sort of man Gabriel despised with particular intensity. Bekker was no run-of-the-mill killer. Thousands had suffered at his hands, although he kept them clean these days, delegating the dirty work to others.

And Gabriel D'Ange…. He never left anything to chance. Never *improvised*. His schemes were always meticulous and utterly ruthless. And he'd been trying to get to Bekker for centuries now. Jorin was the one man who'd managed to elude him. Which meant he had something up his sleeve that he wasn't sharing.

Gabriel had Vivienne's cuff. The fact that he'd worn a glove to touch it meant he hadn't used it yet, but God only knew what he intended — and what Balthazar would be walking into if he accepted Gabriel's invitation.

"What are you going to do?" Lucas asked, fingers straying unconsciously to the scar on his face.

Bekker had given him that when he left him for dead as a young child.

Yes, Balthazar thought wearily, that's an excellent question. *What the hell am I going to do now?*

The grandfather clock in the hall chimed four o'clock as Balthazar stared into the banked coals of the fire, unable to sleep.

If he did go to the Picatrix Club, there was a fair chance he wouldn't walk out again. Balthazar had many enemies among the Duzakh, not all of them dead, unfortunately. One might recognize him despite the mask. He was a tall man, taller than most. That alone would set him apart.

If he didn't go…. Well, Balthazar didn't truly believe Gabriel would punish him for it, that wasn't his style. But it wouldn't earn him any goodwill either. And Lucas Devereaux was like a son to him. If there was a chance to see Bekker dead….

Balthazar rubbed his forehead.

A true existential dilemma.

Not to mention the damned cuff.

If not for me, Gabriel would have lived and died on his father's farm, likely by the ripe old age of forty or so, and that would have been the end of it.

Balthazar had been on a recruiting trip for Neblis, searching for children with the spark to wield a talisman. Only one in a thousand mortals had it. Those who served the Persian king wore the cuffs of the Water Dogs and those who served Neblis wore the chains.

It wasn't something Balthazar was proud of it, but he'd done it. And one day he'd found himself in a tiny village near the sea, leading one of these children from a thatched hovel to the horse Balthazar had left tied to an apple tree. Gabriel's parents had been both deeply religious and desperately poor. Balthazar purchased the boy with minimal fuss, promising a vague apprenticeship. His mother wept when they left but Gabriel himself was dry-eyed and full of questions.

Balthazar trained him personally in the arts of necromancy. He was clever and fearless, and at first Balthazar thought he had great potential. But he soon revealed a rebellious streak and his own moral code that no number of beatings could break. They just made him harder. More obstinate.

And yet even after Neblis was dead and her dark lords scattered across the globe, Gabriel had never come after him.

Balthazar suspected it was because he too had worked against the Duzakh.

Honor among thieves.

Now he rose and and pressed a hidden panel near the fireplace, revealing a cache of talismans he'd collected over the years to hide them from the Duzakh. It was his life's work, a way of atoning for the wrongs he'd committed and, in all honesty, continued to commit.

He lifted a set of necromantic chains, running the links through his fingers. Taken during the Purge, when Balthazar had seized the opportunity to part some of the worst of the Duzakh from their source of immortality. The iron was cold and heavy in his hands, shimmering with a fey light.

He'd served Queen Neblis for two hundred years. Stealing children was the least of his crimes. The things he'd done for her....

Well, they would earn him a place in the Pit for all eternity.

Balthazar did not fear death the way ordinary people feared it. No, the thought of what waited in the afterlife brought the sort of terror that dried one's tongue and left the palms slick with icy sweat.

He had boltholes no one would ever find, perhaps not even D'Ange. All his instincts screamed at him to have nothing to do with this. He'd come to London in the first place because he intended never to return.

But he had made a promise a very long time ago, to a man who had believed in redemption.

That he would try to be good.

Balthazar returned the chains to their place and closed the panel. He made the sign of the flame, fingers brushing forehead, lips and, lastly, heart. Then he trudged off in search of something suitable to wear to a party.

CHAPTER 23

"The man's a wraith," Vivienne muttered.

She sat in the conservatory at Park Place with Alec, who reclined on the sofa, his bad leg stretched out on an ottoman. He held the afternoon post in his hands.

"Cyrus found nothing useful about D'Ange in his archives?" she asked. "No clue as to where he might be?"

Alec shook his head. "Nothing more than we already knew."

"What about the strong room? Was anything else missing?"

"He hinted at it, but didn't specify what. Only that it wouldn't be a danger to us."

"Hell," she muttered.

Alec sighed and scanned a second letter. "Harrison Fearing Pell and John Weston sent a note from New York, offering their aid."

They'd worked with Pell and Weston on the Clarence case, forging a bond of friendship with the pair of young investigators at the American division of the S.P.R. Harry in particular was exceedingly clever, Vivienne thought, but she very much doubted D'Ange had crossed the Atlantic.

She forced a smile. "It's kind of them, but I don't think there's much they can do that Henry Sidgwick and all his agents aren't already."

Three long weeks had passed since they'd returned to London from Ingress Abbey, with no more word from Gabriel D'Ange and no sign of Anne. Nathaniel was still recovering at a hospital in Bucharest, but his last letter had been hopeful that he would be strong enough to return to England by April or May.

Alec and Vivienne made a full report to both Henry Sidgwick and Inspector Blackwood of the Dominion Branch. Blackwood had offered them men to watch the house, but Vivienne refused. Their only hope was that D'Ange might try to contact them again, arrange for some sort of a deal, and she didn't want to scare him off.

Every day was an agony of waiting. Alec bore it with his usual stoicism, but Vivienne was starting to come apart at the seams.

Before she met Alec, she'd been bonded to another. When that daēva died, Vivienne had lost the will to live. If not for the children who'd been left in her care, she would have ended it. And when she took a necromancer's blade between the ribs at Gorgon-e Gaz, it came almost as a relief. Her name had been Tijah then.

Achaemenes ... Alec ... had bonded her against her will to save her.

It was a bitter irony. Under the Empire, daēvas had always been the ones with no choice in the matter.

She'd hated him for a while. But Alec Lawrence was hard to hate.

Now she'd take that blade a thousand times over if it would keep him safe from D'Ange.

And she wondered where he would be if he'd chosen differently.

"Viv," Alec said softly. "Don't dwell."

She lifted her head. "Sorry."

"What are you thinking?"

"Nothing."

Alec held her gaze for a moment more, then looked away.

He wouldn't let her smoke in the conservatory, said it was bad for the plants, but she kept thinking of the pack of Oxford Ovals on her bedside table.

Vivienne heard footsteps and Quimby's flushed face poked into the conservatory. "My Lady," he hissed. "There's a visitor, he wouldn't wait."

Alec frowned.

The butler quickly read out a card resting on a small silver tray. "Count Balthazar Jozsef Habsburg-Koháry—"

At that instant, a tall man filled the doorway, olive-skinned and sleekly attractive.

"Don't mind the title," he said with a charming smile. "Just Balthazar will do."

Vivienne's rage was so acute, it took her a long moment to react. She leapt to her feet and slammed him into the wall, a knife materializing at his throat. From the corner of her eye, she saw Quimby beat a swift retreat.

Balthazar's gaze narrowed. He glanced at her bare wrist. "Missing something?" he murmured.

The knife edge pressed deeper, at the edge of drawing blood. "You *bastard*—"

"Let him go, Viv," Alec said with a touch of impatience. "He doesn't have it. He wouldn't be here if he did. I want to hear what he has to say."

Since the Clarence case in New York, Alec had been favorably disposed towards Count Koháry. Vivienne saw things differently, but she knew he was right. She scowled and took a step back. "Talk, necromancer."

"I'm not a necromancer," Balthazar said, straightening his coat in a leisurely fashion that made her want to murder him all over again. "Not anymore."

"Then how is it you're still alive?" Her voice lowered. "I know you're an old one. We've determined that much."

"There are other talismans to prolong life," he said cagily. "I'm not here to discuss that." He swallowed. "I'm only here to tell you the name of the man who stole your cuff. Gabriel D'Ange."

"We know that already," Vivienne snarled.

Balthazar regarded her. He smiled. "But did you know where he's going to be tonight?"

She took a step back, still wary, if less inclined to kill him on the spot.

"A place called the Picatrix Club. It's owned by a man named Jorin Bekker, though he's rarely there.

"Bekker," Alec murmured. "I know that name." A look of hatred crossed his face. "We nearly had him in Berlin that time, do you remember, Vivienne?"

She nodded grimly. She knew exactly who Jorin Bekker was.

"The Club is named after an eleventh century book on magic and astrology originally written under the title *Ghayat al-Hakim*," Balthazar continued, removing his hat and tossing it on a side table. "His own private joke."

Vivienne stared at him. "I don't *care* about that. Tell me about D'Ange."

Balthazar handed her an invitation. "I have no idea where he's staying in London, but he told me he planned to attend. He's been trying to get to Bekker for … let's just say a very, very long time."

She scanned the engraved script. "And why should I believe a word you're saying?"

He shrugged. "Don't. I'm just clearing my conscience, such as it is."

"How did you learn he had the cuff?" Alec asked.

"He showed it to me. Gold with a winged griffin, yes?"

Vivienne looked up sharply. "So he has it with him." She paced to the French doors, watching Balthazar's reflection in the glass. "What do you know about the Order of the Rose Cross?"

Balthazar gave a small shrug. "They're maniacs." A bark of laughter. "Necromancers on some divine mission from God, if you can fathom it. Assassins, above any law except their own. They've killed kings and popes and hundreds more people you've never heard of." His voice softened. "Once you're on Gabriel's list, he'll hunt you down if it takes him forever. So I hope you fully appreciate the risk I've taken in coming here."

"I do," Alec said in a friendly tone.

Vivienne said nothing. She was thinking. "Why is he going to the Picatrix?"

"Like I told you, he wants Bekker."

"I have no objection to that. But I want my cuff back!" She didn't mention Anne. The less this man knew, the better.

Balthazar gave a slow nod. "I'm sure you do." He reached for his hat. "Well, good luck to you both—"

She rounded on him. "Where are you going?"

Balthazar placed the hat on his head and adjusted the brim. "Home. I have a party to dress for. Black tie, you know."

"Oh no, you're not simply walking out of here...." A pause. "You're going?"

"I have a personal score of my own to settle with Bekker." His lips thinned. "May I have my invitation back now? I'll need it to get in the door."

Vivienne snatched it away from his hand. She looked at Alec, who nodded.

"Take me," Alec said.

Balthazar laughed, long and loud. "And let Gabriel know I betrayed him? Not a chance."

Alec Lawrence's temper finally roused. "I'll be discreet. But we'll never get near him without an invitation.... Unless you have another one?"

"Sorry. I'd give it to you if I had." He paused. "What did you do to him anyhow?"

"It doesn't matter," Alec replied wearily. "It was a long time ago."

Balthazar gave a small shake of his head. "Time means nothing. D'Ange doesn't forget." He eyed the invitation. "It'll never work anyway. He obviously knows you."

"It's masked, isn't it?"

Balthazar's gaze hardened and Vivienne saw a hint of the man beneath the well-groomed façade. "Don't make me regret coming here."

Vivienne swept to the door, blocking it. "You'll take Mr. Lawrence as your guest or I'll alert the Dominion Branch that there's a soiree of necromancers taking place in London tonight. I think they might be interested." She smiled. "As a bonus, I'll put out the word that you're their informant."

Balthazar stared at her for a long moment. "You don't play nicely, do you?"

Vivienne waited. He reached into his pocket and Alec tensed, but Balthazar only produced a heavy gold pocket watch. He glanced at the time, then snapped it shut with a sigh.

"All right, then. I was planning to bring my man Lucas Devereaux, but Mr. Lawrence is roughly his height and build." He eyed Alec's cane. "You'll have to do something about the leg though. Like I said, D'Ange doesn't forget."

"I'll bind it," Alec said. "That works for a while."

Vivienne pointed to a wicker loveseat and Balthazar dropped down with a sigh.

"What do you know about this Order of the Rose Cross? How many will be there?"

"There are only eight members at any given time. D'Ange is their leader. He told me the ranks had been winnowed, though he usually has a few hopefuls waiting in the wings."

"Two died in Gran Canaria," Alec said. "They'd followed me there on holiday."

Balthazar crossed his legs, one arm stretched along the back of the loveseat. "So counting D'Ange, you can expect four or five, I'd say. For a fish as big as Bekker, he'll muster the troops."

"I met a man with stumps." Vivienne held up her pinky and ring fingers. "He claimed he lost them chopping wood."

"Oh, yes," Balthazar replied. "Johann Constantin Andreae. Gabriel's most loyal foot soldier." He laughed. "But he didn't lose them chopping wood. It was during the Purge of 1782. Constantin was surrounded by revenants sent by another necromancer. One bit off two of his fingers before Gabriel beheaded them."

"Charming," Vivienne muttered. "Let's move on. The Picatrix. Have you been there?"

"Once or twice."

"Is there a back way in?"

Balthazar nodded. "The garden. It will be guarded, naturally, but there's a public park beyond the wall if you want to stay close."

Vivienne did.

"You can't bring any weapons," he said to Alec. "Not a damned toothpick. We won't get a toe inside the door if you do."

Alec held up open palms.

"What exactly do you intend?" Balthazar demanded.

Alec shrugged. "I'm not sure yet. But I'll keep you out of it."

"For God's sake, just be discreet," Balthazar said, rising and reaching for his hat. "I don't relish the thought of D'Ange discovering I'm the one who brought you there."

Alec murmured his assent.

Count Koháry turned back at the door, his expression unreadable. "I'll send Lucas with instructions about where and how to meet beforehand."

When he was gone, Vivienne looked at Alec. "Do you trust him?"

"It doesn't matter. We're out of options."

"I don't like you walking into a roomful of necromancers wearing a daēva cuff," she muttered. "In fact, I loathe it."

Alec said nothing. They both knew his was locked in place, the key centuries lost.

She let out a breath. "All right. The much larger problem is what you'll do with D'Ange if you manage to get him alone. Much as I'd like to, we can't just kill him even if he has my cuff. Not until we know where he's holding Anne."

"Cyrus said he has his own rigid sort of honor," Alec said. "It's true. I didn't know him long, but I had the same impression. Perhaps we can use that to our advantage."

Vivienne pondered it for a moment. Then a gleam appeared in her eye.

"Here's a thought," she said with a sweet smile. "Why don't we borrow a page from D'Ange's own little playbook?"

CHAPTER 24

Balthazar fitted the demi-mask to his face and regarded the gaudily painted jester staring back at him in the shaving mirror. The crooked nose was concealed, along with most of his coal-black hair. Save for the dark eyes, he could have been anyone.

Balthazar curled his lips in a suitably grotesque leer.

His smile died. It would do.

He wore an evening dress suit with tails and a black tie, which he now made a minute adjustment to. Might as well go out in style.

Like Gabriel, Balthazar had always stalked his prey from the shadows, pretending loyalty to various factions of the Duzakh while undermining them all at every turn. It was a razor's edge, but he'd walked it unerringly for centuries.

Time to choose sides, old friend.

It almost came as a relief. The confrontation had been inevitable.

"Are you ready, my lord?"

Balthazar could see half of Lucas's face in the mirror behind him. Close-cropped hair turning prematurely grey at the temples and a little waxed moustache that drew attention away from the scar bisecting his jaw. Lucas was only twenty-seven, but he'd been with Balthazar since he was four years old. Balthazar had raised him as his own, paying for elite boarding schools and other, more specialized training.

"As I'll ever be," Balthazar replied.

Lucas fixed a feathered eagle mask with a sharply curved beak to his own face. His mouth was a tense line. Seeing Bekker dead was Lucas's dearest wish. Balthazar knew he was unhappy about the decision to allow Alec Lawrence to take his place.

"I'll bring the carriage round."

Balthazar glanced at his cache of talismans, then resolutely turned his back on it. There would be no smuggling of weapons, magical or otherwise, into the Picatrix Club. Bekker was too careful for that. Balthazar just hoped Alec Lawrence had received the message — and didn't try anything unforgivably stupid before Bekker was dead.

He donned his silk-lined top hat and trotted out the front door. They took a winding route through London, passing through the genteel bustle of Picadilly and on to less savory districts. When the carriage reached a tangle of narrow alleys, the wheels slowed. Balthazar heard a soft thump. Then it rolled forward again, setting a course for Queensgate near the Royal Horticultural Society.

A line of footmen waited outside the Picatrix Club. Alec Lawrence, now wearing the feathered eagle half-mask and similarly attired in a coat and tails, climbed down from the driver's bench and opened the door for Balthazar, then followed him through a wrought-iron gate as one of the footmen took charge of the carriage. Alec walked without his cane and Balthazar detected no telltale limp. They exchanged a quick glance as the front door was opened by yet another footman.

There was no plaque or anything else to signify the nature of the townhouse. It could have been any of a dozen discreet gentlemen's clubs, with a whiff of cigar smoke in the air and walls of dark-paneled wood.

But the six men who waited inside the vestibule, all masked as fantastic, nightmarish animals, proceeded to conduct an exceedingly thorough search of their persons before they were permitted to go any further.

"Easy now," Balthazar murmured as one of them groped through his trouser pockets. "We've only just met."

The man showed no reaction whatsoever. He had a job to do, and by God, he was going to do it.

Balthazar saw Alec tense as rough hands ran over the cuff around his wrist, then yanked his sleeve up. Bekker's minion examined it with a slight frown and let the shirt fall back into place.

Balthazar suppressed a smile. The silly bugger had never seen a bonded cuff before. Not surprising since so few were left, but he had no idea a daēva was in their midst. *Bekker's getting sloppy with his training.* In Balthazar's time, every necromancer worth his chains knew exactly what that cuff meant — and to run in the opposite direction.

Once through this checkpoint, they were ushered into a much larger room with an ornate vaulted ceiling and row of windows overlooking a balcony and garden beyond.

Perhaps a hundred men stood whispering in little knots. There was no food or drink on offer. The Duzakh didn't trust each other enough for that.

Balthazar nodded his head toward an open space near the raised dais in the center of the room. They stood for a moment, listening to the low murmur of conversation. Through the eagle's mask, Alec's eyes roamed the crowd, seeking out his quarry, but Balthazar saw no sign of D'Ange, or Bekker either.

Perhaps a quarter of the men had brought their human captives, imagining the display gave them status and prestige. These would be the youngest necromancers. In fact, Balthazar knew the slaves would only prove an encumbrance if disputes broke out — as they often did. The captives wore iron collars around their necks and their eyes were blank as dolls. Balthazar sensed Alec's revulsion and fully shared it.

But now wasn't the time for heroic gestures. Balthazar's sharp gaze swept the crowd. Despite the array of freakish masks, he knew a few of the oldest ones well enough to identify their names.

"Kir Nazari," he said softly to Alec. "The one who keeps raising his hand to his face and then stopping himself. He has a scar on his nose he strokes when he's nervous." Balthazar nodded his head at another necromancer, morbidly obese, in a mask with curling ram's horns. "And that's the one who gave him the scar."

Balthazar's gaze moved onward … and flicked back. A man had appeared at the edge of the room. He was of medium height and build, notable only for the fact that he'd disdained a tie and tails, wearing a plain wool coat with silver buttons. He wore the mask of a panther. Balthazar's neck prickled as the man turned his head and Balthazar saw the dark blond hair, tied back at the nape with a black ribbon.

Gabriel appeared to be alone.

Alec noticed an instant later. Balthazar felt him tense.

And then the whispering grew as Jorin Bekker entered through a side door, surrounded by a cadre of flunkies. He walked slowly to the dais at the center of the room.

Bekker held his hands up and waited for perfect silence.

"Welcome, friends," he said. "Welcome to the Picatrix Club."

He had a slight Belgian accent, his voice high and sweet like a child's. In truth, he looked no more than sixteen, a slender youth who might have been handsome if not for a certain reptilian quality to his features, a covetous hardness around the eyes. Longish hair swept back from a high forehead and small, full lips. Bekker did not wear a mask. He was signaling that he had no fear of revealing his face. He had no fear of *them*.

"It has been a long century since last we gathered, but I believe the time has come to set aside our differences. Do we not all enjoy wealth, power, immortality? Yet some among us became greedy, forging alliances outside of the Duzakh. And that, my friends, led to our downfall." He paused. "We must reinstate a ruling council, bring order." A crooked smile. "We are like large predators, each requiring a designated range in which to feed. But that cannot be accomplished without...."

Alec's finger tapped impatiently against his trouser leg. Gabriel hadn't moved, only stood listening like the rest of them.

"So what I propose is this. We have some newer members, but precedence must be given to—"

And suddenly Alec was moving, making his stealthy way through the crowd toward Gabriel. Balthazar bit back an oath and stepped forward, catching his sleeve.

"Just wait, for God's sake," he muttered.

Alec pulled free and continued on, inexorable. There were a few mutters of irritation as someone's shoe was trodden on. Gabriel glanced over his shoulder. His eyes met Balthazar's through the panther mask and he gave a tiny nod. Of course, Gabriel would recognize him instantly.

But he hadn't noticed Alec Lawrence yet.

On the dais, Bekker's speech was gaining momentum.

"... the Duzakh will be reborn, stronger than it was before, and with mechanisms in place to settle...."

Balthazar made another futile snatch at the back of Alec's coat. And then they both stood directly behind D'Ange. He caught and held Alec's eyes through the eagle mask for a brief moment.

Don't. Balthazar mouthed. *For the love of—*

Alec Lawrence leaned forward to Gabriel's ear and whispered something in French. Balthazar couldn't make out the words but he'd learned to read lips during the Purge, a useful skill at gatherings such as this one.

What Alec had said was this:

"You have my sister, you *fucking bastard*, so why don't we step into the garden and settle the matter like gentlemen?"

Sister? Balthazar thought.

Gabriel stiffened. He ignored Alec completely and turned to Balthazar.

"I'll kill you for this someday," he said softly.

Not a threat. A simple statement of fact.

Balthazar closed his eyes, suddenly wearier than he'd ever been in his life.

I should never have come here. I could have been halfway back to Spain by now.

Gabriel half-turned to Alec. "I'll be glad to," he hissed. "Just let me have Bekker first."

Alec gave a curt nod.

And so they stood shoulder to shoulder while Bekker droned on and Balthazar could hardly believe no one else noticed the murderous tension between the two men. Alec's hands were balled into fists. Gabriel's hung loose and open at his sides, but his perfect stillness conveyed the posture of a predator about to pounce.

And then Balthazar realized that Bekker had finally stopped talking. Despite the masks, he stared unerringly in their direction.

"We have a special guest tonight." Bekker paused. "Gabriel D'Ange."

An unhappy murmur rippled through the crowd of Antimagi.

"Here we go," Balthazar murmured.

Gabriel shouldered his way to the center of the room and stood before the dais.

"It's been an age since we met," Bekker said. "You look the same as ever."

There was some sycophantic laughter, but not much. The room held its breath.

"I understand you've brought me something," Bekker said. "A gift."

"Oh, I did. Would you like to have it now?"

Bekker licked his lips.

Three of the Order of the Rose Cross materialized in the side doors, leaving the main entrance at the back of the room unguarded. They held crossbows. Balthazar recognized Constantin immediately by his missing fingers and burly shoulders, but he didn't know the others. This didn't surprise him. The nature of the Order implied a fair amount of turnover. Gabriel D'Ange and Johann Constantin Andreae were the only ones who had survived since its founding.

But Gabriel didn't usually mount a frontal assault.

Bekker gave a thin smile. Then one of the Order loosed a bolt. It struck the necromancer standing next to Bekker. He frowned slightly, raising a hand to pull it out … and screamed, a horrible cry. He fell from the dais, heels drumming on the ground, his face turning an ugly shade of purple.

There was a surge as the Duzakh started backing toward the open doors.

"Nobody moves," Gabriel snapped. "*Nobody.*"

The room stilled.

"*Sanctus arma,*" Balthazar whispered with a note of awe.

Alec shot him a look.

"Forged during the Crusades." He spoke rapidly. "Weapons supposedly blessed by Saint Michael himself. Most were lost. Whatever the hell they're made of, they'll kill a necromancer. But they're almost impossible to find anymore."

Balthazar watched intently. Gabriel was full of surprises.

"You *fils de put* slaver." Gabriel tore his mask off and spat on the polished parquet floor. "Jorin Bekker." The name was spoken in a clipped, ringing tone and Bathazar wondered how many men had heard their own names spoken in such a way, and how many had heard Gabriel's voice as their last sound on earth.

"I sentence you to death in the name of the Saints and the Holy Father for the crimes of rape, kidnapping, murder, profiting from the blood and sweat of innocents…."

The litany went on.

Bekker didn't try to run. He just regarded him with those flat sharklike eyes.

When Gabriel finished, a pregnant hush fell on the room.

"I don't want the rest of you," Gabriel said quietly, his gaze never leaving Bekker. "*Get out.*"

There was a brief, pregnant pause, followed by a stampede for the back of the room. But too many of them reached the doors at once and they couldn't all fit through.

So naturally, they started killing each other.

Balthazar saw one of the Order shoot a necromancer with human captives and unlatch the collar and bracelets, freeing his slaves. These poor souls were shoved through a side door just as a revenant tore through the floorboards, a heavy iron blade in its gore-caked fist. Gabriel kicked it away with contempt.

"*Donné!*" he barked, throwing out a hand.

His protégé tossed him the chains. Gabriel whipped them around the neck of one of Bekker's bodyguards and snapped it. Another vicious jerk and the head popped off and rolled across the floor, coming to rest at Balthazar's feet.

That's when things officially went to *merde*.

Gabriel and his chains were a graceful whirlwind of death, but Balthazar lost interest in watching him when a pair of revenants exploded through the floor directly in Balthazar's path. Viking warriors risen from the grave, with eyes of silver and the pallor of yesterday's fish. He grabbed a gilded chair and brandished it like a lion-tamer. One crushing downstroke later, Balthazar stood with half the chair in each hand. He was wondering what he ought to do with the pieces when a crossbow bolt whizzed past his left ear. The revenant toppled.

Balthazar whispered a quick prayer of thanks. Then he

scooped up its broadsword, beheaded the other, and tried to find an exit that wasn't clogged with bodies.

Gabriel was still single-mindedly carving a path to Bekker, his mouth set in a grim line, and Balthazar had to wonder why Bekker hadn't fled. He stood still as a statue on the dais, watching the melee around him, watching as his bodyguards fell, one by one, and Gabriel slowly advanced.

If he drained a necromancer as old and powerful as Jorin Bekker, D'Ange would gain decades of life. Maybe more.

The room was starting to empty, either because the men inside it were dead or they'd had the wits to bring a talisman of Traveling. Gateways were opening in the spilled blood all over the room, necromancers leaping into them, half with their animal masks askew. It was like some surreal, hellish scene from a Hieronymus Bosch painting.

Where was Lucas? Vivienne? Balthazar took a step toward the windows fronting the balcony and saw Constantin rush up and seize Gabriel's arm. Gabriel shook him off, raging in French so rapid Balthazar couldn't follow it. Apparently, things weren't turning out the way they were supposed to. Gabriel turned away....

And Constantin reached into his cloak, unsheathed a sword and drove it straight through Gabriel's back.

Balthazar froze, shocked to his marrow.

D'Ange blinked rapidly as a foot of steel erupted from his chest. Quick as a snake, Constantin withdrew the blade and stabbed him again. And yet again.

The sword looked ordinary enough, if forged in the old way, double-edged with a cruciform hilt now dark with rust, but Balthazar knew it had to be *sanctus arma*. He waited for the inevitable scream, but it never came.

Blood ran from Gabriel's mouth. He sank to his knees, his face disbelieving.

Constantin swung the blade back to take Gabriel's head from

his shoulders when one of the Order — a loyal one, apparently — slammed into Constantin and dragged him down. The man was already dying from a dozen wounds. Constantin finished him quickly. He stood and turned back to Gabriel, now braced on all fours, head hanging low.

And Alec Lawrence stepped between them.

"He's mine," Alec snarled, a bloodied revenant blade in his hands.

Constantin scowled and raised the sword, but his new master beckoned sharply. "He's good as dead," Bekker snapped. "Leave him."

Constantin cast a final look at Gabriel and Balthazar knew exactly what he was thinking. *Better safe than sorry.* But Alec still stood over D'Ange and Bekker was snapping orders. Constantin spun away, striding to one of the open doorways where Bekker's men stood guard. They all vanished, presumably to a Gate.

Gabriel fell to one side, unmoving.

What did he offer to make you betray your mentor? Balthazar wondered with a strange bitterness. He should have been grateful that he wouldn't be hunted like a dog for the rest of his life, but he felt … sad. They didn't make them like Gabriel D'Ange anymore.

And then Balthazar was swept into the melee again, wondering where the hell the reinforcements were.

Old grudges were settled at the Picatrix Club that night and new ones born. Everywhere Balthazar turned, he saw flickers of black lightning, heard the roar of revenants as necromancers died. He kicked one from his broadsword, adjusted his cuffs, and took a moment to survey the scene. Balthazar had always thought the term *bloodbath* to be hyperbole, but in this case….

Alec Lawrence had hold of Gabriel's boots and was hauling him toward the balcony to the garden. One of Gabriel's arms dragged limply above his head, trailing the chains locked around his wrist. His face was a death mask.

But he hadn't gone into the usual convulsions, the instantaneous suffocation, and Balthazar felt a superstitious thrill of fear.

What *was* he?

Alec crouched down and injected something into Gabriel's thigh. Then he stood, swaying a little on his feet. His bad leg had started to buckle. The eagle mask was long gone and he looked exhausted. Balthazar guessed Alec had been occupied protecting his prize.

He failed to notice when Gabriel's eyes fluttered open.

With a savage groan, Gabriel sat up and whipped the chain around Alec's ankles, yanking it taut. Alec crashed to the floor. D'Ange had something in his fist, a talisman of Traveling, and the two of them sank into the slick of blood.

It happened in an instant.

"Where are they?"

Balthazar turned. Vivienne stood on the balcony, wild-eyed, Lucas at her side.

He could tell she already knew, but he answered.

"Gone."

A police whistle sounded in the street. Vivienne screamed, an animal sound, and Lucas stepped forward, blade sweeping to behead a revenant as it shuffled toward them. Balthazar gently took her arm.

"He's gone, Vivienne. We have to get the hell out of here."

He dragged her back out the French doors and down to the garden below, where a dozen more bodies sprawled in the grass. It was clear now what had them taken them so long to arrive.

Vivienne was trembling as they ran to the carriage and Lucas leapt into the driver's bench and shook the reins.

"I'll kill him," she whispered as they hurtled through the dark streets. "Mark me, Balthazar."

He glanced at her face and wondered if D'Ange had finally met his match.

CHAPTER 25

Vivienne refused Balthazar's offer of a glass of brandy, staring at him with an unreadable expression.

So he drank alone while she paced the study and Lucas watched out the window to make sure they hadn't been followed back to Mayfair.

"Is he...?" Balthazar let the question dangle in the air.

"Still alive?" Vivienne replied in a hollow voice. "Yes."

That came as something of a surprise.

"And I presume you can find him?"

She gave a hard nod, then pressed her palms to her eyes. She looked dead on her feet.

"I have to get home," she said. "I need my scimitar."

Balthazar knew she'd lost the sword she brought to the Picatrix. He held up the bottle. "Sure you won't—"

"I don't want any of your bloody *brandy*," Vivienne snarled. "I want...."

"Alec back," Balthazar said in a soothing tone. "Of course. Where is he?"

Her eyes lost focus and Balthazar knew she was following the thread of their bond.

"Not far … in the direction of the Channel," she murmured. "It has to be France."

"No great shock there," Balthazar said. "We can Travel—"

"I'll lose him in the Dominion. The bond doesn't work beyond the veil." Her head slowly turned. "What do you mean, *we?*"

"I'm going with you. Mr. Devereaux will come, too."

Balthazar glanced at Lucas, who nodded.

"Why?" she demanded.

Because I'm not letting you walk into Gabriel's lair alone.

Because I owe you a debt, though you don't remember my name and I sorely hope you never do.

Balthazar sighed. "Because I'm not having him after me for all eternity. I'd prefer to be there when you settle it. One way or another."

Vivienne hesitated, but she was in no position to turn down his offer. "We need to take a ship. It's the swiftest way."

"My man can arrange for passage. We'll hire horses on the other side."

Lucas let the curtain fall. "I'll ride down to the docks," he said curtly, still brooding over Bekker's escape. "Find out what's leaving first thing in the morning."

Which wasn't far off now. The sky outside was lightening to dawn.

Lucas strode from the study and Vivienne made to follow. Tendrils of hair had sprung loose from her braid. A streak of blood across one dark cheek made her look like some warrior-priestess from ancient Kush. "I have to go home. I need weapons—"

Balthazar smiled.

He led her up to the attic and unlocked a door. Vivienne stared for a long moment.

"This is quite a collection you have, Balthazar." She strode into the room and surveyed the gleaming array of swords and daggers, curved sabres and nimble rapiers.

"Why is Gabriel punishing you?" Balthazar asked, curious, as he watched her roam the large space, running her hands over the hilts, lifting the blades and testing their weight. "What did you do?"

"I don't want to talk about it," Vivienne snapped.

"All right." Balthazar chose a katana sword from the wall and examined the edge. "Will you at least tell me how he managed to take your cuff?"

"He drugged me," she muttered.

"Ah." That might explain the aversion to brandy.

"D'Ange pretended to be an abbot," Vivienne admitted. "He was so convincing. He made me like him. Trust him." She shook her head. The prospect of revenge seemed to be reviving her spirits. "It was a flawless performance until the end. He even spoke English with a Hungarian accent!"

Balthazar gave a mirthless laugh. "That sounds like Gabriel. He specializes in getting to people who can't be gotten to. And his schemes are often … elaborate. I suppose it keeps him entertained."

Balthazar thought about Bekker, about the trap he'd laid knowing D'Ange couldn't resist coming for him. He'd said Gabriel was *good as dead*.

But that wasn't quite the same as *dead*, was it?

Balthazar had a feeling Jorin Bekker would learn the difference soon enough — assuming D'Ange scrounged up yet another of his feline lives and survived Vivienne.

"I always thought all his talk about being chosen by God was … well, I thought Gabriel was a bit insane," he said to her. "But the *sanctus arma* didn't kill him. And I'm not sure what that means."

She shrugged. "Perhaps it's not what you think."

"Perhaps."

Yet Balthazar had known both men for centuries. Constantin would never be so foolish as to think an ordinary blade would finish Gabriel D'Ange. And if he tried, he'd damned well better succeed.

"There's one proven method," she said tightly. "Cleave his head off."

Balthazar nodded, feeling oddly conflicted. Vivienne's reticence made it difficult to say who was at fault in the situation. And he wasn't at all certain the world would be a better place without Gabriel D'Ange. *Safer*, yes. There were many who would dance a jig on his grave. But still….

Holy Father, I'm getting soft in my old age, he thought, wishing he'd brought the bottle upstairs with him.

"I doubt even Gabriel could come back from that," Balthazar agreed softly, replacing the katana in its brackets.

Vivienne lifted her skirts a few inches to strap a stiletto to her ankle. "What does the Church think of him?"

Balthazar laughed. "Oh, they've officially disowned him. He can't be controlled and Rome won't tolerate that. But he has … sympathizers. Mostly among the lower ranking clergy."

"The brothers at Saint George's knew what he was. They went along with it." She let her skirts fall. "He was after Bekker at the Picatrix?"

Balthazar nodded.

Vivienne's jaw tightened. "I'd almost admire the bastard if he hadn't done what he did. But now…." She trailed off.

There was no need to finish the thought.

It was war.

PART IV

"There is no bombast, no similes, flowers, digressions, or unnecessary descriptions. Everything tends directly to the catastrophe."
   —*The Castle of Otranto*

CHAPTER 26

Anne was reading one of her books on mathematics when she heard a creak somewhere in the house below. She leapt out of bed and ran to the head of the stairs.

Gabriel leaned against the wall, halfway up. She could see a trail of bloody handprints behind him.

Anne rushed down the stairs and threw an arm around his waist. He sagged against her but didn't seem to see her. He looked ghastly, his eyes wild. She hauled him up to the second floor, step by painstaking step, as he ranted incoherently in French. Anne eased him into his bed, panting from the effort of nearly carrying him the last twenty paces.

Gabriel looked at up at her, his pupils tiny pinpricks. Anne had seen it before in the rougher parts of London. *Opium.*

"You're knackered," she muttered.

Then she unbuttoned his coat and her heart turned to ice.

Gabriel smiled through red teeth as she fetched wet cloths and cleaned the gore away, tried to bandage the terrible wounds with strips of cloth she ripped from the shirt hanging over the chair. They kept bleeding through so she wound them tight as tourniquets. At least he seemed beyond pain.

"God sent me an angel," he whispered, so low it was almost inaudible.

The sight of him was more than she could bear.

Why wasn't he healing? What had been done to him? And *who* had done it? She felt a cold rage far worse than any he'd ever driven her to.

Anne stayed up all night watching him, cooling his forehead as he muttered deliriously in his sleep, raising water to his lips and making him drink. The next morning, when the sun rose, he looked a little better, but she was shocked to see a streak of white in his hair.

Gabriel's eyes opened. They had a mad light. Then he saw her and his gaze softened.

"Anne...."

"You're home now," she said soothingly. "Drink some water."

She held the cup to his dry lips. He winced as he swallowed.

"Tell me what happened."

Gabriel face grew hard. "I was betrayed. Constantin sold me out. It was ... a mess."

"Is he the one who drugged you?"

Gabriel looked away. "It doesn't matter. Bekker is gone. It could take years to find him again." His jaw tensed. "But I'll hunt them down, every one of them." He struggled to sit but she gently pushed him back down again.

Anne touched the white in his hair. "You're aging, Gabriel."

"The fight at Picatrix drained me," he admitted. "And the price of healing."

"What do you ... need?" Anne swallowed. "I have years to spare—"

Gabriel gave her appalled look. "You? No! Never." He gazed at her, his eyes narrow. "You say it's wrong for me for prey on mortals, to steal their lives. So I won't. But if you don't bond me, soon I will die, just like the poor, tragic Beast."

His words triggered that instinctive fear. Could Anne truly trust him with everything that she was?

"I thought you were supposed to be Beauty," she snapped irritably.

"Yes, but now I'm losing my good looks," he joked with a weak smile. "It will be Old and Ugly and the Beast."

Anne didn't find this amusing in the least.

Gabriel slept again. He slept all day, a sleep as deep and still as the enchantment of her rose cameo. In the evening, Anne came back and sat on the bed. Seeing him at the very edge of death made her realize how terrified she was of losing him.

She kissed his forehead and curled up next to him, listening to his soft breathing.

And she dreamt she was running next to a huge, dark shadow, running through the trees as a stag leapt into the underbrush ahead. It veered away and she let it escape, only running, running through the endless forests of the night.

The moon was high and full when she woke, flushed with strange, feverish longing, and reached for Gabriel.

The bed was empty.

Anne went down to the entrance hall and sat on the stairs, waiting for him to return.

Just before dawn, the door eased open. Gabriel strode into the house wearing only his skin. He had a smudge of dirt on his face and leaves caught in his hair.

He halted when he saw her. He looked full of life again. Unmarked and strong. A man of no more than thirty-five, although she could see the faint streak of white in the moonlight.

"Tell me what it's like," she said in a low voice.

He drew a deep breath. Exhaled. "It takes me out of my head. There is no thought. Nothing but…. My beating heart, the sounds, the smells. The earth beneath my feet, the stars above. My body."

She moved to him and ran a hand down his lean flank. The muscles twitched beneath her palm.

Gabriel pulled back, his face cold. "Don't," he said roughly. "I swore to myself I wouldn't touch you." His gaze flicked to the rose cameo. "Not like this."

"Then you have no choice." She stared at him defiantly, tugging at the ribbon on her cotton shift and letting it fall to the floor. A chill from the open door swept across her skin. "Release me, Gabriel."

His eyes lingered on her small, high breasts, her softly rounded belly, then lifted to her face. Without a word, he pulled her to him, one arm around her waist, the other fumbling at the cameo around her neck and then…. Anne shivered as strength and power rushed into her body. She slid into the Nexus, her senses sharpened to a fine point.

She heard the blood pumping through his veins — and could have reversed its flow with a thought, freezing the powerful muscle of his heart.

She felt earth resonating in his bones — and could have snapped them all, one by one.

The only thing on this earth stronger than a necromancer was a daēva.

Gabriel stepped back, watching her with wary eyes. She knew he'd just been betrayed by the one man he trusted above all others.

Anne didn't hesitate. She stepped forward and pulled his mouth down to hers. It was a soft, tentative kiss at first. He cradled her head with one hand, pulling her deeper into his mouth, the other exploring the line of her hip. Gabriel lifted her in his arms, his breath ragged, and took a step for the stairs.

"No," she whispered, aflame with desire for him like no other man she'd ever known. "Right here. Now."

Gabriel looked down at her, as hungry as she was. *Hungrier.*

He backed her against a tapestry, the rough weave pressing

into her shoulders. Gabriel lowered his head, nuzzling her neck. "Wrap your legs around me, Anne," he murmured in her ear. "Hold me tight."

She threw her arms around his shoulders and Gabriel lifted her up to straddle his hips, his hands cupping her buttocks, his thumb brushing her swollen sex.

"Mmmm, like this, Anne?"

"Yes," she hissed. "Yes...."

His teeth grazed her neck as she arched into him. A finger teased her open, slid inside.

Anne's breath hitched, a sharp, convulsive gasp. She reached between them and circled his velvet flesh with her hand, eliciting a growl of pleasure. Anne tried to guide him inside her but he slapped her hand away.

"No, no.... Not so fast, little beast."

Gabriel lowered her down, but only the tiniest bit.

"I've wanted you for so long," he murmured. "Dreaming of you. Your smile, your ears...." He took a lobe between his teeth.

He suspended her above him, giving her himself a fraction at a time as he always had, ignoring her pleas with an iron discipline that she wanted to shatter into a thousand pieces.

And then, after long minutes of this outrageous teasing....

"I've taken all I can hold of you," she gasped.

Gabriel stopped. She pressed her face to his damp neck, half-wild from the deep, aching throb of him between her legs. He lowered his head and kissed her, a lazy, eternal kiss. Then his hands remorselessly guided her down again, his voice coaxing and thick with need.

"Just a little more, Anne.... Only a little...."

Gabriel exhaled a shuddering breath as he thrust home.

His head fell back, exposing a column of pale throat, and Anne kissed the place where the Beast had nearly torn him open, felt the hot vein pulsing just beneath the skin, tasted the salt of his sweat.

Only to stay like this forever....

Small tremors ran through him, every muscle ratcheted tight, palms rough against her bottom as his hips moved in a slow grind.

"All of me," Gabriel whispered, his voice uneven. "Will you take it all, Anne?"

He meant not the part of him that pressed her to the wall but his madness and passion and his bloody, bloody hands.

Yes. Yes. Yes, she whispered back. *I will.*

The chill air raised her breasts to hard peaks and they brushed his chest, only the slightest touch, but it broke her. Waves of pleasure so sharp they might have been pain wracked her body, cresting and building again. She clamped down on him and he cried her name, howled it through the empty halls of Chateau de Saint-Évreux.

Gabriel's legs were shaking like autumn leaves as he eased her down and buried his face in her hair. He braced one arm against the wall, the other pulling her close. He smelled like the forest, like pine and moss and cool streams.

And sex.

He gave a hoarse laugh. "Okay, I could wait another three hundred years for that."

She took Gabriel by the hand and he allowed her to lead him up the stairs, docile as a child. When they reached her bedroom and crawled beneath the blankets, she thought he would collapse into slumber. But he started kissing her again, cupping the curls between her legs, stroking her with a practiced hand.

Anne gave a low laugh. "I'm sore, Gabriel. It's been ... a long time."

"My poor darling." He didn't sound very sorry. "For me as well. I'll have to make it better then." Gabriel took the rosy bud of a breast in his mouth, his weight pressing her into the goose-down mattress. Anne ran her hands down the taut lines of his back, the hard curve of his buttocks.

"*Nom de dieu*, Gabriel," she whispered in his ear. "You were nearly dead last night. Haven't you had enough?"

His brown eyes lifted to hers, gentle and warm. The Father Gavra eyes, Anne thought — though there was nothing saintly in the look he gave her.

"I'll never have enough of you, Anne. Never enough...."

His tongue returned to her breast, then moved down with excruciating slowness, finally parting the tender flesh between her legs. She slid her fingers into his hair and gripped it as she felt herself nearing the precipice again.

And will he take all of me?

Anne sat up, her cheeks flushed, pulling away from his mouth. "Not so fast, *mon Belle*."

This time, she made him lie on his back and she had her way with *him* exactly as she pleased, sometimes sweet and slow, other times hard and brutal, toying with him as mercilessly as he had done with her, until they both lay in a spent tangle, the blankets hurled to the floor and the bed having moved a good four paces from where it started.

"Tell me about *The Chymical Wedding of Christian Rosenkreutz*," she said, tracing his full lower lip. Gabriel employed that lip to great effect when he sulked, or curled it in scorn, but now it was soft and pliant beneath her fingertip.

He glanced at her. "You found it?" He gave a purring sigh. "It came to me in a vision. A beautiful dream of a better world." He was quiet for a moment. "I don't remember much about my early childhood. It was so long ago. But I have a single memory of standing on the shore of the Bay of Biscay, the water lapping at my feet. I must have been very young. It's one of the things I liked about this place when I bought it. The view of the water."

Gabriel's voice grew drowsy. "After I deserted from Neblis's army, I came home to Gaul. My family was all long dead but I had nowhere else to go, so I stayed, watching the Roman Empire fall and Christendom rise under the Emperor Constantine. For a long time, I lived aimlessly, day to day."

Anne laid her cheek against his chest, listening to the soft beat of his heart as he idly stroked her hair.

"I tried to hunt only evil men, rapists, murderers and the like. I haunted the lowest wine sinks where such creatures were most often found. I grew soulless, Anne. Despairing. Empty. Was I truly any better than my victims? And then one day, I was in Rouen and I passed the great cathedral there. Something made me go inside."

"I've seen it," she said softly. "It's beautiful."

"Yes. In truth, I was trying to find the courage to end my life. Seeking some final forgiveness for my sins before I did the deed. I knelt down in the pews and prayed." He laughed. "I wasn't even sure who it was I prayed *to*, but in the hush of that great building I sensed a ... presence. A presence of grace. Of unconditional love. My burdens lifted. I felt reborn, a child of God again, and resolved to follow a new path. So I joined the Knights Templar. You know the rest." He paused. "And you, Anne? What did you do after you were freed?"

And she told him of the years she spent traveling among the ancient cities of the world with Alec and Vivienne, sealing and closing the twelve Greater Gates to the Dominion, until she grew restless and started to go her own way.

"Gabriel?"

"*Oui?*"

His voice was very heavy now.

"I want to bond you."

The hand stroking her hair tensed. She felt his heartbeat speed up.

He rolled to his side and looked her in the eyes. To Anne's surprise, he seemed hesitant.

"Are you sure it's what you want? It can't be broken, Anne. Only by death."

"Or transference to another," she pointed out, though that would be … unimaginable.

He looked away. "Or that."

She touched his cheek and turned him back to face her. "I am, Gabriel."

He nodded, his voice ragged at the edges. "If that's what you want, Anne, I'll give it to you."

CHAPTER 27

Alec saw a candle in the darkness. Heard approaching footsteps.

Gabriel D'Ange.

He carried a bucket in one hand. D'Ange set it down and gave it a kick. The bucket slid across the stone floor, water sloshing over the edges. Alec cupped his hands and drank deeply. Christ, he was thirsty.

"So," D'Ange said in a low voice. "Here we are."

They stared at each other for a long moment.

"All this over a wooden *cross*?" Alec burst out. He slowly shook his head. "What the hell is wrong with you? You could have just asked—"

"That's not the point. I invited you into my house. You sat at my table, ate my food, drank my wine, and then you robbed me when my back was turned!"

"You were a murderer," Alec said coldly.

"And what are you? Two of my brothers are dead. Good men. They wouldn't have touched you. They had orders only to follow."

"And not be taken alive. You left me no choice." Alec calculated the length of the chain, but D'Ange stood just out of reach. "Then you sent wights—"

"I didn't," D'Ange snapped. "I hate fucking wights! That was the *fils de put* Constantin. I'm sure he'd already gone over to Bekker."

Alec stared at him. "Where's my sister?" he demanded. "If she—"

"You'd be a dead man if not for Anne's sake. You should have left me alone. Left *us* alone. I might have given you the other cuff back." He looked away.

Alec sensed an opening. "I have the cross. Safe. It's yours."

Gabriel turned and studied him for a long moment. He seemed … torn.

"*Putain*," he muttered, more softly. Alec's hopes rose. Then he shook his head. "No. I don't want it anymore."

"Where is she?" Alec demanded.

"Anne is here." His gaze flicked to the low ceiling, an almost guilty look on his face. "Of her own accord." A pause. "I want something else." His eyes rested on Alec's cuff. "You can find another set somewhere. And you'll be freed once I'm gone."

Alec felt a chill, bone-deep. "It doesn't come off."

D'Ange reached into his pocket and Alec tensed, expecting a knife. But he held up a key.

"It's a funny story. There was a market in Kabul, an old woman selling a tarnished gold bracelet. I recognized the griffin. Useless without the match, but I wasn't about to leave it there for anyone to find. It came with a key though. From what I remember of the Immortals, all the keys were identical so they could be switched if the daëva fell in battle." He took out a pair of gloves and slid them on. "Shall we test my theory?"

Alec backed away as far as the chain would allow.

D'Ange stepped forward, moving on the balls of his feet.

"Don't make me hurt you. This doesn't have to be hard—"

Alec let out a wild laugh. "No?"

"No. I'll even give you the one I have. You only have to find a match."

"They don't fucking exist anymore!"

He shrugged. "I found one. You just have to look hard."

He was close now, so close....

The chain slithered across the floor as Alec readied himself.

CHAPTER 28

Anne ran the crushed velvet skirts through her fingers, a small smile on her lips. She'd found the dress laid out on their bed. Not black like the one she'd worn when he kissed her hand in Strasbourg that evening so long ago, but forest green with a row of tiny pearl buttons, and she knew Gabriel was telling her that the past was dead, gone, and they had only the future before them. One bright and sweet with promise.

She wanted to thank him for the gift, but he wasn't in the kitchen or the music room or any of the places he usually went. And then she finally found him in the old ruined chapel, where mourning doves nested in the crossbeams and ivy clung to crevices in the ancient stone. Anne paused in the doorway. Soft light spilled through the stained glass window at the far end of the nave.

Gabriel was on his knees before the altar, head bowed.

And for an instant she saw the Knight Templar of six hundred years ago, the white tunic with the red cross, a long blade at his hip, praying on the eve of battle, and Anne almost envied him his faith. His unwavering certainty.

She lived in a different world, less certain but one with its own delights. She *had* seen that mermaid in the Zambezi River, and fairies, too. And she longed to share it with him.

Anne watched him for a moment more, then retreated to allow him privacy.

She returned to the house and filled the big claw-footed tub with water warmed from the barrel he always left near the hearth. She'd nearly slipped into a doze when she heard him enter behind her.

Anne lazily bent one knee and let it fall to the side, hoping to goad him into getting in the tub with her. But instead of touching her body, his hands filled her wet hair, lifting it, combing it with his fingers. Warm breath tickled her ear.

"Come away with me, Anne. Tonight."

She turned her head. "Where?"

"Anywhere. I don't care."

"And your cross?"

"Let him keep it." Gabriel paused. "But we can't stay. They'll come looking. I bought this place in my name. They'll find it. And I ... I don't want to fight them, Anne. They might not believe you chose the bond freely, whatever you say."

Anne knew the truth of this. Vivienne in particular had always been overprotective. Anne indulged her, but she was no child. She would send a letter. Let everyone cool down a bit before she told them face to face.

"I would go anywhere with you, Gabriel," she murmured. "Anywhere at all."

"Mmmm."

The water sloshed gently in the tub as he soaped a cloth and ran it across her belly.

"I'll cook for you every day, make you fat and happy. There's a place I know, oceans away. White sand and the greenest water you ever saw. I'll catch you fish."

A slow, aching burn filled her as his knuckles grazed one breast. "And how will we get to this place?"

"A ship will come tonight. I'll ride into town and make the arrangements."

She felt him move to stand and caught his wrist. "Don't go."

Anne heard a smile in his voice. "Poor darling. So hungry again?"

"Yes. Starving."

He bent down and kissed her, a kiss that promised all sorts of things ... later.

Anne sighed. She touched his cheek. "I'll bond you under the moon and stars. On the tower."

Gabriel laughed. "All right."

He kissed her once more and she heard his light steps retreating down the stairs, the faint thunder of his horse as he galloped down the road.

Anne lay back in the warm water, drowsy and besotted with thoughts of what it would be like to have him afterwards. She had no fear of him anymore. She trusted Gabriel utterly to hold her power with an open hand ... and to teach her how to change her form.

You'll have all my gifts.

But Anne knew that wasn't why she was bonding him. She would do it if he was a pauper with nothing but the rags on his back and not a single ounce of his own magic.

She fell asleep in the bath and woke some time later, her skin pimpled with goosebumps. The sun had set and a full moon was climbing above the forest as she dried off and dressed in a simple shift. Anne glanced at the dress laid out on the bed but decided to wait.

Gabriel had always spoiled her with his cooking. Her own skills in the kitchen were clumsy in comparison — mainly because fire in close proximity could be deadly — but she could at least set the table and make it look nice. Anne gathered lavender from the garden, then set off for the kitchen in search of a vase.

She hadn't lingered there when she'd gone looking for him before. A quick glance through the door had told her he was elsewhere. Now she went inside and started searching the cupboards. She found a porcelain ewer she thought would do nicely, and turned to leave when her gaze fell upon a heavy oaken door, and single drop of dried blood on the floor before it.

Gabriel must have taken a cloth and tried to clean it up. Yet a trace remained, a dark stain on the doorjamb.

He had told her he always Traveled through a pond in the woods. That he didn't like opening gateways from the Dominion into his own home. But of course he couldn't have when he returned from London.

He would never have made it that far.

It's only Gabriel's, she thought. *He was dying....*

Yet Anne felt the first stirrings of a terrible, nameless dread as she pushed the door open and saw more droplets winding down into darkness.

She felt a sudden urge to turn around, to go back upstairs, open a book, and pretend she'd never seen it.

To leave well enough alone.

But she couldn't.

So she padded down the stairs in her bare feet, following the trail deep beneath the castle to places she had never gone before. There were old casks and barrels stacked against the walls, and bits of rusty armor. Rolled-up carpets with nests of mice that skittered and squeaked at her footfalls.

Several heavy oaken doors later, the trail ended in the wine cellar.

Where she found Alec sitting against the wall in chains with a split lip and truly spectacular black eye.

And Anne's first treacherous thought was not *My poor sweet brother*, but rather, *What did you do to him to make him chain you up down here?*

She hurried forward and knelt down. Alec wordlessly drew her into his arms, holding her for a long minute. Then he pulled away and searched her face.

"He said you were here of your own accord … Is that true?"

She brushed the question away. "How badly are you hurt?"

Dried blood coated the floor. The chains.

"Most of it's his."

She drew a deep breath. "Tell me what happened."

"I was at the Picatrix Club—"

"Are you the one…." Anne swallowed, her throat dry as dust. "Are you the one who stabbed him?"

Alec snorted in disgust. "I didn't lay a hand on him except to inject him with morphine. I found him on the floor and I was trying to drag him out to the garden. Viv was supposed to be waiting there."

She closed her eyes. She wasn't sure what she might have done if Alec had said yes.

"I would have if I'd had the chance," he added, "but we were swept apart. It was chaos, Anne."

"You shouldn't have taken his cross." She frowned. "It was wrong."

"It was impulsive. I sure as hell wish I hadn't now." Alec stared at her. "Whose side are you on?"

"Yours," she replied automatically, but it wasn't true. She felt torn in half. "Did he use the chains to drain you?"

"No."

Anne studied the length of black iron links, her skin crawling, and saw that the bracelet worn by the necromancer was around Alec's ankle and the collar worn by the slave had been fixed to one of the stone support columns.

"He did this to you *after* the Picatrix?"

She thought of the condition she'd found Gabriel in. It was hard to believe.

Alec's face hardened. "He's an animal, Anne. I've never seen anything like it. I'd hit him with a full syringe!"

That wouldn't stop Gabriel, she thought. Not right away, at least.

"But couldn't you just have used the power on him—"

Alec held up his arm and pushed his shirtsleeve back. She saw a band of white skin ... and no cuff.

And the truth hit her like a hammer blow.

"He took them. Vivienne's and mine both. He hasn't used them yet, but you have to help me get them back!" The raw desperation in his voice would have broken her heart if it hadn't just fractured into a thousand pieces.

"I'll handle Gabriel," Anne said in a voice she barely recognized.

Anything else she could have forgiven. *Anything*. But this....

"Be careful. If you'd seen him at the Picatrix.... Are you even listening?"

"What did he say? Exactly?"

"That he didn't want the cross anymore. Only the cuffs. That I could go find another set." Alec's eyes narrowed. "You don't trust him, do you?"

"Of course not," Anne snapped.

"Vivienne is close, I can feel her. She'll be here soon—"

Anne stood and brushed off her skirts. "I'll get them back for you, Alec."

"Anne. Damnit, Anne! Come back...."

She strode through the lower level of the castle and emerged from the kitchen just as Gabriel entered through the front door. He was humming *Rosa del ciel* from *L'Orfeo*.

"Darling," she said with a smile. "Oh, is that supper?"

He had a cloth bundle under one arm, a loaf of bread sticking out the top.

Gabriel's face lit up when saw her. He pulled her into a kiss and Anne's fury mounted at the flush spreading across her skin.

Pure animal lust, she thought savagely.

Gabriel pulled back, his gaze wary. "Are you all right, Anne?"

Her smile widened. It was the same smile she'd worn when she wanted to make him talk to her.

"I'll just run along and dress, shall I?"

Gabriel gave her a last long look. "I'll meet you in the tower then."

"I'll meet you there."

She went upstairs and swiftly searched both bedrooms, finding nothing. He must have them on him.

Anne stared at the green dress for a long minute. Then she put it on, moving like an automaton, and sat down in front of the vanity. She twisted her hair into a chignon and pinned it up.

A single tear ran down her cheek. Anne brushed it away. Steeled herself.

Gabriel was waiting in their old dining room in the tower. A simple meal had been laid out on the table, things he'd bought in town. Bread, cheese, a bottle of wine.

How handsome he looked in his dark coat and snowy white shirt. She wondered how she could ever have thought him plain.

Gabriel pulled her chair out, then sat down across from her. He seemed on edge.

"I have to tell you something, Anne." A pause. "Don't be angry at me."

"Don't be angry at you?" She raised her eyebrows. "I wonder what it could be?"

She stood, bracing her palms on the table, and leaned towards him.

The narrow ring of gold in his irises seemed to gather the candlelight. Gabriel grew very still.

"Could it possibly be the fact that you made love to me while my brother was lying shackled in your *wine cellar*?"

"Anne—"

She summoned a wind, sending the plates smashing against the wall. "Where are the cuffs, Gabriel? Vivienne is coming here and she'll rip you to pieces. Give them to me."

"You betrayed me," he growled, his chair grating back as he sprang to his feet.

"No, you betrayed *me!*"

Another gust knocked Gabriel back a step. A crack zigzagged through the stone between his legs.

"I'll tear this tower down," she seethed. "Bury us both."

He threw his arms up. "Go ahead!"

"You stole their cuffs—"

Gabriel pulled out a leather bag and threw it at her feet, his accent thickening as it always did when he grew angry. "Fucking keep them, I don't care. I just want you, Anne!"

She grabbed the bag and feinted for the door. He moved to block it and she ran up the winding stairs to the top of the tower, Gabriel in pursuit.

Anne backed against the parapet as he exploded from the doorway. Gabriel stopped ten paces away, breathing hard. His face was very pale. When he spoke, he'd mastered himself — if barely.

"When you first came here, I purposefully avoided you. I didn't want to look at you, speak to you. I was ... afraid of you, Anne. I'd never stopped thinking about you since the night we met." He started to pace. "I just wanted to get rid of you." A sharp gesture. "Finish it. So I sent two men to track down your brother but I had no idea he'd left on holiday. I only discovered later they'd all gone off to fucking *Gran Canaria.*"

Gabriel rarely cursed. It was a measure of his extreme agitation that he did so now. "Then Vivienne appeared at Saint George's asking about you. She traveled with a man, but it wasn't Alec Lawrence. What were the odds? They were never apart!"

Anne knew the truth of this. Bizarrely, her first thought was, *Good for you, Alec, taking a holiday without her.*

"I had no quarrel with Vivienne," Gabriel continued. "I tried to make her leave, but she was relentless. Then she found your bracelet. It must have fallen off when I carried you back through the passages. She confronted me. And I thought of a better way to punish Alec."

Gabriel smiled and for an instant Anne saw the harsh executioner who had passed judgment on so many of his fellow men.

"To bond my brother?" she demanded.

"No," he said softly. "*Worse.* To keep the cuff and let the threat that I *would* hang over his head for all eternity. Never knowing when I might choose to put it on and sever him from the Nexus. Cause him unbearable agony." Gabriel shrugged. "I wouldn't have actually done it. I wish to be bonded to *him* as little as he wishes to be bonded to *me.* But he wouldn't know that."

Anne slowly shook her head. "You are the Devil."

"Am I?" Gabriel scratched his ear. "Ah well, it seemed a fitting punishment at the time. But then I came to know you." He sighed deeply and looked up at the sky. "How to explain? You made me remember what it's like to be … human again. Just a man."

She waited, listening with crossed arms.

"So I told myself, *no!* He's your brother. I should show … mercy." He said the word with a touch of wonder, as though it was some bird with exotic plumage he'd never seen before. "And I tried to, I tried, Anne, but when he attacked me at the Picatrix, I stopped caring. I thought I'd take his cuff too and use them myself." He sighed. "Then I started to feel bad again. I was going to tell you before—"

"You lying bastard," she growled. "You wanted my power."

"If I wanted that, I could have forced you! I just…. I wanted you to stay with me, Anne. It was the only way I knew how—"

"You have no idea what the bond means to him. To Vivienne. It's not like your *chains.* It's a marriage of two souls! Without it, they'll both die as surely as if you slit their throats yourself." Her jaw clenched. "In truth, you know almost *nothing* about the bond, Gabriel. You don't even know it can be used by one bonded to track the other. I never betrayed you. You betrayed yourself by bringing Alec here.

"But that's not what…." Her voice nearly broke. "How could you ever imagine for one second that I would trade their happiness for my own? You don't know me at all, Gabriel."

And that was the worst of it.

Gabriel looked remorseful. "I'm sorry." He took a step toward her. "Anne, I—"

Anne Lawrence wasn't the sort to slap a man. She made a fist and punched him hard in the face. Gabriel rocked back on his heels. He touched his lip and his fingers came away red.

"*Mon petit bête*," he whispered brokenly. "I just love you so fucking much."

Anne grabbed his coat. And then her mouth was on Gabriel's, his blood on her tongue, and she felt the wordless despair of the damned. She still wanted him despite his stupidity and recklessness. God help her, she still wanted him more than she'd ever wanted anything in her very long life.

Gabriel pulled away, his breath ragged. "Come with me, Anne. Leave the cuffs. Just come. The ship is waiting." He glanced out at the Channel, where a pinprick of light floated on the dark water.

"I *can't*."

"Then kill me!" He pulled a dagger from his belt and tore his shirt open, offering Anne the hilt. "Go on, do it! Carve my heart out. I won't resist!"

From another man, the demand would be ridiculous melodrama. Anne knew Gabriel meant every word.

There was a crash at the base of the tower, like a heavy oaken door rebounding against a wall.

His head snapped toward the door as footsteps rang faintly on the stairs.

"Get behind me, Anne," he said softly, and she sensed his hackles rising, knew more blood was about to be spilled. He'd endured too much in the last days. It had broken his self-control.

And who would she try to protect?

She gave him a push toward the parapet, sick with dread. "Just go, Gabriel!"

"Not without you!" His voice lowered, his eyes pleading. "You love me, Anne. You know you do."

Yes, her heart whispered. *And I would watch you kill my brother and his bonded, or them kill you, and there would never, ever be a way back. But perhaps I can still save you....*

A sob tore from her throat. Anne grabbed the blade from his hand and drove it between his ribs to the hilt. Gabriel let out a hissing breath. He braced a hand on the parapet. His face turned to ash.

Tears streamed down her cheeks. "I don't love you. I want you gone. Now!"

The look in Gabriel's eyes was a blade to her own heart. He threw his head back and ... changed. His form seemed to shimmer. To blur at the edges. She blinked and in that brief instant, Gabriel was gone.

A great cat, tawny with jagged black stripes, crouched on the parapet.

A reflection of the man inside.

Gabriel's soul was a fierce, terrifying, beautiful thing.

The heavy hindquarters bunched. Anne reached out, her fingertips brushing silken fur as it leapt over the edge. She gave a sharp cry and leaned out as far as she could, but the ground far below was lost in gloom.

"Anne!"

She dimly saw Vivienne and Alec and two strange men swarm onto the parapet. Anne picked up the bag with the cuffs and thrust it into Vivienne's hands.

"I have to go," Anne whispered, not trusting her own voice. "Don't follow."

She pushed past them all and dashed down the winding stairs, barely hearing the voices calling her name.

What if she was wrong?

What if he was too weakened?

The tower stood a hundred paces high.

Anne ran into the courtyard, terrified she would find a broken body sprawled on the flagstones, but the bailey was empty.

Empty save for a trail of blood leading out the postern gate to the steep path that wound down to the shore where they used to walk together.

She fell to her knees and wept bitterly, but Anne would never permit them to find her that way. So she stood and turned her back on Chateau de Saint-Évreux, walking out the gate and down the road, her skirts dragging through the dewy grass on the verge. It was still dark but dawn wasn't far off. Her legs carried of their own accord, her mind lost in a labyrinth of memories.

Small things, but precious to her.

Gabriel chopping wood in his shirtsleeves, whistling a jaunty tune.

Gabriel sitting cross-legged on the floor with a needle and thread mending clothes or cleaning his boots while she read aloud to him.

Gabriel.

Killer. Lover. Soldier of God ... and baker of birthday cakes with pink rosettes.

The memories drowned her.

It was the first time she'd been happy and she hadn't had the sense to realize it.

Each day brought a new surprise. He had an ocean of blood on his hands ... and a phobia of spiders. She'd found him standing sheepishly on a chair one morning, a razor in his hand and soap on his face. He'd refused to come down until she carried the creature outside, cupped in her palm and trying hard not to laugh.

"It's the legs, Anne," he confessed to her afterwards. "The tiny hairs…." Gabriel had given a convulsive shudder.

She understood it would take years to truly know him. Each time she peeled away a layer, there was one another waiting beneath.

And oh, how she wanted those years.

She'd never even asked his last name.

After a while, Anne saw the gates in the distance, wrenched half off their hinges. She had no idea where she planned to go. Only to keep walking until she ran out of road.

And then a sound made her turn.

A low, despairing howl.

The sound did not come again, but she marked the direction. She entered the forest, walking until she spied a stone structure through the trees. Anne went inside.

It held a barred animal enclosure, spacious and with fresh straw on the ground that was littered with gnawed bones. A second cage, covered in a length of oilcloth, sat empty to the side. Gabriel must have planned to bring it with them.

The beast sat on its haunches in the darkest corner. When it saw her, it growled deep in its throat.

A man-eater.

And what would become of him now that his master was gone?

A savage, uncaring pity rose up in her. Anne filled herself with wind and earth, filled herself to bursting. The cage door flew from its hinges, clattering against the stone wall. She held her ground, not blocking the way but unafraid.

Part of her would welcome his jaws around her throat.

The Beast of Gévaudan stared at her for a long minute. Then it crept into a shaft of pale morning light.

A wolf, but like no wolf Anne had ever seen. It was easily three times the size and with silver eyes like mirrors. A majestic creature. Its haunches bunched ... and it sprang past her, arrowing away without a backward glance.

She watched it vanish through the trees.

"Go find her," Anne whispered.

PART V

"That which is done out of love always occurs beyond good and evil."
   —Friedrich Nietzsche

CHAPTER 29

SUNDAY, MAY 19

T he morning the master of Eridge Castle finally arrived
home was one of celebration.

It had taken two full months before Nathaniel was strong
enough to make the journey from Bucharest. He still walked with
a slight limp, but Alec had made him a present of a sword-cane,
which he now leaned on as they made their way to the dining
room.

"You spoil me, Alec," Nathaniel murmured with a flirty smile.
"You'll have to teach me to use it properly."

Alec grinned. He enjoyed Nathaniel's teasing. If his preferences had been different…. Well, the Viscount of Nevill was a
strapping specimen. And a very dear friend.

The cook, Mrs. Abernathy, made a bang-up English breakfast
for him, with eggs and bacon and kippers and toast with her
homemade strawberry jam. They gathered at the table and dug
in. Nathaniel was already hatching plans to whisk them all away
to the World's Fair in Paris, where the new Eiffel Tower had been
unveiled, though he said the lifts to the top weren't quite
ready yet.

"Someone will have to carry me up the stairs," he declared. "Any takers?"

Alec laughed and poured a cup of tea.

"He's going to milk that leg for all its worth, mark my words," Vivienne said. "Lazy lord."

Nathaniel smiled, then sobered a bit. "So D'Ange is gone?" He buttered a piece of toast and took a bite.

Vivienne nodded.

"Will you try to find him?"

"No," Alec replied firmly. "We promised Anne we'd let it rest."

Nathaniel arched a blond eyebrow. "Sounds sensible."

Vivienne shifted a little, but gave another reluctant nod.

Anne had brooked no argument from either of them on the matter.

"And this Picatrix Club?"

"Shut down," Alec replied. "Though the man who owned it, Jorin Bekker, was long gone by the time officers from the Dominion Branch stormed the place." He glanced at Vivienne. "Happily, D.I. Blackwood never discovered we were there that night. He would have been ... displeased we cut them out."

To say the very least.

Nathaniel blew on his coffee. "You say a necromancer actually *helped* you?"

"I still don't trust him, but I do think Koháry spoke the truth when he said he stood against the Duzakh," Vivienne conceded grudgingly.

"I saw him kill at least four at the Picatrix," Alec said, folding his napkin with a contented sigh. "One had captives. He freed them and saw them to safety."

"His man Devereaux held his own in the garden." From Vivienne, this was high praise. Her face clouded again. "He's far more than Koháry's servant. I intend to keep an eye on them both. "

"Hmmm, I'd like to meet this Count Koháry someday," Nathaniel murmured.

Vivienne laughed. "He's exactly your type. Groomed to a fault and charmingly oily."

"Your mind always crawls straight into the gutter, darling." Nathaniel beamed. "But I still love you." He went to the sideboard and helped himself to more bacon. "So D'Ange killed Adrian. And he was the *pricolici?*"

"That's what Anne says."

She'd barely spoken of what had occurred at the Chateau de Saint-Évreux. Neither of them had pressed her about it.

"But how did he come to be a beast?" Nathaniel wondered aloud.

"Not a clue," Vivienne replied.

Lord Cumberland reached for the jam, a merry glint in his eye. "Well, good riddance. He belonged to a bad breed, and we are quite content to be freed from him and his kindred. Aren't we, Vivienne?"

She gazed at him fondly. "Indeed we are." She glanced at the empty chair. "Where is Anne, anyhow?"

Alec shrugged. "She said she was going for a walk in the park."

Balthazar dragged the comb through his raven hair, parting it on the left and smoothing it down with a palm. He was freshly shaven and wore an elegant grey morning coat. He leaned into the oval mirror.

Save for the faint line at the corner of his mouth, he looked perfectly presentable for a little afternoon romp.

He'd been a very good boy since the Picatrix Club, but he was starting to feel … tired.

A fair number of the Duzakh had perished that night, but not all. And the ones who had escaped were the most dangerous. The old, clever ones. Like Balthazar.

He'd only caught a quick glimpse of Alec's sister on the tower before she vanished. A lovely woman.

And D'Ange.... Well, Balthazar had been relieved he was already gone.

If not, they might all have ended up like the Calico Cat and the Gingham Dog, he thought with amusement.

It was a silly little limerick called *The Duel* Balthazar had often recited to Lucas when he was a young child. The words returned to him now.

The gingham dog and the calico cat
Side by side on the table sat;
'Twas half-past twelve, and (what do you think!)
Nor one nor t' other had slept a wink!
The old Dutch clock and the Chinese plate
Appeared to know as sure as fate
There was going to be a terrible spat.
(I wasn't there; I simply state
What was told to me by the Chinese plate!)

The gingham dog went "Bow-wow-wow!"
And the calico cat replied "Mee-ow!"
The air was littered, an hour or so,
With bits of gingham and calico,
While the old Dutch clock in the chimney-place
Up with its hands before its face,
For it always dreaded a family row!
(Now mind: I'm only telling you
What the old Dutch clock declares is true!)

The Chinese plate looked very blue,
And wailed, "Oh, dear! what shall we do!"
But the gingham dog and the calico cat
Wallowed this way and tumbled that,
Employing every tooth and claw

In the awfullest way you ever saw—
And, oh! how the gingham and calico flew!
(Don't fancy I exaggerate—
I got my news from the Chinese plate!)

Next morning, where the two had sat
They found no trace of dog or cat;
And some folks think unto this day
That burglars stole that pair away!
But the truth about the cat and pup
Is this: they ate each other up!

"Now what do you *really* think of that?" he finished softly.

Balthazar turned as Lucas appeared in the doorway.

"Are you going out, my Lord?"

Balthazar finished buttoning his shirt. "I have a luncheon appointment. It's not far. I'll walk."

Lady Tottenham's husband was a Member of Parliament who was rarely home. They'd met at the theater three nights previous.

"I've contacted the estate agent," Lucas said, trailing his master down the staircase. "He found a potential buyer for the house."

Balthazar paused at the door, one hand resting on his silver-tipped walking stick.

In truth, he should have left a month ago. Gabriel knew where he lived. Yet he happened to like the teeming metropolis of London. The restaurants, the clubs, the parties — high and low.

The women.

Balthazar was suddenly weary of hiding in the shadows like vermin. If D'Ange decided to carry out his threat sooner rather than later... What was it the French said?

"*C'est la vie*," he murmured.

"My lord?"

"Cancel the contract." Balthazar put his hat on and smiled. "I think I'll stay for a while after all."

CHAPTER 30

Anne strolled through Saint James Park, her parasol folded. It was one of those rare, fine mornings, the sky as blue as a robin's egg and flowers blooming brightly in their beds.

The spring weather had attracted Londoners from all quarters, some having picnics in the grass, others letting their children run and shout in the open parkland. She chose a path around the lake, searching for a vacant place to sit in solitude.

And for an instant she saw a man in a black coat through the trees, his back to her. Her pulse quickened, but when he turned his face … Anne gripped her parasol and continued walking.

She'd never spoken a word to anyone of the Beast of Gévaudan, but she kept a guilty eye on the newspapers, scanning their pages for reports of animal attacks on the French coast.

There were none. She thought perhaps the Beast had grown accustomed to its diet of deer and rabbits and no longer hungered for the flesh of men. She only hoped that would remain the case.

And on sleepless nights, of which there were many, she found solace in imagining him running through the ancient forests with the mate Gabriel had tried unsuccessfully to capture. If his she-wolf still lived, Anne knew the Beast would find her.

She'd lingered at Park Place, needing be to near those she loved. Vivienne and Alec had tried to distract her, each in their own way, her brother with his laboratory and Vivienne by dragging her out to parties.

They had such passion for each other. Too much, perhaps, to become lovers. Yet Anne sensed a new tenderness between them, as though old walls had cracked — if not tumbled down.

Neither would admit this, of course.

Henry Sidgwick had offered her an assignment in Brazil following up on sightings of a *curupira*, little fairies with orange hair and backwards feet. Anne turned it down.

She was starting to feel the old restlessness, but she had stayed in London.

Just one more week, she'd told herself the day before. *Then I'll go.*

Now she found an empty bench beneath the willows and sat down, her heart beating a little faster as took the letter from her pocket.

It had arrived in the early morning post and she'd been sure to get to it before anyone saw. In fact, she'd been keeping a close eye on the post.

She studied the exquisite penmanship, the exotic postmark.

It was the second letter to arrive at Park Place, although the first been addressed to Mr. Alec Lawrence and was delivered three days after Gabriel leapt from the tower. It was dated the day of her birthday, just as he had promised her.

The language was curt, but in essence it said exactly what Gabriel had claimed. That he would trade Vivienne's cuff for the rose cross and set Anne free. Further instructions would follow. The signature was a harsh scrawl.

This letter was different. It was addressed to her and the script had been formed with care, with many flourishes. She raised the envelope to her nose and fancied she could smell coffee and flowers and a hint of *him*.

Anne had waited to read it until she was alone. She glanced around, half expecting Gabriel to be watching, although she knew in her heart he was far away.

The page contained three lines.

Even broken in spirit as he is, no one can feel more deeply than he does the beauties of nature. The starry sky, the sea, and every sight afforded by these wonderful regions, seems still to have the power of elevating his soul from earth.

La vie est un sommeil, l'amour en est le rêve, Anne.

Yours always, La Belle

She recognized the first passage. A quote from *Frankenstein*, the last book she'd read aloud to him. It was her favorite for the scientific bits and his for the terrible pathos of the monster.

As for the second, the words were simple enough to translate, even with Anne's rusty French.

Life is a long sleep and love is its dream.

Something sweet and deep stirred in her as she watched the young mothers pushing prams and couples strolling arm in arm.

It didn't feel like a final parting.

It felt more like ... an invitation.

Anne examined the stamp. She smiled and tucked the letter in her pocket.

AFTERWORD

Dearest Reader,

The next book in the Gothic Gaslamp series, *The Necromancer's Bride*, follows Anne and Gabriel (Balthazar, too) and is on sale now at most online booksellers. Take a moment to sign up for my newsletter at katrossbooks.com so you don't miss any new releases!

And if you're curious about how Vivienne Cumberland met Alec Lawrence, the history of the daēvas, and Balthazar's checkered past, you can take a journey back to ancient Persia in the Fourth Element Trilogy where these characters first appear. Book #1 is *The Midnight Sea*, I hope you'll check it out.

Cheers, Kat

ACKNOWLEDGMENTS

Warm thanks as always to Laura Pili, my muse and first reader.

To the lovely team at Acorn, and to Christa Yelich-Koth.

But my greatest debt is to Poe, Shelley, Walpole, Radcliffe, Lewis, Stoker and all the other dark dreamers who invented the Gothic novel. This book would not exist without you.

ABOUT THE AUTHOR

Kat Ross worked as a journalist at the United Nations for ten years before happily falling back into what she likes best: making stuff up. She's the author of the Fourth Element and Fourth Talisman fantasy series, the Gaslamp Gothic adventures , and the dystopian thriller Some Fine Day. She loves myths, monsters and doomsday scenarios.

www.katrossbooks.com
kat@katrossbooks.com

ALSO BY KAT ROSS

Gaslamp Gothic
The Daemoniac
The Thirteenth Gate
A Bad Breed
The Necromancer's Bride
Dead Ringer

The Fourth Element Trilogy
The Midnight Sea
Blood of the Prophet
Queen of Chaos

The Fourth Talisman Series
Nocturne
Solis
Monstrum
Nemesis
Inferno

Some Fine Day